AMANTHA

by
Sarah Aldridge

A&M
BOOKS
1995

Printed in the United States of America.
First Edition

Cover design by Judy Merrill
Typeset by Muriel Crawford

Library of Congress Catalog Card Number: 95-77329
ISBN 0-9646648-0-1

TO
TW

Part I

On the western shore of the lower Chesapeake Bay, in southern Maryland, in the nineteenth century there was a large estate that went by the name of Godwin's Chance. Its title deeds dated from the time of the Stuart kings of England and throughout most of its existence it was a profitable supplier of tobacco for the European market. The house and home grounds, no longer used by the owners as a dwelling place, were difficult to reach. In fact, the condition of the roads was such that the easiest means of approach from the outside world was by boat. It survived the Civil War with little damage.

Shenstone was the family name and the heir in 1880 was Godwin Shenstone, who had a French mother and had spent a good deal of his boyhood in France. Like his immediate forebears, he was a banker in Baltimore, but he spent very little time there, preferring to cultivate his business interests in Europe. Now in his late thirties he was still not married.

The Leggetts, on the other hand, though equally long-established in the vicinity of Annapolis, were lacking in a gift for financial success and lived on the remnants of a family fortune that had been a good deal diminished by the Civil War. One of them, in fact, Clyde Leggett, died penniless five years after Appomattox of the effects of wounds he had received in General Early's army. Since his wife had died before him, he left his only child Amantha to the charity of his brothers and their wives, who shifted her about from one to another during her growing up so as to equalize the burden. In 1885 she was eighteen years old, a vivid beauty and just out of finishing school. She came back to Baltimore to stay with her Uncle Ralph and Aunt Katherine, who had no daughters of their own.

Amantha knew that they expected she would marry soon and well. It was a wish she joined in with, since she was anxious to achieve the independence of being a married woman. Money entered into the matter, she realized, though she had little conception of money except as something

1

necessary to supply the comforts and luxuries that she took for granted. She had not been trained to any special skill. Her relatives assumed that a girl of her background would not earn money.

On this morning the warm sunlight of a September day shone into the room of the tall, narrow Baltimore house where she sat at breakfast with her uncle and aunt. As Uncle Ralph wiped the crumbs from his chin and gathered up the letters by his plate, Aunt Katherine, who was studying the society column of the morning paper, said, "I wondered when he was going to put in an appearance."

"Who?" asked her husband, without much interest.

"Godwin Shenstone. It says here he arrives from Paris on Monday."

"Must have come to oversee the trading of his tobacco crop. He always comes for that. He sells most of it in France."

"Martha Downing is bound to have a reception for him. I'll see him there. I believe I'll take Amantha with me."

Amantha, aware of the thoughtful look in her aunt's eyes, stood at the window fiddling with the tasseled window curtain pull. She had heard Godwin Shenstone discussed before. He was very handsome, very wealthy, very worldly, she had been told. He mingled in the best society in Baltimore, London and Paris. Thirty-eight seemed pretty old and she wondered why he had never married.

* * *

Amantha's Aunt Katherine sat in a corner of Mrs. Downing's drawing room with a middle-aged friend and observed the throng.

"He is extremely clever," she remarked, her gaze dwelling on the robust, handsome man standing directly across the room from her. "He never makes the mistake of being a Frenchman when he is here. Yet I know he thinks civilization ends in the middle of the Atlantic."

"You mean Godwin Shenstone," said her friend. "It is ridiculous how the women pursue him. Of course he'll end by marrying a

Frenchwoman and he'll marry money. All the Shenstones think of money first."

Silently Aunt Katherine agreed with her.

In the carriage going home Uncle Ralph said, "I was talking to Godwin Shenstone. He was telling me about a German — I think his name is Benz — who has invented a self-propelled carriage. He says it has an internal combustion engine and eventually he thinks something of that kind will have a commercial future."

"If Godwin thinks so, it will be so." Aunt Katherine's tone was tart. "He is never mistaken where there is money to be made."

"Can't see it myself. It will be a long time before such a thing could be reliable enough to replace horses. How can you supply fuel for it? It is a pipe dream."

"I don't suppose it will remain so," his wife replied." I suppose you must have a large streak of selfishness to prosper the way he does."

Her husband was at once on the defensive. "Oh, he's pretty sharp when it comes to making money. But I must say this for Godwin: nobody has ever accused him of making an unfair deal or failing to live up to his end of a bargain."

"That's because he can always outguess his opponent."

"Oh, Aunt Katherine!" Amantha's fresh young voice breathed the words softly. Her aunt glanced toward her in surprise.

"Why, what is the matter? Everybody knows that Godwin Shenstone is always out for number one."

"Oh, Aunt Katherine!" Amantha repeated. "I'm sure he is very good and kind!"

"Good heavens above, Amantha! You don't even know the man!"

"He has beautiful eyes."

Her aunt examined her face as carefully as she could in the passing light of the street lamps. "You danced with him once, I know," she said in a kindly tone. "Did he give you such a soulful look?"

Amantha did not respond and her aunt said nothing further. The next

3

morning she noticed that her niece was unusually quiet and unresponsive. The silly girl, she thought; still dreaming of last night. Is she smitten by Godwin? Eighteen was an age when girls were apt to fall in love, sometimes with very unsuitable men. What a foolish age. She was glad she had not got to go through all that again. She remembered that once she had thought she would gladly die if Ralph did not ask her to marry him. Well, she had no real complaint of him as a husband but now she was far from considering him the marvel of the universe she had once thought him to be.

Her train of thought was interrupted by Amantha, whose voice was filled with a strange timidity. "Aunt Katherine, are we going to the theater this week?"

"Why, I don't know. Is there a play you especially want to see? If so, I'll have to inquire if it is suitable for you."

"There is a French company here. I think they are giving a play by Moliere. Mr. Shenstone said he thought they would be quite good. It would be good practice for my French."

Her aunt noted the obvious gloss of self-improvement that Amantha had added to justify her interest. So it was true. Amantha had fallen in love with Godwin Shenstone. Her tone was kind when she said, "Godwin praises anything French, my dear. His mother gave him a bias that way. I think it is he you want to see, isn't it? Well, my child, I must warn you. He has no interest in you. You will make yourself unhappy over the impossible."

Amantha's dark blue eyes filled with tears. "Oh, Aunt Katherine! He did act as if he liked me! He told me all about France and what a wonderful place Paris is."

Aunt Katherine looked at her critically. Undoubtedly she was a very pretty girl, with a fresh, perfect complexion and sparkling blue eyes and soft brown hair. Any man would respond at once to the pleasure of talking to her. Aunt Katherine sighed. It was a phase to be got through, she supposed. Her tone was testy as she said, "You need not go to the play to

4

see him again. He will be here a week from today at my home."

"Oh, Aunt Katherine!" Amantha's eyes opened wide with delight. "I didn't know you knew him so well."

Aunt Katherine made a slight sound of disgust. "You mean, you did not know that I had any means of capturing him for an hour. Well, there is one thing I will say for him. He does his duty by his family obligations. After all, his Shenstone grandmother was my mother's first cousin, so he does not choose to ignore me when he comes to Baltimore. But, Amantha, child, do pay attention to me. I do not think he is interested in you. He may not even remember you."

* * *

"This is my niece," said Aunt Katherine drawing Amatha forward with a firm hand. "She is my husband's brother's daughter."

The cool hazel eyes considered her politely. Amantha felt a flood of heat rise through her body to her face. He was just as she remembered him: a medium-sized, well-built man, fresh-skinned, with close-lying hair and a mustache.

"I believe she met you at Martha Downing's last week," Aunt Katherine added.

"Ah, yes. How do you do, Miss Leggett?" The bland voice was the same. He did not betray the fact that he did not remember her and she could not be sure that he had forgotten her.

She stammered a question about his stay in Baltimore. A slight flicker of amusement showed in his eyes. He replied readily, "I shall not be in Baltimore very much. The reason I come each year is to see about my tobacco crop at Godwin's Chance. So I shall be there most of the time."

He was gracious, he was patient in answering questions about his plantation, about the success of his tobacco crop, questions he must have answered frequently in the two weeks he had been in Baltimore, and he displayed no haste in leaving. He also seemed not at all disconcerted by

5

Amantha's lingering gaze, for she found it impossible to keep her eyes off him for long. The cheerful, imperturbable face, the firmly set jaw, the alert, restless glance fascinated her. He was altogether unlike anyone she had ever encountered.

When at last he announced he must go, her heart sank and the beginnings of despair took possession of her. She asked impulsively, compelled by the urgency of her heart to find an excuse for seeing him again, "Do you play tennis?"

He looked at her in surprise. "Lawn tennis? Why, yes. Do you play?"

She blushed as she blurted out, "Yes. I was the best player at my school." She explained hurriedly that the fashionable school to which she had been sent was among the first to adopt the new game, imported from England, as a sport for girls. She had excelled in it, developing a passion for it with all the uncomplicated ardor of adolescence.

He was smiling now. "And do you play it now, here in Baltimore?"

She explained that there was a club where there was a court and the young people of her circle were allowed to play there on certain days.

He was watching her with an interest he had not shown before. "Do you play mixed doubles?"

"Sometimes," she answered eagerly, and then added with a boldness that surprised herself, "I think I could arrange some, if you would like to play. Tomorrow afternoon, if the weather is good?"

"Tomorrow afternoon, if the weather is good," he replied promptly.

It was fair the next afternoon and he came, as arranged, to fetch her and take her to the club. She had read in novels about girls who were deliriously happy. That must be her state, she decided. In spite of her exalted feelings, she played well and Godwin seemed to enjoy himself. Afterwards he went with her and her friends to Aunt Katherine's house and Aunt Katherine served lemonade in tall iced glasses — Godwin, she saw, was handed a mint julep — with sandwiches to take the edge off the appetite the vigorous game had given them. The conversation was the happy, inconsequent chatter of the very young. Amantha came out of her beautiful haze only when Godwin announced he must be going. A sudden shyness overcame her.

"You're going away now?" she managed to ask, afraid of the answer.

Godwin gave her another attentive look. All afternoon she had sensed approval in his manner, approval of the way in which she played, of her competence in arranging the afternoon's sport, in the directness with which she had responded to his remarks. Now she was suddenly self-conscious again.

"I am going down to Godwin's Chance. I don't know just how long I shall be there." He turned away to say goodbye to her aunt, "Au revoir, madame." He made a gesture as if to kiss her hand. It was the nearest he ever came, in her phrase, to "acting the Frenchman."

"Perhaps we shall see you again in Baltimore before you go abroad again," she suggested, aware of the despairing gaze that Amantha had fixed on his face.

"Perhaps."

He was the last to leave and as the door closed on his back, Amantha exclaimed, "He's just wonderful!"

"Godwin? Well, I hardly think so. But he can be very charming. You must not be misled by that, Amantha."

Her Uncle Ralph came in then and Amantha withdrew into reverie. She was struggling with a confusion of feelings. Godwin's nearness aroused an excitement in her body she had never experienced before. The talk among the other girls at school had enlightened her to some extent as to the nature of the physical relationship between a man and a woman but she found it hard to envisage the details, especially when she observed the studied primness of the older women among her aunt's friends. It seemed to her that any physical act that sought to appease the unformed longing in her body required a greater freedom of spirit than her elders would be capable of. Godwin fascinated her. It seemed to her that he would be capable of anything and the very fact gave her a sense

7

of alarm in being close to him.

"Do you think, Aunt Katherine, that he will come to see you again?" she asked suddenly, out of the blue.

Her aunt, startled, made a gesture of impatience." Who? Godwin? Good heavens, Amantha! By now he has forgotten you exist!" She paused to consider the stricken look on Amantha's face. She drove on, convinced she must be as ruthless as possible for the girl's sake. "You must believe me, Amantha. He is a man of the world and, I think, enough of a gentleman not to take notice of you unless he had serious intentions. I don't even know if he is really thinking of getting married at all."

"It seems he is," Uncle Ralph's voice interjected in their conversation. "At least, I hear that he has remarked somewhere along the line that it was time he married."

There was silence while his wife digested what he had said. "If he is circulating that bit of information, he will have every woman in town hanging about his neck."

Uncle Ralph shrugged. "Maybe he is just trying to stir up some excitement."

"He will succeed." Aunt Katherine turned briskly to the drooping girl near her. "Come, Amantha, help me pick up in here. Dicey has enough to do in the kitchen."

But she learned from several friends that what her husband had said was true. Godwin Shenstone had let it drop that he was looking for a wife and everyone assumed that he would bring to this enterprise the same knack for efficiency and organization that he used in his business ventures. Undoubtedly he had definite ideas about the requirements that must be met. It was even suggested that one reason for removing himself to Godwin's Chance for a week was to allow the news to spread and the field of choice to be arrayed for his return to Baltimore.

"What surprises me," said Aunt Katherine to Martha Downing candidly, "is that he has come to Baltimore for the purpose. I had always imagined he would marry in France."

8

"I think you misjudge him a little, Katherine. He does have a strong family feeling and he may well feel that he wants an American wife, from among his own sort of people."

"Well, I'm sure he will want one with a good dowry and not too independent."

Mrs. Downing sighed. "Katherine, you make him sound impossibly calculating. It is true that we cannot expect him to be governed by fancy. It is not in his nature and he is not an inexperienced boy. But I think he will want an amiable girl."

Aunt Katherine, seeing her own skepticism unwelcome and realizing that even with her elderly friend Godwin's charm was at work, said nothing further. For the balance of the week she avoided the subject at home and strove to ignore the wan looks and lack of appetite of her niece. Since forthrightness had had no effect on Amantha, perhaps a deliberate silence would be better.

She was astonished one morning when the maid announced that Mr. Godwin Shenstone was in the parlor and wished to see her. She found him standing in front of the swept and empty grate, looking fresh and cheerful in a tweed suit.

"Cousin Katherine," he said at once, "I hope this isn't inconvenient."

"Why, not at all. But I scarcely expected to see you again this year."

He smiled and there was an ingratiating overtone in his voice. "I realize that I have somewhat neglected my kin. I must plead the press of business affairs that have preoccupied me for the last ten years. Now I seem to have a breathing space and I find I have some amends to make."

Aunt Katherine looked at him more closely. This seemed to her a little fulsome, for their family connection had never provided a very close bond. She waited for him to say something further.

"In fact, you may be very much surprised at the reason for my coming to see you now. I have come to ask you if I may pay court to Amantha."

"Amantha! Why, Godwin, she hasn't got a penny to her name!"

The frankness of her response brought a frown and a slight flush to his face. He must often hear inadvertently, she thought contritely, of the mercenary motives that were always attributed to him. She wished she had had the presence of mind to restrain her tongue.

But he said with dignity, "I have plenty to offer the girl I marry. What I want is an amiable girl who can learn to have some regard for me."

That would be no problem, she thought. But a certain coldness settled around her heart. "Well, really, Godwin, you surprise me beyond all saying. But I think you must realize that Amantha is quite taken with you. She is a very innocent girl and you must make allowance for her lack of sophistication."

"Oh, I do!" he said cheerfully. "It is part of her charm. I find it flattering. She is very young. This is just as well, since I believe I have a better chance of happiness with a girl I can teach, who has everything to learn about life. I am used, you know, to the French view of these things."

Aunt Katherine did not answer at once. The dismay that she had first felt was renewed by what he said. Of course, mere romance was no basis for the serious business of marriage. She had often said so herself. But there was a season for all things and first youth is the time for the generous warmth of feelings that do not count the cost. There was nothing in Godwin's words or manner that gave promise of anything but the most careful balance between reason and emotion. This could stifle the most ardent love.

In the end she said, "I confess I am unprepared for this, Godwin. But, of course, I have no objection and I am sure that Ralph will not have either. Please to remember, though, that we are not her formal guardians. In fact, she has none, since she inherited no property."

"That," said Godwin easily, "is a matter of no consequence in this situation."

* * *

10

The train to New York pulled out of the Baltimore station. The October day was fair and mild and the autumn sunlight had shone upon the wedding party as they came out of the church of Saint Michael and All Angels. Amantha, watching the small knot of her relatives standing on the station platform recede into the distance, waved happily. The wedding had been entirely according to precedent. The wedding reception had been gay and noisy. And now she was on the first stretch of her honeymoon with Godwin.

Mrs. Godwin Shenstone. She felt her wedding ring through her glove and glanced briefly up at — yes —her husband, savoring the title on her tongue silently.   He stood beside her wearing his usual noncommittal smile, raising his hand for one more farewell to the people on the train platform. She felt his other hand seek her elbow and turn her gently but firmly toward the door of the coach. He had taken a drawing room for the trip to New York and now the porter appeared in the narrow passage and ushered them into it. Amantha, her senses acutely open to a thousand new impressions, felt a little shiver of exquisite enjoyment run through her. It seemed incredible that everything could be so perfect — the perfect husband, the perfect setting for a perfect married life. She was used to train travel. A good part of her childhood had been spent in boarding schools, with train journeys to and from the houses of her various uncles at the beginnings and ends of holidays. But these journeys had been by coach, in care of the conductor, with sandwich lunches to stave off the pangs of hunger. This was very different — the obsequious porter, the attentive husband, the delicate meal served with flourishes in the privacy of the drawing room.

She raised enchanted eyes to gaze at Godwin. He had helped her off with her wrap and was now removing his own topcoat. He gave no sign of excitement or unusual happiness. He sat down in the armchair closest to her and took a small, thin cigar from a case in his pocket. She had learned, in the course of the month that had elapsed since he first presented himself as her suitor, that he smoked these expensive little Cuban

11

cigars. They gave a distinctive scent to his clothes. Since he was the only man she had ever known who used them, the scent had become, for her, part of him. If he noticed the shining adulation in her eyes as she gazed at him, he did not indicate that he did, but was busy lighting his cigar. She said finally a little timidly, "We are going to Paris right away?"

He glanced at her briefly and nodded." We shall be in New York, at a hotel, for a couple of nights. Then we shall sail for London, where we shall spend a few days. After that, we cross the Channel and spend a short while in Paris. You will want to add to your wardrobe. But most of our honeymoon will be in Italy, at Rapallo. I expect that we shall stay quite a long time there. You will like it. Rapallo is in a very beautiful part or the world."

At his calm words the little shiver of excitement went through her again. Really, it seemed to be too good to be true. How many of the girls she knew would thrill to this golden future laid out before her. The fact that he never deviated from his cool, detached manner did not trouble her. She was used to taking people as they were. During his month's courtship he had kissed her several times, on the mouth, with closed lips, brief but firm kisses. Once, when overcome with delight at a bouquet he had brought her for an evening party, she had impulsively flung her arms around his neck. He had disengaged himself with good-humored chiding, saying the time had not come for such things. There was an exactness in his measurement of the right degree of warmth for any occasion that she had learned was as much a part of him as the assurance with which he dealt with all his social and business affairs.

Now she exclaimed, "Oh, Godwin! This is all so wonderful! I am the happiest girl in the world!"

She jumped up and leaned over to kiss him. This time he did not restrain her but shifted his position in order to draw her down on his knees. Deliberately, with his hand at the nape of her neck he drew her head down and returned her kiss. She felt his tongue thrust firmly between her lips and into her mouth. Surprised and yet eager, she opened her lips to receive it, fascinated and excited by its moist, warm presence. Then briskly he withdrew it and with a firm but gentle pressure pushed her onto her feet.

"Why, Godwin! Nobody ever kissed me like that before!" She stared at him, excitement making her cheeks pink.

He looked up at her with a self-satisfied smile. "I should think not. Let's have a little champagne." He reached for the bottle standing in an ice bucket.

Two glasses of the bubbling wine made her laugh hilariously at anything he said. His own imperturbability was unruffled and his manner remained that of a tolerant, patient teacher. When she demanded that he kiss her again, he did so, with the same lingering deliberation. As the train approached New York the wine began to make her drowsy and it was in a haze of ill-defined euphoria that she obeyed when he told her to put on her hat and coat and follow him from the coach into the train station and thence to a cab.

This was a dream, she told herself, as the cab found its way through the enormous, pushing, noisy crush of people and vehicles that seemed to overflow the narrow streets. They arrived finally at the hotel, a staid place in a comparatively quiet street. As they followed the porter carrying their bags down the long carpeted corridor, she thought again, this is really happening. Here she was, a married woman, caught up in the bustle and lively confusion of the great world. She thrilled to the idea already beginning to see herself in retrospect as an inexperienced child, aware of life only as reflected in other peoples' lives and in the books she read.

In their room, Godwin said, "I think you had better have a rest. I have some business to attend to. We'll have supper in our room here later."

"But, Godwin, are you going to leave me here alone?" There was sudden panic in her voice.

He made a gesture of impatience." You are perfectly safe. And as I said, I think you had better have a rest."

In spite of her excitement, it was not long after the door had closed behind him that she found herself dozing in the chair. The wine, on top of the strain of her wedding and the reception overtook her and in a few minutes she lay down on the chaise lounge and fell asleep. She did not awaken until the sound of the opening door roused her and she opened her eyes in bewilderment to see Godwin come into the room. The daylight had sped and dark filled the room. He lit the lamp with the many-colored glass shade and sat down in the armchair close to her.

"Did you rest well?" he asked in a kindly voice.

Amantha nodded and yawned. She was still drowsy but with a pleasurable sense of well being.

"Are you hungry?" he asked next, and suddenly she felt ravenous. "I'm starved."

He held a hotel menu out to her and asked what she wanted to eat. It was the first time she had ever ordered a meal and the acknowledgment of the fact brought again the thrill of awareness of herself as a grown woman with the power of command. In the end, she followed his suggestions for a meal and when it came ate with relish, untroubled by the critical air with which he examined each dish as he lifted its cover. When they finished he drew out one of his little cigars and lit it. She lay back again on the chaise lounge.

Eyeing her attentively, he said in a bantering tone, "How do you feel, Mrs. Shenstone?"

The purposeful playfulness in his manner made her instantly aware of the unacknowledged question that had lain in abeyance throughout the day. Instinctively she knew she had stepped very close to the moment when the half-understood physical act of coupling with this man to whom she was now legally bound must take place. The same panic she had felt when he had announced he was going out returned, this time to linger a while longer. Something of this must have shown in her face, because with elaborate casualness he turned his attention away from her and spoke of their sailing two days hence.

"I have chosen to go on the French ship," he said, "because it will be an introduction for you to French manners and the French language. You know French, don't you?"

"Oh, yes," she replied eagerly. "I've had years and years of French in school. But I expect I'll find it difficult to talk to French people. They are very impatient, aren't they?"

He shrugged. "At first you will find it difficult. But you will get used to it. One thing you must remember. French people, especially those of good class, are not as outspoken as Americans. You will have to learn to be more careful how you act and speak."

The reminder that he was older, infinitely more experienced and critical subdued her rising exuberance. He had rung the bell for the waiter and presently the man came and removed the remains of their dinner. He got up from his chair and walked about the room, picking up small objects from the tables and setting them down again, glancing at her from titme to time. Then he came and sat on the edge of the chaise lounge beside her. The little panic returned to tease her as she became aware of the warmth of his body against her leg.

"You are going to need some help in dealing with French dressmakers," he said matter-of-factly. "I have written to a friend of mine, the Comtesse de Brieux. She says she will be delighted to help you choose your wardrobe. I'm afraid that's something I can't do much about myself."

"Oh, Godwin! Does she speak English?"

"Of course. But you must make an effort with French."

He sat beside her, talking in a desultory way for an hour or more, unhurried, unconcerned with any problem that might arise. Amantha, wide awake after her afternoon nap, watched him expectantly. All at once he leaned over and kissed her firmly on the lips. She felt his hand pass under her arm and press her breast. Her heart began to beat wildly as he kept his mouth against hers and worked his tongue between her lips. A long shiver passed through her body and a sensation of warmth spread

15

through her. Then he sat up again and smiled down at her. There were bright glints of light in his eyes and his hands continued to search over her body. Their touch raised her excitement to a fever pitch. She wanted to throw her arms around him and press herself against him and yet a confused shyness held her back. Godwin said softly, "I'm sure that you would be more comfortable without all those clothes on. I'd rather see you without them. Why don't you go and take them off?"

Still smiling, his eyes were fixed on her with the new sort of gleam in them. He made a gesture towards the bedroom. She looked at him in astonishment. She was well aware of her body. She had even examined herself naked in stolen moments before a looking glass. She knew her body craved physical pleasure, the unmentionable joy created by eager fingers and the resulting flood of warmth through aroused nerves, though the ways in which this was to be obtained remained only half-known . She knew that this was something one never acknowledged, something sought in one's bed alone, in the dark, safe from all inquiry. That anyone, much less a man, even one calling himself her husband, should suggest that she undress and appear naked before him, plunged her into a sudden turmoil of conflicting impulses.

Godwin's smile had grown a little quizzical. "Well, are you going to do as I say?"

In an excited rush she got up and went into the bedroom. She stood for a moment undecided in the middle of the room, half eager to obey him and strip herself forthwith, half anxious to escape from the necessity of doing so. Fumbling, she took off her dress and corset and shoes and stockings. Then in her chemise she stopped, overcome by indecision. As she stood thus she was suddenly aware that Godwin had come into the bedroom and was watching her. He was clad in his dressing gown, his legs bare beneath the hem of the dark, brocaded cloth. The same smile was still on his face.

"Don't be frightened," he said in a soothing tone that did not altogether agree with the brightness of his eyes.

16

She stood unable to move as he came over to her and put his arm around her, his fingers gently feeling her flesh through the thin chemise. As if mesmerized, she obeyed the urging of his arm as he propelled her to the bed and pushed her down onto it. In an instinctive movement of self-protection, she closed her eyes as he withdrew his arm from under hers. Then she was aware of his body as he lay down beside her and pulled her against him. Again he kissed her as before and his hands traveled down her back. She struggled briefly, in panic, as his fingers sought between her thighs and she became aware of his penis thrusting against her. Still she resisted as he mounted her and then suddenly as the eager warmth flooded her, she yielded and felt a sharp pain as he drove into her and carried her with him past his own climax.

A few seconds later she opened her eyes, aware of his weight on her stomach, his head against her breasts. He raised his head and drew himself up in the bed beside her. The light was still on by the bed and she saw him look down at her thighs. His smile returned, a discreet, well-pleased smile, and then he leaned over and kissed her gently. "You won't mind it so much after this," he said.

He settled himself down comfortably beside her after putting out the lamp and within a few minutes his regular breathing told her he was asleep. She raised herself on her elbow and looked down at him in the half-gloom. There he was, his body warm against hers, so recently so unbelievably intimate with her, and now so calmly distant. This, she thought, was the goal to which all the excitement of the last weeks had led up to. All the half-understood, half-imagined things that had filled her personal world now were resolved. She was no longer a virgin; she was a married woman. No one now would assume that she was ignorant of the common physical act that was the center of human life. All the unspoken or half-explained things she had been aware of in childhood and adolescence were now clear. But with this new experience came a new perception: the protecting cloud of her innocence had been breached and she was now vulnerable — to what she could only vaguely foresee.

As the excitement of her sexual arousal faded and her thoughts became more coherent, she felt a growing sense of disappointment. She tried to understand this, eager to clarify her own feelings. She had expected something else, something further. Instinctively she knew that Godwin had been very considerate of her and that his carefulness was something she should appreciate and probably would value more as time went on. But what troubled her was the fact, obvious to her now, that their physical joining had brought him no nearer to her. He was as remote, as unfathomed, as he had been before. No doubt, as he had assured her, she would learn to enjoy intercourse with him. But would it always be as with a stranger?

At last she lay down beside him and fell asleep. When she woke he was already up and dressed, sitting in the sitting room reading the morning paper. When he heard her stir he put the paper down and came into the bedroom and, coming over to the bed, leaned over and kissed her, firmly but without lingering. He had ordered breakfast, he said, and it would be up whenever she said she wanted it. She was hungry and eager to get out of bed and dressed. She noted the approval on his face as he returned to his paper to wait for her to be ready.

He was an attentive escort to her all that day, a gallant squire at dinner in a famous, old restaurant and at a witty and sophisticated play afterward. In their bedroom once more he was again the competent, capable lover. Less absorbed in her own inexperience this time, she covertly watched him as he approached her. Unpracticed as she was, she was aware that he was adroit, self-possessed, anxious to please her. This was obvious in the gentle skill with which he fondled her, the appreciative smile with which he admired her body. He was always naked when he got into bed with her. The only article of covering he used was a condom and he explained its purpose to her. He did not intend, he said, that she should start a family immediately and he took this means of protecting her. He stated these facts simply, as if he took it for granted that his own decision was sufficient, without any inquiry concerning her own wishes.

18

* *.*

The clear gray light of an early November morning flooded the paths and flower beds of the Tuileries Gardens. Amantha, on her first walk in Paris, was surprised and enchanted by the liveliness of the scene that she had read about chiefly as the background to the French Revolution. London had been grave and calm in those neighborhoods she had seen, and the spirit of history, of the remembrance of famous people, seemed suited to it. But to her Paris was an incongruous setting for things of the past. It seemed too full of the effervescence of day by day life. She tried to express something of this to Godwin.

He smiled at her, a smile of an indulgent and understanding uncle. "Paris is much more than a background for the Terror, though I suppose that is mostly the way you would have heard of it."

They had traveled across the Channel the afternoon before and he had taken her dining and for an evening view of the Seine. This morning he had said at their breakfast of croissants and coffee in their hotel room that he would take her for a first view of the sights that every American should see. At lunch, at a famous restaurant which he named, she would meet Mme. la Comtesse de Brieux and go with her for a first visit to the dressmaker. In spite of the matter-of-factness of his tone, a surge of excitement overwhelmed Amantha. She was indeed walking in the Tuileries Gardens, on the arm of her husband, due to meet a countess for the first time and have dresses made by a famous couturier. A year ago she would have thought this all sheer fantasy, delicious fantasy but quite unreal.

She glanced at Godwin. He seemed unconcerned, unruffled by any anxiety, any anticipation. Of course, to him nothing of this was new, with the exception of the fact that he was now a married man with a wife for whom he was responsible. A two-week acquaintance with him as a constant companion had made her aware that his practiced charm was the polish that came from considerable experience of women. She had known from the beginning that his was a sophistication beyond that of her family circle of elders. Aunt Katherine, whose Southern background held its own share of euphemistic disguise of the inconvenient, had nevertheless sometimes shown that she mistrusted his social adroitness, gained from his French mother and his years of mingling with well-to-do and cultivated foreigners. But Uncle Ralph had bluntly said that Godwin, to his knowledge, had never let anybody down who relied on his word.

Amantha, eyeing him covertly now, said "Godwin, don't you feel a thrill at being here with me? I know you're very familiar with all this, but it is different, isn't it, here with me?"

He gave her an alert glance, aware of the appeal in her question. "Of course, my dear. I have never walked about Paris with a wedded wife — my own, that is." He gave her a brief gleaming smile that flattered her to the core, and added, "And I'm fully aware that every man who passes us turns around to look at you."

She laughed gaily. He never failed to come through when she appealed for special attention. This had become a happy sort of game which she could play at any time, when the tone of their tete-a-tetes seemed to be growing too sober.

The luncheon in the subdued, dignified atmosphere of the old restaurant came as a pleasant contrast to the bright cheeriness of their morning's sightseeing. She was amused to realize that in the last two weeks she had learned to recognize and view with tolerant interest attitudes on the part of other people that were obviously alien to her own. She glanced around the restaurant. Godwin was engrossed in a conversation with the waiter concerning their meal. The countess, he said, had not yet come.

"Does she have a husband?" Amantha asked. "Or is she a widow?"

"Her husband isn't able to appear in society. He is an invalid."

"Oh, dear! That can't be very nice for her."

Godwin made a slight, noncommittal gesture with his hand. The maitre d' hotel had come to their table and murmured something in his ear. He got up and said, "Excuse me for a moment, Amantha. I must go and meet our guest."

Some minutes passed while she sat alone at the table, still fascinated by the scene around her. She did not realize that Godwin was coming back to her until he was there accompanied by a woman who wore a fashionable fur wrap. Her attention abruptly turned from the observation of strangers to focus on the newcomer.

She had not thought, ahead of time, what she expected the countess to look like. Her first feeling was of surprise that the woman before her was still young, though older than herself. She was a slender, blond woman whose fine-textured skin glowed softly with a delicate bloom. Her pale gold hair was swept up from her forehead. The mild grey eyes looked at Amantha from under straight eyebrows. The delicate nostrils of the thin, high-bridged nose quivered a little. Her bearing was that of someone used to attention, to the protection of friends and servants.

Amantha struggled to remember the French formula for greeting a stranger to whom she was being introduced, which Godwin had been careful to drill her in. The countess's voice was pitched higher than her own and her voluble French flowed over the three of them as they seated themselves, smoothing the awkwardness of introductions in a public place.

Suddenly the countess, observing her hesitation and placing on it her own interpretation, switched into a fluent but faintly accented English, in which her voice became a little more shrill.

"This is your first visit to Paris, your husband tells me, madame. It is an experience, is it not?"

Immediately Amantha became aware of a number of things. The countess was a beautiful woman in a style quite unfamiliar to her. She wore a pervasive but unobtrusive scent. She was dressed with an air of fashion that was at the same time discreet and marked. Her most commonplace remark and gesture displayed an elegance that Amantha had never before seen. And she was highly nervous, as if she was keyed to a

21

fever pitch by some strong emotion.

Amantha, hearing the English phrases, found her tongue and strove to suppress the schoolgirl and act the part of a married woman. "I am looking forward to this afternoon, madame. It is very kind of you to help me choose a wardrobe. I am sure Godwin has told you that I have never had such an opportunity before."

Contrasted with the sophistication of the countess's manner her own statements seemed bald and awkward, and yet there was no use her trying to imitate the other's adroitness, since she would not have succeeded.

The countess paused briefly while her grey eyes looked directly into Amantha's without betraying any emotion. "You are very young, my dear. That, of course, has its compensations. Your husband tells me that you have no mother or sisters." When Amantha nodded, she went on. "I do not know, exactly, how American girls are brought up —" she did not conclude her obvious thought but left the phrase in the air, as if in invitation to Amantha to supply her with an explanation.

"Oh, I've got aunts," Amantha said, smiling readily. "They've done their best for me." The candor of her response seemed to relax the countess's nervous tension. She smiled as she said, "Then I shall think of you as my younger sister. We shall understand each other better that way."

Amantha, used to having her life arranged by those older than herself, agreed. The conversation then flowed onto other things and she was content to follow the lead that Godwin and the countess provided. Godwin said presently that he would leave them when the meal was finished. He took them from the restaurant to the countess's carriage, waiting in a side street, and then said au revoir with much bowing. Amantha had never seen him so ceremonious nor so absorbed with someone else as he seemed to be with the countess and she found herself watching him as she would a stranger. The countess was now smiling and more relaxed. She would, she said to Godwin, deposit Amantha at the hotel when the visit to the dressmaker was over.

22

"Do you live in Paris, madame?" Amantha asked, as the coachman urged the horses into motion.

"We have a house here, but I come only for visits," the countess answered, her gaze still fixed on Godwin's back retreating down the street. "My husband's health requires us to live in Italy much of the time. At first, this was a penance to me. Now I am accustomed. Or perhaps age has made me more resigned."

Amantha was aware that the gleam in her eyes was ironical. Indeed, no one would think of age where the countess was concerned. The thin face with the clearcut jawline, the fine, fresh skin, the sensitive mouth, all spoke of a young woman still far from the threshold of middle-age. The countess was perhaps as much as fifteen years older than herself. The implication in her words must be that it was not age but the trials of marriage that had brought resignation. Since Amantha knew nothing of the circumstances of the countess's marriage except that the count suffered from ill health, she decided to make no response.

The countess said, "It is sad that you do not have a family to love you. I, too, have lost my parents. It makes one feel very much alone."

Amantha tried to explain that she had been orphaned so young that she had really no sense of loss that was not compensated for by dutiful aunts and uncles.

"It is not the same thing," said the countess, shaking her head slowly. "Even a husband cannot provide all the affection one needs."

"You don't have children?"

There was a pause before the countess answered, a pause during which she cast another glance at Amantha. "No," she said, and then as if she had been going to say something further and had changed her mind, she repeated, "No."

By then they were at the dressmaker's, where the doorman bowed low and addressed the countess by name. It was obvious from the way in which she was greeted by the women assistants that she was well-known in this establishment.

23

Then each day in the two weeks that followed the visit was repeated and Amantha grew used to the concentrated seriousness with which the questions of dress were considered by the countess, by the couturiere and all her assistants. Godwin had said that she would need clothes for country living but that gowns for the evening would also be required. Evidently their sojourn in Italy would involve dinner parties.

She quickly got into the habit of asking the countess for enlightenment on the mysteries of French social customs. In doing so, she soon discovered that she fell easily into an intimacy with her that was closer than that she had with Godwin. Occasionally the countess betrayed a moment's astonishment at her naivete and ignorance, but she checked herself at once and hastened to explain with the careful explicitness of a conscientious governess. As their familiarity with each other grew, she gave Amantha brief lectures on the accepted behavior for a young married woman. Amantha, who had known only the easygoing rules of a closely-knit Southern social group, accepted her tutelage docilely The countess might sometimes be shocked at her gaucherie, but she never laughed at her or ridiculed her ignorance. She seemed to take her role of elder sister with the utmost seriousness.

One day the countess said, as they were about to leave the dressmakers, "I took the liberty of asking your husband whether I might take you to my house after our visit here. He is, I think, busy this afternoon and said he would come to fetch you later. Will you come with me?"

Amantha, flattered, said, "Oh, yes, I should love to," and followed her to the carriage. The question arose vaguely in her mind about what opportunity the countess had had to talk privately with Godwin, but the thought faded as they drove along through a district of old houses to the hotel de Brieux. Half a dozen generations of de Brieux had lived in the old mansion, set back behind an elaborate iron railing. Inside, amid the plush-covered chairs and settees, the dark old portraits, the massive chandeliers, the heavy tapestries, she was conscious of the mustiness of a house never fully aired. She was struck by the way the countess's pale beauty seemed to glow against this dark background, almost as if a halo of light emanated from her.

The countess led her to a small sitting room in which the white and gold furniture and walls covered in chinoiserie wallpaper gave a less somber air. She sat down on a small settee covered in petit point and placed her hand on the seat beside her. "Please sit here," she said. She was speaking in French now. Amantha was acquiring quickness and a greater store of words in the language and the countess lapsed more and more into it when they were alone.

Amantha sat down beside her. The diamonds and sapphires in the rings with which the countess's slim white fingers were laden flashed as she moved her hands.

"Amanthe" — from the beginning of their friendship she had gallicized Amantha's name — "it is true that you know very little about your husband, isn't it?"

Amantha, taken by surprise, did not respond. The countess went on, "I do not mean his family, his origins, since he comes of the same milieu as yourself."

"He's Aunt Katherine's cousin," was all Amantha could think to say.

The countess's grey eyes were fixed on her as if she sought to understand this allusion. "But he is much older than you. He is much more experienced, he has lived much longer as a man than you have as a woman."

Amantha said hesitantly, "Why, I suppose so." She returned the countess's scrutiny with questioning eyes.

A sigh escaped the older woman and she turned her gaze away. Amantha, aware that she was distressed, quickly began, "But, madame —"

The countess interrupted her. "You must call me Leonie when we are alone." She stopped and, looking down at her hands, brooded for a few moments. Then she looked up and said, "Amanthe, I find I cannot say to you yet what I want to say, what sometime I must say to you."

"But why not?"

"Because it will make you dislike me — hate me."

Amantha's dark blue eyes widened in astonishment. "Why, I couldn't do that! You've been too kind to me."

She barely heard the countess's low-voiced "Mon dieu" and was further surprised when she got up from the settee and walked quickly across the room to stand by the piano that almost filled one wall.

"Nevertheless, Amanthe," she said then, "the time may come when you will find it difficult to forgive me — perhaps impossible. But, now, enough of this."

And she rang for the servant to bring some wine and small pastries.

Frequently, after that, they ended their afternoons together at the hotel de Brieux. Amantha's mind sometimes reverted to this conversation and she was tempted to ask for an explanation, from Leonie herself or from Godwin, but an unaccountable shyness held her back. It was true, the countess and Godwin were much closer in age than she was to either of them. They shared a cultural background that was strange to her. These facts made her hesitate to demand from either of them explanations they did not spontaneously offer. -She found a tendency in herself to brood sometimes on what the implications of this might be. Neither of them had made any mention of the length of time of their acquaintance or how they had met. Godwin had said that he acted sometimes as the Comte de Brieux's man of business. The count, he said, was well known as a scientist; but he had little taste for business affairs. Perhaps that was the connection. When she got this far in thinking about them, Amantha found that she hesitated to go on. Was there something she feared?

She grew used to not seeing as much of Godwin as she had before. In the mornings he often was away from the hotel for several hours. In the evenings they invariably went out to dinner or to the theater or the opera in company of Godwin's friends. Godwin seemed to prefer the French people he knew to Americans. He said there were too many Americans in Paris these days who had nothing to recommend them except

26

the sudden fortunes they had made in the years since the end of the Civil War. Her command of French grew rapidly. The knowledge of French social customs that Leonie instilled in her gave her a quickly evident assurance. She was surprised at her own adaptability. She soon learned that a decorous flirtatiousness was expected of her by her French dinner and dancing partners and that Godwin approved of the ease with which she responded to them. He seemed unaffected by any jealousy of the attentions such men paid to his pretty young bride.

Alone with him in their bedroom she soon learned certain other things about him. He was attentive, expert in love-making, but he hated anything unusual. And it was always to be he who made the first advance. One evening, when the wine and the dancing had awakened in her a need for satisfaction, she had made a timid overture. He had responded, after a first hesitation, with kindness. But the gentle disapproval he had conveyed made upon her the impression, she realized, that he had intended it to make. The incident made her sharply aware that there was a barrier between them, across which he did not intend her to come.

She already knew that she knew little about his life, his beliefs, his true opinions, his most deep-seated prejudices. She found now that he did not expect her to learn about these things. She understood nothing of his business transactions, on which his considerable fortune was based. She did not know what his political outlook was, either at home or abroad. He made it plain that he did not consider either to be a subject for a woman to concern herself with. Women, she learned, in his eyes could be clever, knowledgeable, well-read, talented in music or the arts, competent in some sports, but only within a strictly limited scope and never to a degree sufficient to compete with a man.

"In other words," Amantha thought, rebellious when she had run up against his will on one occasion, "I can be a clever child but nothing more. He can teach me to be an agreeable companion for him, but I am not to have any ideas of my own."

He did not explain his sometimes hours' long absences and when she asked about them he shrugged and carelessly replied that he had affairs to attend to before they left for Italy. Amantha, unwilling to cloud her own contentment, dismissed the matter and spent the time writing letters to her relatives and friends, letters that had become long overdue in the bustle of her first weeks abroad. When she came to write Aunt Katherine she described in detail her new wardrobe, the dressmaker's establishment, the countess, the sights of Paris. Reading the letter over before she posted it, she was suddenly struck by the vast difference that now existed between herself here in a Parisian hotel and the girl who had mooned so desperately over Godwin in her aunt's house in Baltimore. Then she had believed herself hopelessly in love with a super-being — that was the only word for her concept of Godwin then. Now she was the much cooler wife of a man who still pleased her and who had opened up to her new worlds of sensual pleasure and social interest but whom she saw now clearly as a man, a human being she scarcely knew after weeks of intimacy. Slowly she closed the envelope and sealed the flap.

* * *

On the train to Rapallo there was a small, grey-haired woman in their compartment who struck up a conversation with Amantha when she heard her speaking English to Godwin. She was a German, she said, the daughter of a Heidelberg professor and the widow of an Italian and she liked to practice her English.

"It is true, signora, that this region around Rapallo is a beautiful paradise, one of the most heavenly spots in the world."

Amantha nodded politely. She was growing accustomed to the polyglot character of many Europeans and had decided that she herself would make an effort to imitate their facility with languages. Otherwise, there were so many human experiences that would be hidden from her.

It was a fine, sunny afternoon. The warmth and brilliance of this corner of Italy banished the wintriness of Paris. The train from Genoa

28

slid swiftly along through the farms and orchards. Probably, she thought, there was very little difference in this tidy landscape and the same countryside in the prosperous days of the Roman empire.

"It is a luxurious garden, signora," the little woman continued enthusiastically, "even in winter. People come here to live the whole year round. Do you stay in a pensione, madame?"

Amantha glanced briefly at Godwin. It was the sort of question she had learned to refer to him if possible, even when she knew the answer.

"We have a house near Rapallo," he replied promptly. "Perhaps you know it. It is below the high road, on the sea front. The Villa Delfina."

A bright smile lit up the woman's face. "Of course, signore! I pass it every day. You are signore Shenstone?"

Godwin acknowledged the fact with a nod. "My wife," he said, with a gesture toward Amantha.

"So young!" the woman exclaimed. "Forgive me, but I thought she must be your sister or your niece."

Amantha noticed that tact had restrained her from saying daughter. Godwin did not in fact look old enough to be her father, though he was more than twice her age. The thought amused her, for now she felt much less the school girl than she had been a few weeks before. Godwin's face showed no expression and the woman continued, "It is your honeymoon then. For I know that signore Shenstone has been a bachelor until lately."

Godwin cocked an eye at her but still said nothing.

"You have lived here a long time?" Amantha asked politely.

"Twenty years, signora. My husband was a pharmacist popular with visitors, especially Americans. He spent a few years in America as a young man. You did not know him, signore Shenstone, but he was well known to your neighbor, M.le Comte de Brieux. He was often called to the Villa Margherita when M.le Comte had an attack of asthma. Poor man! He suffers so much!"

There was genuine compassion in her voice, Amantha noted, even as she felt surprise at hearing the de Brieux name mentioned. She glanced

29

again at Godwin, but he was still looking at the little woman and seemed unconcerned. He had not made any reference to the fact that they would soon again encounter Leonie after she had left Paris. Nor had Leonie herself. It seemed to Amantha a strange omission and in her newly acquired sensitivity to the meaning that might lie beneath the surface of commonplace remarks, she wondered if there was a significance to it. When they alighted from the train at the trim flower-bordered station and were in the carriage that awaited them, she said as casually as she could, "You did not tell me that we would see Leonie here."

He said blandly, "I thought I had mentioned that they have the villa next to ours at Rapallo. Look out there at the glimpse of the sea, Amantha. This is really one of the most beautiful views in the world."

There was no stress in his manner and the scene of blue sea framed in luxuriant trees and shrubs was fine enough to account for his abrupt turning of the conversation, yet even as she admired the view her mind registered the fact that a hidden significance must lie in his failure to mention their neighbors. For she was certain that he had made no such mention and that he knew that he had not.

The carriage climbed the slight hill to the gates in the white, bougainvillea-draped wall of the Villa Delfina. The pebbles of the curving drive shone glaringly white in the brilliant sunlight. Amantha said nothing further about the de Brieux. She was conscious now of a need to take stock of herself, of making a reckoning that she felt she had been postponing for the last few days in Paris — as if she had been turning away from facing something that was daily more intrusive in her life, as if she had been saying to herself," I'll think about that when we get to Rapallo." Now she was at Rapallo and the information that the countess was her neighbor brought the subject directly into the foreground of her thoughts. She felt a twinge of impatience, in the midst of the sensuous luxuriance of the scene in which she was enveloped, to get on with her consideration of it, as of some puzzle with which she had been presented, the solution of which was vital to her well being. Leonie, she remembered, had spoken only of Italy. She had never specified the name of the place where she lived with the count, and in taking leave of her in Paris, she had merely remarked that no doubt they would soon meet again.

This feeling was submerged for a while by the very weight of enchantment in the setting of the Villa Delfina. The white house with its tall, wide windows and stone-paved loggias looking out beyond palm, orange and lemon and fig trees, grapevines, beds of luxuriant flowers alive with bees and butterflies, to the sparkling sea, filled her with a sense of unending abundance. The warmth of the blinding sunlight intoxicated her. She was used to the milder beauty of Chesapeake Bay, the great expanse of its waters fringed with low-lying vegetation, often hazed over with a humidity that in the summer sunshine was sultry. This scene had sharper, more vivid colors, combined with assiduous cultivation. It seemed more amenable to man's control, more subservient to human life.

Walking about the house and the gardens, she was overwhelmed, as she had so often been in the last few weeks, by a sense of the miraculous that she, an orphan and penniless and until now completely dependent on the good will of relatives, was the mistress of such a domain, free to wander freely among the flowers, savoring the magnificent setting, while servants took care of the unpacking of her belongings, the preparation of food, the attendance on any wants she might indicate. She found it incredible that all this should be at her command. Or at least at Godwin's. It was through Godwin, of course, that she enjoyed all this. In a hundred small, scarcely noticeable and perhaps unconscious ways he impressed this fact on her. Perhaps unconscious. She paused to reflect for a moment on this facet of the situation. Certainly he never made a parade of his power over her. He simply took it for granted that decisions and choices were always for him to make, that she would be only too ready to accept those he did make. And so far she had been only too ready to accept them, still too astonished at her change of circumstance to raise an objection even to herself.

The Italian servants at the villa were eager to confront her with their household questions. And also frankly curious about their master's bride. With her growing astuteness she realized that her youthfulness made them bold in addressing her and in measuring her malleability. They were used to Godwin's firm hand. Their first interest, she knew, was in discovering whether he intended to turn over that authority to his new wife. She was aware that her own ignorance and lack of experience in managing any servants, much less such sophisticated, expert ones, threatened danger. Godwin, she decided, would continue in control. So she made it as obvious as she could from that first day that she referred any question to him. He seemed to accept the situation matter-of-factly and patiently resolved each dilemma.

She wanted to ask him a number of questions of her own   but bided her time. She had begun to wonder if he did indeed intend to spend days and weeks together in this retreat, entirely away from the business affairs that had appeared to occupy him off and on during their stay in New York, London and Paris. It was clear to her that he was a wealthy man with varied interests, whose wealth was growing through astute and watchful management. This fact lent color to the assumption made by all her relatives and friends in Baltimore that he had married because he wanted to establish a family, to beget children to inherit that fortune. And yet, if this was true, why did he take such precaution to prevent her from conceiving? Nor did he ever make any allusion to the possibility that she might want a child.

In the evening, as the darkness came across the water, lamps were lit in the spacious, austerely furnished rooms. They ate elaborately, waited on by several footmen and maids, and later strolled together up and down the long loggia that overlooked the water. The moon was almost full and its light filled the garden, alive with the night sounds of birds and insects, full of strong shadows. Beyond, on the water, it sparkled with a subdued, ghostly sparkle. Amantha, wearing one of her new Parisian gowns that just cleared the floor and was overlaid with heavy lace, pulled Godwin's arm closer to her side under the light woolen shawl she had wrapped around her to ward off the night chill. Obediently he responded by tightening the muscles of his arm and leaned over to kiss her.

"You have enjoyed yourself today?" he inquired.

"Oh, yes," said Amantha. "I must learn Italian so that I can talk to the servants and the tradespeople without an interpreter."

They took another turn up and down the loggia, pacing slowly in amicable silence. What, Amantha wondered, did Godwin think about in those long silences when they were alone together? She was sure she was not in his thoughts. Once she had tried to tease him, asking him if he was too absorbed in his business affairs to think any more of her, now that they were married. He had not been amused and she let the matter drop. He was, she had learned, touchy about his money and the attention he gave to it. He had inherited a good deal and had increased that inheritance considerably. But he did not like to talk about it, at least with her. Goodhumoredly she accepted his attitude. After all, he was generous to a fault and never stinted anything when he thought it would please her.

Her attention was recalled to the moonlit scene by Godwin, who freed his arm from hers to put it around her waist. He stood still and turned her to face him, drawing her close and kissing her several times. She felt desire stirring in him in the close embrace and felt her own rising in response.

Later, in bed, he caressed her with greater intensity than usual, as if he was at special pains to assure her of his desire for her. As he kissed her and his hands strayed over her body the sudden thought occurred to her that he sought thus to erase any idea she might have that his interest in her had waned, that she had any reason to doubt his devotion.

In the first light of morning she was drowsily aware that he stirred and left her side. When she was dressed and came down to the loggia to the table where breakfast waited, he came in from the garden, looking fresh and well exercised, and bent to kiss her fondly before sitting down. It was obvious that he was in a very good mood. She spoke at once of the

33

idea that had entered her head earlier.

"Godwin, do you suppose that signora Tagliacci would tutor me in Italian?"

He looked at her in blank amazement. She was amused. For the first time, she had been able to take him completely off guard, even if only over a trivial matter. She was sure he would remember that she had spoken of learning Italian and he himself would probably propose a tutor, but that she should take the initiative in suggesting who that tutor should be would not occur to him.

"Signora Tagliacci?" He was still at sea.

She said calmly, "The little woman on the train, the widow of the pharmacist. I know she is German, but Germans are very thorough and I have a good ear for languages."

She said this confidently. It was one of the things she had learned to do in the last month: to speak confidently, as if she expected no demur.

"Oh, oh, yes," he responded. "Why, I suppose she might be interested. She probably would like to earn some money. I shall inquire."

Amantha smiled to herself but said nothing further. Godwin was very characteristically Godwin. He would accept her suggestion but he took it for granted that he would be the one to carry it out. He finished his cup of coffee, kissed her again and, saying that he would be back for lunch, walked briskly away down the loggia.

Yes, Amantha thought, as she watched him going away, she did need to take stock of herself. When she thought back to herself as she had been in Aunt Katherine's house in Baltimore a short two months ago she had a sense of remoteness, as if she were contemplating someone else. She remembered vividly her first acquaintance with Godwin, her awe and then her adoration of him as an extraordinary being who would never deign to notice her, much less return the passionate love he aroused in her. She remembered also the blissful astonishment she had felt when he had returned from his stay at Godwin's Chance and had told Aunt Katherine that he wanted to marry her. In her new speculative mood she wondered what could have happened, in that brief period while he was away and she languished in forlorn hopelessness, to have changed the utter indifference he had certainly shown before he left Baltimore into the purposeful eagerness with which he returned to court her.

She had learned, since then, that he compartmentalized his life. What he did in the day, with other people, was strictly divided from what he did when he returned to her. At first she had not realized that, during those first episodes in bed, his whole being was not involved, as hers was. Now she saw that there was some part of her that stood apart, that was not overpowered. He was no longer the pivot of her existence, as he had been when she married him. He was the source of her luxurious life but he was no longer its essence. She really did not know him at all. At first she had asked him questions, artless questions. Did he like this? Didn't he like that? Was he lonely before he met her? He had no close relatives, no living parents, brothers or sisters, aunts or uncles, who could tell her about his life before she met him. In Baltimore he was known only in his outward guise. And he himself gently but firmly turned aside any effort she made to learn about his inner life directly from himself.

That, she decided, was what had somewhat quenched the ardor of her first days with him, had checked the spontaneous, wholehearted love she had felt for him in the few weeks before they married and during the first days of marriage. It was as if he had created a sort of space between them that thwarted all attempts of hers to get near him in any but a physical sense. It left her with questions. Did he really love her? Or had he simply chosen her to be the sort of wife he wanted? He certainly seemed pleased at how she had proved that she could fulfill his requirements. But did she know what all his requirements were?

"He wants me for something." The idea was so definite that she said it aloud. It was something he was willing to pay a good price for, in bed and board, a correct husbandliness. She could not reproach him with a grudging spirit in paying it. He enjoyed their lovemaking and he was anxious that she should also. But the satisfactoriness of last night's intercourse, she suddenly realized, had become lately somewhat rare. Why? The question lingered in the back of her mind even as she got up, made restless by her reflections, and walked out into the garden. For the first time since well before her marriage she felt idle and bored with her idleness. The Italian lessons would be a welcome distraction. She hoped they could be arranged soon.

When midday came and the servants were setting the table in the room that gave onto the loggia, she heard the sound of carriage wheels on the drive and guessed it must be Godwin returning. The sound of voices coming into the house told her he was not alone. A woman was with him and she realized in a few moments that he had brought signora Tagliacci with him. Her brief surprise quickly vanished. It was like him to proceed promptly and efficiently to carry out any plan he had decided upon.

He appeared in the arched doorway to the loggia, standing aside to let the woman pass before him. He said, "Amantha, here is Signora Tagliacci. I believe she can be persuaded to teach you."

The little German woman came briskly toward Amantha with her greeting, "Buon giorno, signora." How alien she looked in this setting, thought Amantha, so neat and quick moving in the luxuriant languid warmth. The twenty-odd years of her sojourn in Italy had not changed by one iota her character as the daughter of a Heidelberg University professor. Her eyeglasses glinted as a shaft of sunlight struck the lenses. "I shall be delighted to be your teacher," she said, with a smile clearly intended to convey the idea of humbleness mingled with condescension. She had often, she explained, as they sat down to their meal, even while her husband was living, tutored foreigners who wanted to perfect either their German or their Italian.

Amantha gave a merry little laugh. "I'm afraid, signora Tagliacci, that this isn't a question of perfecting. I can say buon giorno and that is about all."

Signora Tagliacci made a little tutting sound. "You will make very

36

quick progress. Anything can be mastered quickly if the will to learn exists." She was already the teacher. "When would you like me to come?"

"Why," said Amantha, who had given no thought to the matter, "how about right after lunch, for a start? Or do you usually take an afternoon nap?"

The German shook her head. "That is a custom I have never adopted. I should be delighted to begin this afternoon. I am looking forward to teaching you. Someone so young, so vigorous. Oh, no, signore, no more! I shall be tipsy." She stopped Godwin from filling her glass by holding her hand over it. Politely he withdrew the bottle of wine.

But Amantha had caught her glance as it rested for a moment on Godwin and then shifted to herself. She is wondering how much difference there is in our ages, she thought. Aloud she said, "I have an Italian dictionary but no grammar or reading book."

"We do not need anything for a first lesson. But I can recommend some books for you to get."

"Tell me what they are," Godwin said. "I am going into the town this afternoon and I can buy them."

Signora Tagliacci laid aside her dessert spoon in order to open her handbag and search for a pencil. Godwin signaled to the footman and the man presently laid a pad and pencil on the table by her.

Presently, when they had had coffee on the loggia, Godwin rose and bending over to kiss Amantha, said, "I'll be back in time for dinner. Arriverderci, signora. The carriage will be here to take you home when you are ready."

The German woman fluttered gratefully about him as he bowed and left them. "How charming he is and how fortunate you are, signora Shenstone!" she exclaimed, still gazing admiringly at Godwin's departing back. "American men make very indulgent husbands, I have noticed."

"Do they?" said Amantha. "I'm afraid that I'm not well enough informed about Europeans to be able to judge."

"Indeed they do. They do not seem to expect so much of their wives."

"In what way?" Amantha's question was asked idly.

"Oh, in every way! You are perhaps too young to realize this. For you are very young, aren't you, my dear — a pampered young bride." Amantha looked at her with curiosity. Noticing the shrewd eyes, she maintained as impassive a manner as she could. She herself was, she realized, as much an oddity to the German woman as signora Tagliacci was to her.

Signora Tagliacci turned to the subject of Italian grammar. Amantha was at once aware of a sharp difference between her method of teaching and what she had been used to in the girls' school she had attended. Obviously signora Tagliacci was going to demand a much greater degree of attention and industry.

Presently signora Tagliacci broke off the lesson. It was not a good thing, she said, to prolong this first session to the point of fatigue. Amantha agreed and suggested that they stroll down the garden path to the wall that protected it from the sea. There was an unobstructed view of the water and of the curving wall, green with mold and parasitic plants and overtopped by drooping shrubs and tree branches. Amantha leaned her elbows on the rough stone coping. The dampness made the spot cool in the afternoon warmth. Behind them an old, semi-circular fountain, in which stood a much crumbled figure of a cherub in the midst of ferns and water lilies, splashed softly.

Signora Tagliacci, standing beside her, remarked, gesturing to where the wall curved further out around a little promontory, "That is the Villa Margherita. Do you know the Count and Countess de Brieux, signora?"

"I met the countess in Paris. My husband knows them well and she helped me to get some new dresses made. I have never met the count. He was not in Paris."

"Oh, no, he would not have been. He never leaves this spot. Travel is too fatiguing for him. Occasionally the countess goes to Paris. I expect she gets a little bored with this perpetual villeggiatura." She added, smiling, "There is a new word for you. It means exile in the country."

Amantha automatically smiled back but made no reply.

Signora Tagliacci went on, "Then you must pay a call on Mme. de Brieux. I'm sure you will enjoy each other's company, especially whenever your husband is away."

Amantha glanced at her but still did not respond. So signora Tagliacci took it for granted that Godwin would not always be at the Villa Delfina.

When signora Tagliacci had gone, riding away in the carriage which Godwin had sent back for her, Amantha sat on the loggia in thought. How long and how well did Godwin know the de Brieux? Especially how well did he know Leonie? Am I jealous? Amantha asked herself. Am I looking for something because I am jealous? All at once she felt very far away from her life in Baltimore. She was embarked on an unknown sea with no idea what her destination might be. Only Godwin could give her any clue and for the moment, at least, he appeared to her to be such a stranger that she could not contemplate asking him so intimate a question.

They ate dinner that evening by the quiet glow of lamps with low-turned wicks which the servants set about the room. Godwin had kissed her perfunctorily when he arrived back late in the afternoon and had gone at once to the room he used as an office or study. They had met again only after they were both dressed for dinner. Now they sat opposite each other at the narrow table with the ornately carved legs and heavy lace cloth.

"Well," said Godwin, "how did the Italian lesson go? I brought the books signora Tagliacci recommended."

"I enjoyed it. She can tell me a lot about the customs here, as well as the language. Things I want to know."

Godwin laughed briefly. "Life in Baltimore isn't quite adequate as a guide for Italy, is it?"

"Naturally not." Amantha felt annoyed at his tone. He had never before implied any criticism of her background.

He seemed aware of something jarring, because he replied immediately, half-apologetically, "The Italians — and the French, for that matter — are not accustomed to a simple approach. It is the result of hundreds of years of sophistication. They don't understand if you are too forthright. They approach things indirectly. And they tend to look for hidden meanings."

"They tend to be superstitious, too," said Amantha bluntly. "I thought Southerners were superstitious enough, but they can't hold a candle to these Italians. Do they really live in such fear of devils as they seem to?"

Godwin, aware that a real irritation underlay the brusqueness of her tone, said soothingly, "I believe they do have a very lively horror of the supernatural. What happened today?"

"Oh, when I was dressing I knocked a bottle off my boudoir table and my maid had a conniption. She made me understand that it was an ill omen, since it happened, according to her, without explanation."

"Well, you'll have to get used to this. But you don't have to adopt their superstitions."

"I'm not likely to," she said shortly.

Godwin looked at her down the length of the table. "I don't expect you will. You're a pretty levelheaded girl."

They exchanged a long look. It was the first time —this seemed a day for first times, the thought passed quickly through her mind — that they had been face to face like this, more as equals and she not simply the untutored recipient of Godwin's wisdom. He smiled as he lowered his eyes, as if he was genuinely pleased by her self-assertion.

After a pause Amantha said, "Signora Tagliacci pointed out to me the Villa Margherita from the bottom of our garden."

Godwin gave her a quick glance, "We are invited there to dinner tomorrow night. I was about to tell you this. De Brieux is feeling better than usual."

"What is the matter with the count?"

40

Godwin gave a slight shrug. "It is hard to say. He seems to suffer from a number of things, including asthma. He has been ill for years."

"Is he an old man?"

"Old? He is a number of years older than Leonie, but I do not know his age."

"You have known them — you have known her — for a long time, haven't you?"

He raised his eyes to look at her directly and steadily. "Yes," he said emphatically.

The following evening, when they arrived at the Villa Margherita, the drive and the entrance were lit by lanterns hung on posts and on tree branches. There was no wind and in the still air the garden sounds mingled with the soft splashing of water that poured from the mouth of a stone gorgon's head set in the wall. The Villa Margherita was perched on a higher piece of ground than the Villa Delfina and it was a larger house but so hidden in trees and shrubbery that it was invisible except from the drive and garden or from the sea. This fact lent to it an air of seclusion that apparently suited the invalid who dwelt there.

Godwin stepped down energetically from the carriage and turned to give her his hand. As she took it and jumped down with a tomboyish quickness that belied the satin evening gown she wore, Amantha saw the countess standing at the top of the stone steps, framed in the lighted doorway. They were the only guests, Godwin had told her. She supposed it was for that reason that Leonie had come to greet them instead of awaiting their arrival in the drawing room. As they reached her she kissed Amantha lightly on each cheek and held out her hand for Godwin's. Amantha saw Leonie's eyes sweep her from head to foot, curious, she knew, to see which of her new Paris gowns she had chosen to wear.

Leonie said in French, "You look charming, my dear. I knew that shade of pale yellow would suit you very well."

She took Amantha's arm and walked with her into the spacious room. Her hand guided Amantha across to the gaunt man who sat in a high-

41

backed Italian chair near a fireplace, where a fire was burning to temper the evening chill.

"Philippe," she said, "this is Godwin's bride."

The count gazed at her out of dark, deep set eyes. She judged he would be a tall man if he were standing. His very dark hair showed no grey yet he seemed older than Godwin. He grasped her hand in his own bony, heavily veined one and said in French, in a deep voice, "You will indulge an invalid, madame, and excuse my failure to rise."

He gestured to a settee near his own chair and she sat down beside the countess. Godwin remained standing.

Leonie, sitting upright beside her and facing her, continued in her soft, high-pitched voice, "It will be the greatest pleasure to have you as our neighbors."

Amantha said, as innocently as she could, "I was very surprised when I learned that you lived here. Godwin thinks he mentioned this to me in Paris but I don't remember his doing so."

She purposely did not look at Godwin as she spoke, but at the countess instead. Leonie's gaze shifted away from her as she said, "We are so long established here that I expect he took it for granted that you would know."

There was no emphasis in her manner and then she immediately led the conversation elsewhere. Amantha recognized the skill that she had shown in Paris in avoiding embarrassment. Yet Leonie seemed nervous. Her fine-boned hands moved restlessly, scarcely quiet for a moment. Amantha, sitting beside her on the small settee, was aware of her own physical dominance. She and Leonie were almost the same height. She had first become aware of this at the dressmakers, when Leonie, suddenly impatient with her clumsiness, would jump up from her seat and come to adjust a fold of material or arrange the hang of a garment to achieve the ultimate chic that her own sense of elegance demanded. Now, sitting beside her, Amantha felt the contrast between them —between her own healthy, vigorous, well-rounded youthfulness and the countess's

42

frailer, more delicate body. She was sure that Leonie had never been a tomboy. She must always have been a young lady, demure, immaculate. The habit of a lifetime gave her now a perfection otherwise unobtainable, an aura of fragility, of elusiveness.

The countess turned her palely blond head toward Godwin.

"Your little bride speaks French very well now," she said softly. "She has lost her fear of the language."

Amantha, following her glance, looked at Godwin. His eyes were fixed on Leonie's face. In fact, he had not ceased to gaze at her since he had come into the room. He seemed now oblivious of his wife and his host. Amantha looked at Leonie. Was there the slightest shade of annoyance on the thin face, the least flush on the transparent skin, the smallest tightening of the finely chiseled lips? If so, the shadow passed at once and Leonie's face was as composed as ever. Only her hands betrayed her by continuing to move restlessly in her lap.

"I am learning Italian," Amantha announced.

"A most admirable endeavor." The count's voice came smoothly into the conversation. "The language of Dante."

"And who is your teacher?" Leonie asked eagerly, as if she wanted to escape from Godwin's fixed attention.

"Signora Tagliacci," Amantha answered. "I believe you know her. She said her husband was a pharmacist who attended your husband."

Leonie's eyes flashed briefly. "Of course! Poor man! He died a year or so ago. He was very obliging and would often come himself to bring Philippe medicine. She is a very energetic woman, not content to be idle, though I don't believe she needs to earn money."

Amantha read into her remark an implication that signora Tagliacci was somewhat nosey. "I think she will be a good teacher."

"Indeed, I think that is very likely. She is German and therefore undoubtedly thorough," said the count. "You must have a good ear for languages, madame."

"French was the only subject I ever really liked in school," Amantha replied, smiling at him.

His long face relaxed into a smile. "How young you are! How delightfully young! How fortunate your husband is!"

Amantha glanced at Godwin and saw that his attention was still fixed on the countess. Leonie suddenly seemed less of a stranger to her than Godwin. Leonie looked at her and answered her smile.

* * *

The moonlight was still brilliant as the carriage wheels crunched on the drive of the Villa Delfina when they arrived home. Godwin had been almost entirely silent since they had left the de Brieux and Amantha had made no attempt to rouse him to conversation. He helped her down from the carriage and followed her into the house.

"Shall we sit on the loggia?" she invited him.

"If you like," he said, and sent a servant to fetch glasses and a decanter.

From the loggia they could look beyond the garden out to the sea, bright in the subdued sparkle of the moonlight. Amantha strolled slowly by the waist-high wall, tucking her bare arms into the shawl she had wrapped around her shoulders. Godwin sat quietly at the small iron and glass table on which the glasses and decanter stood. His abstracted face was plainly visible in the radiance and she could see the glowing end of his small cigar brighten as he drew on it.

"The de Brieux have no children, have they?" she asked.

There was a moment's silence before Godwin answered, "No."

"Don't they want any?"

This time Godwin's reply was prompt. "De Brieux is not capable of fathering a child." His tone was brusque, as if he was annoyed.

"Oh! Was that always so?"

Godwin made an impatient movement. "Why are you so curious about them?" he demanded.

Amantha felt a stirring of perverse pleasure in watching his annoyance. "I just thought that Leonie probably would like to have a child."

He seemed suddenly angry. "It is the desire of most normal women."

"And in that sense I am perfectly normal," Amantha retorted, taking pleasure in the opportunity he had given her.

"You are very young. There is plenty of time for all that."

She spoke out. "Godwin, I don't understand you. Everybody thought the reason you were marrying me was because you wanted a family. But I don't think you like children."

His irritation was growing. "You are quite right, I don't."

"Does that mean that you don't intend for us to have any, ever?"

Again he made an impatient gesture. "This is childish. How do I know about 'ever'? At this time I don't intend that we should."

As if one of the goblets on the table had shattered, Amantha felt a sudden rage of rebellion sweep through her. It was the accumulation, she realized at once, of the thousands of small incidents that had happened since they were married, incidents that showed her how inconceivable it was to him that she should have any voice in a decision that affected them equally. A sense of real bitterness followed in the wake of rebellion. She had no weapon against him that would not demolish herself first.

Long after he was asleep beside her, she struggled with the feeling of helpless anger that almost choked her, until at last she fell asleep, after the moon had set.

Godwin was never idle. He spent the mornings in the room he used as an office or study, engaged in business correspondence. Couriers came from Paris several times a week and sometimes there were visitors, businessmen whom he invited to stay for lunch. He was often gone in the afternoon, giving no explanation of his absence. Sometimes he went to swim. At the foot of the garden was a bath house and a small floating dock. He never invited her to join him, and since she could not swim she did not volunteer. She had suggested once that he could teach her to

45

swim but with real irritation in his voice he had said shortly that it was too dangerous, the water against the sea wall being too deep. At some other time and place, he hinted, where conditions were more appropriate, he would do so.

Signora Tagliacci often arrived as he was leaving after lunch. Amantha was conscious of her bright, inquiring eyes, glancing from one to the other of them. It was natural, she supposed, that a woman like the pharmacist's widow, being alone, should have only the affairs of acquaintances to occupy her.

One afternoon the restlessness that increasingly affected her prompted her to suggest to the teacher an outing during the lesson. Godwin, whenever he went out, always sent the carriage back to the villa. Signora Tagliacci had explained to her that there was a famous church and abbey in the nearby hills. But no one she exclaimed, when Amantha suggested that they go there now and see it, ever went out in the heat of the day.

Amantha shrugged. "I am tired of sitting still and it is not so very warm today. Don't you want to go?"

Signora Tagliacci admitted that she would enjoy the expedition and the novelty of it gave her a pleasurable sense of adventure. American women, after all, were not the same, she remarked, as French or Italian.

They visited the abbey, where they were shown a famous miraculous picture that attracted many pilgrims. Returning down a winding narrow road they approached the gate of the Villa Margherita. Signora Tagliacci called attention to the tall iron grillwork that surrounded its garden. Amantha nodded.

"I have been there," she said, and on a sudden impulse added, "Do you suppose the countess will be at home?"

Signora Tagliacci was at once diffident. "I do not know. Perhaps she does not care for unannounced visitors.

"Of course, thought Amantha, always the proprieties. She brushed aside her momentary hesitation and told the coachman to stop and ring the large bell that hung by the gate. The late afternoon had grown still with a drowsy heat. There were bees amid the flowering shrubs. Neither Amantha nor signora Tagliacci spoke until a woman came to open the gate. She greeted them with a wave of her hand as the carriage passed up the drive. The servant at the steps of the villa looked at them with indolent curiosity and then with greater interest as he recognized the carriage. The countess, he said, was at home. He would inform her that they were there.

Leonie came down the curving iron-railed stair behind the footman, her eyes wider than usual, as if she feared some alarming announcement. Amantha said at once, and in English, "I hope you don't mind. Signora Tagliacci and I have been to see the abbey and I thought we would stop for a visit on our way home."

"Of course! Of course!" the countess exclaimed, a look of relief showing briefly on her face. "Come out on the loggia."

It was larger than the loggia of the Villa Delfina and along the garden edge were antique statues with broken noses and blackened legs, fragments from the villa of some ancient Roman, thought Amantha, that had stood on this spot centuries ago. The house cast a deep shadow and in its shelter they sat down on a cluster of chairs placed so that they had a glimpse of the sea over a mass of vegetation. A piece of petit point had been cast down in the seat of one chair, Amantha noticed; so this must be a spot that Leonie enjoyed. A servant brought wine and some little cakes over which signora Tagliacci exclaimed.

The countess said, "You have not seen the abbey before? The painting of the madonna is one of our local curiosities. Godwin should take you there when there is a pilgrimage."

Amantha said, "Signora Tagliacci was telling me about it. I don't think Godwin likes that sort of thing."

"And do you?" There was a laughing friendliness in Leonie's grey eyes.

"Well, really, I don't think I do. But it is all strange to me. This afternoon I was bored with just sitting at home."

Leonie gazed at her for a moment and then looked away. "You find it difficult to occupy yourself when your husband is not with you."

Amantha laughed. "I'm not really that dependent on Godwin. I just need more activity."

The countess's eyes traveled briefly to signora Tagliacci and back to her. Amantha, alerted, in her turn glanced at the Italian teacher. Signora Tagliacci's bright, inquisitive eyes moved quickly back and forth between them.

They all talked then in a desultory way, sipping the wine and nibbling at the cakes. Amantha felt her good humor revived in the warmth of Leonie's manner. But again she noticed the restlessness of her hands and the nervous movements of her body, as if she found it impossible to remain still. When they rose to leave she felt again the contrast between her own youthful robustness and the countess's fragility. Together she and Leonie walked the length of the loggia, signora Tagliacci trailing behind them, and stood for a moment's talk near an open gate in the wall.

The countess gestured down the path that led away into the luxuriant garden. There was a greenhouse, she said, with orchids down there. Some other time Amantha must see them —

Her sentence breaking off in the air caused Amantha to turn and look down the path. A man was approaching wearing a bathing suit, his head down, as if he was yet unaware of their presence. Godwin. Her surprise was so complete that for a moment all she could think was that it was Godwin who was walking towards them.

"Leonie —." He started to speak and then seemed to realize that she was not alone.

The countess gave a high, nervous laugh, with no element of mirth in it. Godwin paused and then walked resolutely toward them.

"So this is where you ran away to," he said to Amantha, with bantering reproach.

A wave of resentment swept over Amantha. It was very quick thinking but she was certain he had not known until this moment that she was not at the Villa Delfina and his remark was made for the purpose of putting off any question she might ask.

"I did not run away at all," she said. "Signora Tagliacci and I went to look at the abbey and since we were passing by here on the way home we stopped for a visit."

A little smile was on his face, as if to say that her explanation was not important. He declined the countess's nervous offer of wine and said to Amantha, "You can give me a lift home, as soon as I have changed my clothes." He crossed the loggia and went into the house.

Signora Tagliacci filled the long silence while they awaited him with sprightly chatter about the legends that were told in the neighborhood. The countess sat down on the low stone wall, her restless fingers feeling its roughness. Amantha stood still, occasionally twirling the parasol she held over her shoulder. In a few minutes Godwin returned, dressed in his usual clothes. Amantha noticed that he did not carry his bathing suit nor the towel. His leave taking of the countess was brief.

The ride back was chiefly in silence. Amantha was aware of signora Tagliacci's eyes, brightly inquisitive, darting from one to the other of them. It was with relief, when they arrived at the steps of the Villa Delfina that she sent the teacher on to her own home in the carriage.

Standing on the top step Amantha asked "Do you often go to visit Leonie in the afternoon?" she asked.

Godwin did not answer immediately. Then he said in a voice that sounded as if he had taken a moment to control his irritation, "I often stop by there for consultation with de Brieux. I have told you that I have undertaken some business affairs for him. Leonie is often lonely. Naturally I sometimes stay to visit with her."

Amantha walked into the house. Where would he go otherwise, where was there for him to go, if he did not go to the Villa Margherita? She remembered vividly the sense of intimacy she had noted at seeing that he kept his bathing clothes at the Villa Margherita and that he had obviously a room set aside there for his use. He had acted, in fact, as if he was as

49

much at home there as in his own house.

In the house Amantha turned to face him. "I see now why you did not want me to go swimming with you."

He made a deprecating gesture. "If you want to quarrel, don't do it in front of the servants."

"The servants," she said sharply, "do not speak English."

His glance was angry. "They do not have to understand our words in order to know that we are having a disagreement."

She turned away from him half in disgust, half in dismay. She knew there was no remorse in his response to her indignation. If he had told her in so many words, he could not have made it plainer that he did not care what she thought of the afternoon's encounter, that he was not concerned about any hurt he might have inflicted. He paid no further attention to her as she left the room and went up the stairs. She paused at the landing to glance back. He had gone to the other end of the room and the footman was serving him a glass of brandy.

In her dressing room she dropped her jacket onto a chair and walked to a window. The sea sparkled in the late afternoon sun. The first shadows of the evening reached out across the water from the steeply rising garden. It was an hour of the day she particularly enjoyed. It had always seemed an especially romantic moment, when she would bathe and dress carefully for the evening, anticipating the hour or so with Godwin on the loggia, lingering over their aperitifs before dinner. Now —

A slight sound caused her to turn around. Her maid stood there ready to help her remove her afternoon clothes. Yes, pampered was the word for it. She was pampered with every material comfort, regardless of how empty life might be otherwise. And suddenly she was surprised by the strength of the feeling of revulsion that enveloped her. Life stretched before her, unknown, unforeseeable — and empty. She turned to let the maid undo her dress.

* * *

Signora Tagliacci corrected her. "No, no, signora. The subjunctive is used in such a phrase. Always when there is uncertainty to be indicated, you must use the subjunctive." She gave a deprecating little laugh. "Americans do not use the subjunctive mood very often, do they? At least, it has been my experience that they always find this difficult in learning another language."

"We're not taught even English with the same discipline," said Amantha calmly.

Something in her manner, she noticed, during these last few lessons seemed to intimidate signora Tagliacci. It was a if the teacher was aware that she was no longer dealing with an untried girl but instead with a woman who knew her own mind. Amantha, watching her, noted the increased obsequiousness with which signora Tagliacci addressed her. It was the German woman's way, Amantha recognized, of covering her curiosity, of guarding against Amantha's own growing sophistication. How much, Amantha wondered, did the teacher suspect about what lay between Godwin and the countess.

Sometimes, with the greatest delicacy, signora Tagliacci probed for information. One afternoon she arrived a few minutes late for the lesson. Amantha, lolling on a chaise lounge on the loggia in the drowsy warmth, felt no annoyance, but the teacher came in with effusive apologies. She had, she said, met Mme. la Comtesse coming out of the church in the side street near the center of town. She seldom saw her now. Before this, she had seen her nearly every day at the early mass.

"She is extremely devout — very generous to charity and very strict in observing holy days. Today is a saint's day and I certainly expected to see her at mass this morning. But, no, she was not there. So I was much surprised to meet her, when I was on my way here, coming out of the church. She must have gone there to pray. Or perhaps she had something

51

important to say to the priest."

"In any case," Amantha cut in, "this is not something we should talk about."

She spoke with more sharpness than she intended, but the woman's obvious intent to prompt some comment from her about Leonie had aroused a quick, ungovernable annoyance. Partly it was annoyance directed against herself. It would be easy to fall into the habit of gossiping with the teacher and she reminded herself that this was dangerous.

Signora Tagliacci was quick to notice her reaction. She went on with some more general remarks, as if she sought to explain her interest in the countess. It was well-known, she said, that the countess regretted her husband's inability to give her children. It was God's will, but it seemed such a pity when there were others who did not want the children they had and even made efforts to prevent their birth. "That is a grave sin for a Catholic," she added.

"Yes, I know that," said Amantha shortly, remembering Godwin's precautions. Her tone of voice silenced the teacher, who nevertheless was obviously intrigued by her manner. Her quick eyes took in the expression on Amantha's face, the decisiveness of her sudden, impatient gestures.

This covert watchfulness grew when Godwin came into the room. Amantha did not show the surprise she felt at his appearance, much earlier than usual. She more sensed than saw the brief annoyance in his manner when he discovered signora Tagliacci to be with her. Evidently something more important than usual had caused him to forget that this was the hour of the daily lesson.

"Ah, signore Shenstone!" signora Tagliacci exclaimed. She always responded with effusion to any encounter with him.

Godwin bowed before he sat down in a chair near them and lighted one of his small cigars. Signora Tagliacci made a point of savoring its aroma. He replied to her politely, but Amantha saw his barely concealed impatience. Obviously he wanted the lesson brought to an end. She said to the teacher, "Signora, I don't seem able to understand the use of the subjunctive in Italian this afternoon. Do you suppose we could postpone the lesson until tomorrow?"

"I am so sorry! Have I fatigued you? Perhaps the warmth of the day has made your head ache?"

Always, Amantha thought ironically, signora Tagliacci attributed any malaise to the warmth of the day. "It is not that. As I have told you, my head never aches."

"How fortunate you are! It must be your American health."

Amantha walked to the hall with her, concealing under a cloak of casual remarks the determination to see her off the premises as promptly as possible. When she returned to the drawing room Godwin had risen from his chair and was strolling out to the loggia. She followed him. He turned at the sound of her step.

"She is always around spying," he complained.

"Scarcely spying," Amantha retorted. "She is simply curious."

He eyed her speculatively while he puffed once or twice on his cigar. Then he said, "De Brieux insists that we go to dinner with them again, this evening."

Amantha waited without speaking.

Godwin went on. "Since he never leaves his own house, they cannot accept an invitation from us, as would be usual. When he feels able he likes to have his friends there — for Leonie's sake, especially."

Still Amantha made no comment, and he went on. "I have been spending quite a little time with him lately. As you know, I have undertaken a business venture for him. Most of the time he pays little attention to business. But he is pretty shrewd. He inherited a fortune and his wife brought him an excellent dowry. He asked me today whether it was true, as he had heard, that I married you without a dowry. He could not believe it when I said I had."

Amantha was silent for a moment and then suddenly asked," Why did you marry me, Godwin?"

Her question startled him. He gave her a swift, brief glance, "That's a strange question for you to ask me," he rebuked her. He looked away from her.

She stared at his averted face. "It might have been strange a little while ago, before we came here. It is not strange now. You know it is not."

He turned away from her and leaned his elbows on the parapet so that his back was towards her. He did not speak.

Amantha plunged on. "Leonie is your mistress, isn't she?"

He straightened with a jerk and glanced around. "What if I said that she has been?"

"And will be again, if she is not now," Amantha pursued.

He did not answer. A thoughtful expression had come over his face, as if he weighed a course of action that only in part concerned her. Finally he asked, "Have you any real complaint about how I have treated you?" The utter reasonableness of his tone struck her so forcibly that she was silent.

She found, in spite of the long thoughts she had had on the subject during the preceding days, that she was not prepared for his cool response to her accusation. He ignored her silence and said, "We're due at the Villa Margherita at eight o'clock."

Abruptly he left the loggia and disappeared into the house. She stayed where she was for a long time, until the deepening shadows warned her that the evening drew on. At first her consternation overpowered her, so that her thoughts lay jumbled in her mind, incoherent, repetitive, then gradually her mind cleared. Godwin had changed since they had arrived in Rapallo, and the change had been caused by the proximity of Leonie. She was certain that they had been lovers. Perhaps —she had heard of such things — he had broken with her before he had come to Baltimore and had thought himself free to marry but the return to Rapallo had once more established the old attachment. In that case, he probably regretted his marriage, resented her. Was that the case?

54

Slowly Amantha turned the question over in her mind. She was surprised to find that some instinct, deep within her, refused to accept this explanation. He did not in fact seem to regret his marriage nor to resent her. Her thoughts brought her back to the same question she had asked herself many times: why had he married her?

At last in despair she gave up the riddle and went to her room and called her maid to help her dress.

This time when they arrived at the Villa Margherita, the countess was not on hand to greet them. Instead the count awaited them in the drawing room.

"Ah, my friends," he said, "I am afraid that Leonie is much indisposed. Indisposition overtook her suddenly this afternoon. Perhaps she will be able to join us later."

Amantha glanced at Godwin. His eyes widened as de Brieux spoke. He murmured sympathetic phrases. He is surprised, thought Amantha. He must have seen her this afternoon.

She brought her attention back to the count. As if he felt the need to make up for his wife's absence, he was more cheerful, more sprightly in his manner. He asked her questions: How was she enjoying her stay; was she now adept in Italian; was her teacher competent? Amantha parried his questions as best she could. Godwin stood silent and gave her no help. But presently she was rescued by the countess, who entered the room still fastening the clasp of a bracelet.

"My dear Leonie," said her husband, examining her with concern, "Are you sure you should not have remained in bed?"

Amantha, as she came toward her to greet her with a kiss on each cheek, noted that she was pale and that her lips were cold. Leonie said, with nervous impatience, "No, I could not stay there. Amanthe, how are you?"

"I'm fine," said Amantha. "I am sorry that you are not feeling well."

"It is nothing," said Leonie. "It will pass." Amantha saw that she shivered a little. Only then did she greet Godwin, obviously forcing herself to assume a calmer manner.

Two more couples were announced, arriving almost simultaneously — French people, old friends of the de Brieux. The men were contemporaries of the count, one a melancholy man with a rusty voice and the other vigorous and smiling, whose black eyes sparkled as they lit on Amantha. He was the Chevalier de Montbrun, she was informed, and he immediately attached himself to her. She soon found he was an accomplished flatterer with a zest for the game of flirtation. It was obvious that he must always thus choose out the youngest and prettiest woman present in order to practice his skill at charming. She found herself responding, finding quick remarks with which to parry his sallies with an ease that surprised herself. He even made her laugh, a merry, wholehearted laugh that drew the attention of the rest of the party. The count looked across at her with the most lively expression she had yet seen on his face. The Chevalier's wife gave a small, uncomprehending laugh. The melancholy man and his serious wife turned their gaze on her as if for some explanation of this unaccustomed levity.

Only Godwin and the countess seemed unaware. They stood a little apart, Godwin's somber eyes fixed on her face, the countess with a hand on the back of a chair, gripping it with white-knuckled intensity.

The same nervous intensity possessed her throughout the dinner. Her voice was pitched a little higher than usual and she talked volubly, often, Amantha saw, without really taking thought of what she said or what was said to her. Amantha, seated next to the count, could observe her clearly at the other end of the long table and also Godwin, who sat at Leonie's left. In the midst of the dinner table banter, which the Chevalier kept up assiduously, Amantha was suddenly aware that their fate rested in her hands. Godwin would be surprised at the idea.

She glanced again at the countess. As if in response, Leonie suddenly returned her gaze. Their eyes met only momentarily. There was a trace of wildness in Leonie's, a look that struck Amantha like a blow — yes, it was a look of despair. Silently and involuntarily Amantha responded to it, "Oh, oh no, you must not despair, whatever it is."

After that, Amantha purposely kept her attention away from that end of the table. Even when they returned to the drawing room she was careful not to observe Leonie. She was thankful now of the Chevalier's inexhaustible chatter. But he fell silent for a few moments and turning to him she saw that he also was observing Leonie. He said, "Leonie is fascinating, isn't she? You will not find anyone comparable to her in our society, even in Paris."

Amantha said, "Is it true that she is not often in Paris?"

The Chevalier replied, "The de Brieux are royalists, you know, monarchists. They go back very far in the history of France, and Leonie's family even further, to Charlemagne. That does not make them popular in the present political climate."

When Amantha did not respond he went back to his cheerful banter.

It was not until the count summoned a footman to bring him a glass of mineral water in order to take a dose of medicine that Amantha glanced around the room and noticed that Leonie and Godwin were nowhere to be seen. On a sudden impulse she said to the Chevalier, "Please excuse me for a moment," and before he could reply she got up and left the room.

She went out on to the loggia, stepping softly and staying back in the shadows near the house wall. She had guessed correctly. The countess sat rigidly forward on a chair close by. Godwin bent over her in an attitude of supplication and concern. They were partly screened by some tall plants in wooden tubs.

Leonie's voice, filled with suppressed sobs, said faintly in French, "But the time is getting so short! I have a horror of the passage of time. How the days fly by! What am I to do?"

Her voice shook with despair. Amantha waited anxiously for Godwin's response. In his voice was mingled an attempt to soothe with a note of desperation.

"I tell you, I will have it arranged in good time! You must not distress yourself like this. You are making yourself ill. You will call attention to yourself."

Against the radiance of the moonlit sky Amantha could see Leonie's hand raised in a peremptory gesture. "Yes, you can speak like that! But it is not you! It is not you! You must speak to her now! I see what has happened. You procrastinate. It is not as easy as you suppose — not so easy to let her know what it is that you expect of her. Oh, Godwin, if she should refuse?"

"She will not refuse." His tone was vehement, as if he was repelling the idea of any failure as much to convince himself as her. "Trust me to show her that she has no real choice. Don't torment yourself with these doubts."

The exasperation in his voice brought a soft moan from her. "Godwin, don't speak so harshly."

Against the luminous night outside the loggia Amantha saw him drop to one knee beside her and take her in his arms. The pale blond head shone in the moonlight against his shoulder.

"Leonie, my darling, my beloved! I will succeed in my plan and in good time. You will not suffer, nor will the child." His voice dropped so low that Amantha could no longer hear his words, but the note of passion, of a lover's longing, echoed in her ears. She had never heard such a tone in Godwin's voice, had never supposed that he could speak so.

A sudden slight sound must have reached his ear, for he stopped abruptly and his head was silhouetted in a listening pose against the faint light. Amantha, alert to her own danger, swiftly withdrew into the small room through which she had come. It was lighted by the lamps in the drawing room and she could hear the voices of the count and his guests. A feeling of unreality had taken possession of her, as if she had watched a play in which the principal actors referred to herself as another character. For she was in no doubt that the "she" of whom they spoke was herself.

She walked back into the brightly lighted drawing room. Now she found it hard to concentrate on the Chevalier's gallantries and he showed that he was disappointed in her lack of response. With a conscious effort she refrained from glancing in the direction of the loggia. The time, which had passed so swiftly before, now dragged dismally by. It was with relief that she presently saw Godwin come into the room. He did not approach her but at once fell into conversation with the Chevalier's wife. Within a few minutes a footman came in and gave the count a brief message. The count turned immediately to his guests. His wife, he said, was now prostrated by her headache and could not bid them good night.

The night, as they returned to the Villa Delfina, was still bathed in moonlight. The sea glimmered and the air was filled with the scent of jasmine and the sleepy sound of night birds. Godwin sitting beside her was silent. She glanced at him and could see by the light of the moon that his face was that of a man who rode alone. A strange feeling, compounded of subdued rage, bewilderment and a sense of forlornness, overpowered Amantha. She shut her teeth against the impulse to rail at him. Under the anger she felt a great determination not to let him know that she had overheard him and Leonie.   Her thoughts were still jumbled, affected by the emotions that laid siege to her heart.

The carriage arrived at the steps of the Villa Delfina. Godwin, with the automatic gesture of custom, took her hand to help her down. Her impulse was to snatch it away but she controlled herself. His warm palm holding hers made a brief bridge between them. He said abruptly, "I shall say good night to you now, Amantha. I am very restless this evening and I must work some of it off before going to bed." He did not wait for any response but turned away and walked down a path into the garden. She knew she would not see him again that night.

In her room her maid was waiting to help her prepare for bed. Her thoughts absorbed her, as she relived the evening, while she went through the motions until the maid helped her into her dressing gown and said good night. Then, at last alone, she sat down by the open window. The fragment of conversation she had overheard could have only one meaning: Leonie was pregnant. But what was it that Godwin must do? What was it that he was to tell her? What was it that they both expected of her? Whatever plan he had made involved her, required her consent. The idea seemed fantastic and yet she was certain of the meaning of their statements.

Her mind pursued these thoughts round and round throughout the night, until in the early morning she at last fell asleep. When she woke, alone in bed, she had a momentary sense of loss. She missed Godwin, missed the feeling of contentment that had become customary. She looked at the patch of wavering light on the ceiling reflected from the water and slowly recalled the evening before and her own endless inquiry into its meaning. When her maid came in she said that signore Shenstone was waiting for her in the loggia.

It was another of the brilliant sunlit mornings of the Villa Delfina. She dressed with special care in a white frock with a dark blue sash the color of her eyes, feeling the need of thus bolstering her self-confidence. There was something portentous in the maid's announcement that Godwin was waiting for her. Ordinarily he would have assumed that the maid would tell her that he expected her to join him for breakfast.

He was seated at the breakfast table, dressed in white trousers and a white shirt, with a red sash around his waist —a cummerbund, she believed the English called it. He wore no coat and his tanned skin gleamed in the shaded light. His head turned abruptly as he heard her step and he got up at once to hand her into a chair at the table, on which stood a coffee pot and cups and some fresh-baked bread. The footman came forward to pour the coffee and when he had finished, Godwin waved him away.

"Good morning, Amantha," he said then, sitting down again. "I hope you slept well."

She noticed that he did not seem as fresh and vigorous as he usually did in the morning. She nodded and waited for him to go on. Now that she confronted him in the daylight she was surprised by her own calmness.

He said, "There is something I must discuss with you, something that must remain forever just between the two of us."

She made no reply and he glanced at her sharply, as if suspicious of her passivity. He went on, "You know, of course, since last night that Leonie is not well."

"She looked quite ill."

He did not speak at once. Then he said, "She is pregnant."

She thought for a moment before she said, "But you have told me that the count cannot father a child."

"He cannot."

"Then the child is not his?"

"That is the case."

"So then —?"

He said slowly, "It is up to me to protect her and the child. She has refused to prevent its birth. That is against her religious principles. The count — no one in her family —must know of the child." When he stopped speaking she said nothing but waited, sipping the hot coffee and milk. He went on, "It is my intention to bring the child up as my own. Which means, of course, that you must be assumed to be its mother."

Slowly Amantha buttered a morsel of bread. She raised her eyes to answer his gaze. "Then it is your child."

He did not look at her as he nodded.

The moments went by while she tried to arrange her thoughts. After a while she said, "When you came to Baltimore, when you left her here in France, you knew she was pregnant. It was your intention even then to do something to shield her. Did you have a plan when you came to Baltimore? Or was it that after you met me you decided upon it. You married me for this purpose — to protect Leonie and the child."

Again he nodded. The turmoil of her own feelings was such that she got up from the table and walked to the low wall that enclosed the loggia.

He spoke to her back. "The thought occurred to me that the right wife would solve the dilemma. Then I met you. You seemed a sensible girl and one to whom I could offer compensations. And you seemed ready to accept me."

Hearing him outline the story in this dispassionate fashion sent a sudden shaft of pain through her. How far from his understanding, then, had the nature of her first feeling for him been! He had seen her simply as a girl emerging from the prolonged childhood of girls of her upbringing, ripe for a man's attentions, flattered and carried away by the intoxication of being singled out by a man who could have chosen any woman for his wife, by being for the first time in her life given the first place with anyone. And since she was a girl without means and with only a good family background and fresh, healthy good looks to offer, he had assumed that she would be willing and ready to obey when he commanded.

"I suppose," she replied, without turning around, "that you thought all this out in Baltimore — or at Godwin's Chance— before you asked me to marry you. You were taking a pretty big risk that I would fall in with your plan."

"Perhaps," he said, and she wondered whether he had not been right in measuring her acquiescence. Could she really have denied him anything, could she really have refused anything for his sake, when he courted her in Baltimore? He could have seduced her, if he had only wanted a passing pleasure, he could have enjoyed the youthful ardor she offered him so eagerly and then have left her to the good will of her relatives. But this was something Godwin would not have done. If he had seduced her, it was for a purpose and with the offer of a solid recompense, the status of his wife.

Her persistence in keeping her back turned to him apparently was trying his nerves, for he spoke again suddenly in an urgent voice. "Amantha, believe me. You will never regret your share in this. You're my wife. I guarantee that you will live a respected and luxurious life as the mother of my child. Even if I die, I will see to it that you are well taken care of. We have a bargain and it is one that will bring you every advantage. I mean it sincerely when I say that as my wife you will have everything you want. You will have nothing to complain of in me as a husband."

She listened to his words through the haze of her own emotions. It was a new thing, she knew, for him to have to plead. She felt a distaste for it, as if it diminished the Godwin she knew and she did not want him diminished. She turned around to face him. He still sat at the table, gazing at her, and she was surprised to see that he actually looked pale. She cast down her eyes and bit her lip. She could not hate him, even as he told her that she was not his chosen beloved but only a means to an end. Plainly, she could not be any more than that, because he belonged to Leonie. Through no act of her own she had been thrust into the closed circle of their love. Or, rather, Godwin had thrust her there, with no thought of her at all. Of course, he believed she must agree to what he proposed. He could not believe that she would refuse.

Though perhaps it was not quite that. He had made his plan in cold blood, choosing her logically and without second thought to play the essential role in his plan. But he had done so unaware that he himself could not be entirely untouched by the situation he created. Leonie had been right. She had seen his weakness. He had procrastinated, when it came to the pinch. He had hesitated, when the moment came for revelation, to admit to her the calculation in his own actions. Godwin was human. He wanted her approval.

Wisely Godwin had sat silent while she mused, awaiting her response.

"You call it a bargain," she said. "Perhaps it is. My Uncle Ralph always said that you never go back on your word."

The barb in her words bit into him and his eyes flashed.

'Nor will I." He rose from his seat and came over to stand by her. He seemed about to take her hand.

She lifted her hands away from him. "I'd just as soon you did not touch me now. I must get used to what you say." He drew back and she added, "You have arranged all this with Leonie."

"Of course," he said.

His vehement statement to Leonie came back to her: "She will not refuse." She looked up to see that his eyes were fixed on her, and she detected anxiety in them. She said slowly, "I must talk to Leonie about this."

He moved abruptly away from her and said angrily, "No! No! I won't have her upset! I forbid you to go and see her!"

Indignation overflowed in her and her eyes flashed. "You forbid me? I don't think so, Godwin."

He was panting from the anger and surprise that held him. He glared at her as if to conquer her rebellion by the sheer force of his will. She stared back at him for a few moments and then realized that she must give him a chance to back away. She walked a few steps across the room and said over her shoulder. "I shall go and call on Leonie tomorrow morning."

She heard no reply and when she turned around, saw that he had left the room.

* * *

She spent the night once more alone in concentrated thought such as she had never experienced before. It was not Godwin who claimed her attention after the first hour or so. She had taken his measure and had come to terms with what her own situation was.

But with Leonie she was in unknown territory. She found she was not jealous of Leonie. From her very first encounter with Leonie in the Paris restaurant, she realized now, there had been a bond forged between them. Was it because Leonie had known from the beginning what the situation was and had seen that they were both caught in a relationship they could not escape?

In the morning, after a breakfast alone, served by the maid in her room, she set out for the Villa Margherita.

The day was not yet too warm. And if she walked down through the garden, she could go through the door in the wall, hidden by vines, which she now knew Godwin used to reach Leonie. The path on the other side led up through shrubs and broken antique statues to the loggia. As she approached she heard a piano played by someone with professional skill and an absorption that projected an intense emotion into the music. There was an opening in the shrubs that enclosed the loggia and she passed through. The music came from a french window that gave onto the loggia. She walked toward it and stood still, listening.

The music came to an abrupt stop. She waited where she stood. A few moments later the tall window opened and Leonie appeared, staring at her with wide eyes. She was dressed in a white dress — purposely voluminous to hide her figure, Amantha now realized.

"Bonjour," said Amantha, deciding to speak French as being probably less trying to the other woman. "Do you mind a morning caller?"

"Oh, no! Not at all!" Leonie's response was breathless with nervousness. "Please come and sit."

She led the way to a sofa covered with gaily colored cushions which stood together with a couple of chairs by a glass-topped table. A light breeze came through the open window and ruffled the sheet music on the nearby piano. Leonie sat down on one of the chairs, turning to face Amantha, who had accepted the suggestion of her gesture toward the sofa.

"I'm sorry to have interrupted your playing," said Amantha." You play wonderfully."

"Don't you play?" Leonie asked, her hands nervously moving over the arms of her chair. There was a false intensity in her voice, as if the question were of real importance.

"Oh, I've had music lessons but I can't play very well," Amantha replied, exaggerating the calmness of her own manner in an attempt to relieve Leonie's nervousness. A small silence fell between them, which was broken when they both spoke.

"I thought I'd better —" Amantha began.

"You have come to see me —" said Leonie.

And they both stopped, looking at each other. It seemed to Amantha that she saw in the wide grey eyes apprehension, chagrin and a sadness. Her eyes moved over the thin face once more tracing its flawless bones, the sharp line of the jaw, the clear-cut eye sockets, the high-bridged nose. Leonie was indeed a beautiful woman with the fine-drawn ageless sort of beauty that would appeal to Godwin. The thin, fair skin with the palest blush over the cheekbones, the arched eyebrows, the narrow lips, the pale gold hair with a silvery down at the hairline over the small ears and the temples — it was a beauty that could not be imitated with cosmetics and which, though it might fade, would never disintegrate. Amantha remembered how it had overcome her the first time they had met, how it had left its imprint on her mind.

A little frown of annoyance at her close scrutiny brought the faintest crease to Leonie's forehead. She said, in a very low voice, "Godwin has told me that you know of my condition."

Amantha nodded as casually as she could. She felt now, alone with Leonie, no real embarrassment. "Yes, he has and he has told me what he proposes to do — what part he expects me to play."

She saw Leonie close her eyes for a moment, as if shrinking from this plain statement of the situation. When Leonie did not speak, she said, "It is a dangerous plan. I do not know much about such things, but I think it will be very risky for all of us, in case anybody finds out about it."

Leonie broke in eagerly. "But he says he can arrange everything! No one needs to know, except the three of us."

"Godwin thinks he can do anything he wants to. He has the means and the determination. But I think he knows that something can go wrong. He won't admit this but he does know it."

Leonie's head dropped and she said in a low voice, "It all depends on you, Amanthe."

66

"Not only on me. Also on you." Amantha paused and then asked, "What about your husband?"

Leonie's head jerked up. "Oh, he must never know! It would kill him!"

"Then let's hope he never learns about it." Impatiently Amantha took off the wide-brimmed straw hat she was wearing and tossed it aside. She saw that Leonie was looking at her in fearfulness. She answered the unspoken question in Leonie's eyes. "Yes, I've come to tell you that I am going to do what Godwin wants me to. I have decided that I will do it because of you and because the child will be yours. I am not doing it for Godwin."

Leonie sank back in her chair. There were tears in her eyes. "Amanthe, do not be bitter against Godwin, I beg you."

Amantha said stiffly, "I don't think I shall ever be able to forgive him. It would not be the truth if I said I did. He has destroyed what I felt for him when he married me. He does not even realize what that was — my whole heart and soul — and that he has destroyed it. But I will always remember that there was a time when I thought him perfect. I was self-deceived; he would point that out to me, you know. But there was once a Godwin that I thought existed and who would never have deceived me."

Leonie stopped her with a cry. "Amanthe, I cannot endure this! I knew nothing of you till he brought you to me. He told me nothing of what he planned to do before he left Paris."

"I know that, without your telling me. I could never believe that you would have had a part in such a deception."

Leonie dropped her face in her hands. "Oh, mon dieu!"

Amantha went on. "I must tell you what I feel, Leonie. There can't be things held back between us. I do not want to quarrel with Godwin. That would be no use to me, to you, to your child. We'll go ahead with his plan. And please don't make yourself more unhappy than you already are."

Leonie raised her head and Amantha heard her say, under her breath, "It is unbelievable — and so young."

Amantha answered, "I am not as young as I was a little while ago."

Leonie cried, "Oh, Amanthe!" But was not able to continue.

Amantha went on, seeking relief in practicality, "Have you accepted the arrangements Godwin says he has made? He intends to give me your child, you know."

Leonie gave a sigh of resignation. "I have no choice," she said sadly. "He is taking a great risk to protect me and I cannot complain of the means he has chosen. But, Amanthe, it is a terrible thing that he has done to you. And to give you the responsibility for a child under these circumstances! Are you fond of children? Do you want any of your own?"

Amantha considered the question. Was she? Did she? "I don't know," she said candidly. "I do know that Godwin does not want me to have any now. I understand why, since he has told me about you. Really it does not seem important to me at present. Perhaps sometime in the future I shall want children." She found it difficult to see herself taking care of a baby. Her closest acquaintance with babies was seeing her young cousins with theirs. Perhaps the neutrality of her feelings would be overcome by the actual presence of the baby.

She raised her eyes to meet Leonie's gaze. "I shall take good care of yours," she said simply. "I'm sure that Godwin will provide everything that is necessary, and I'll see that things are done the way they should be."

Her assurances seemed a little cold even to herself and she felt uncomfortable at the way Leonie turned her gaze quickly away. Leonie's voice was only a murmur when she responded, "The child has no reality yet for me. But I feel so guilty that I have been the cause of bringing a child into the world under such circumstances. It adds to the weight of my sins."

Of course, thought Amantha. Signora Tagliacci had said that the countess was extremely devout. Obviously the reason she had not been

68

going to mass as usual was because her sense of sinning and of the impossibility of confessing what she had done and intended to do. The child now was to her the evidence of sin. However strong her maternal feeling might be — and Amantha could not tell whether Leonie did in fact have any maternal feeling — she would not be able to forget that.

Unable to think of anything to say that might console Leonie, Amantha asked, "But what are you going to do until the baby comes?"

Leonie dabbed at her lips with her handkerchief. "I am going to stay with Tante Melisande. Really she is my great aunt, my father's aunt. She lives in the Auvergne, in a region that is rather remote from modern life. I will see no one there who will be concerned with my condition."

"Won't your aunt notice?"

"No. She is very old, bedridden, and almost blind. In fact, everyone has been expecting her to die for a long time now. She simply lives on. Philippe says it is that she is so disagreeable that even the devil does not want her. He is sadly irreverent." She gave Amantha a wan smile. "And the people in her house won't say anything. They are old servants almost as eccentric as herself. If they notice, they will not be concerned. After all, I am a married woman." She bit her lip as she finished.

"Philippe does not mind your going to stay with her for so long?"

"He does not know how long it will be. I have told him that Tante Melisande is indeed dying. It is not really an untruth," she added hurriedly as if in defense against an unspoken accusation. "She may be dying — she must eventually. I am the only one of her relatives whom she has allowed to come near her for many years. Philippe cannot stand her. He has vowed that he will have nothing more to do with her."

"But he lets you go and stay with her."

"He would not prevent it. That would be unfilial. He would not blame me if I did not go, but he will not stop me, since I feel it is my duty."

"I see. You are going away soon?"

"I must." The same note of distress was in Leonie's voice that Amantha had overheard in the conversation with Godwin. "I cannot hide myself much longer. I live in fear of my own maid. Even Philippe may notice something soon though he seems so abstracted."

Amantha's glance traveled over Leonie's body. Seated as she was, hunched over in the chair, it would be difficult to say that there was anything noticeable in her figure. But she was a slender woman, almost thin, and a moment's forgetfulness might reveal the swelling of her abdomen. No wonder she was so nervous, thought Amantha, watching the fragile white hands moving incessantly over the chair arms.

Amantha said impulsively, "You must try not to be upset."

"Dear Amanthe!" Leonie exclaimed, reaching out to place her hand on Amantha's. "To be so young and to be the victim of another's sins!"

Amantha drew back abruptly. "I'm nobody's victim," she objected, with sudden anger. "Not yours, not Godwin's. You are your own victim."

As she spoke them she regretted the untempered flatness of her words. Leonie shrank back as if she had been slapped. "Do not reject me, Amanthe," she pleaded.

Amantha sprang up and knelt by her, putting her hands over Leonie's, clasped tightly together. She said, "Leonie, I could never reject you." She hesitated, struggling to say the words that filled her heart. "I love you, Leonie. Last night, when I tried to understand all this, I knew that I love you. I love you as I have never loved anyone else, even Godwin.

She stopped and looked up into Leonie's eyes, wide with astonishment. She felt the pulse beating in Leonie's hands under her own.

Leonie said, her breath choked, "Amanthe, mon coeur —"and hid her face in Amantha's shoulder.

* * *

In the late afternoon, at the time Godwin usually returned, Amantha waited for him in the big room that opened out onto the loggia. The decanters and glasses and dishes of hors d'oeuvres were laid out on the big marble table near the french doors, as they were every evening. She heard the sound of the carriage on the gravel drive and then Godwin's voice as he spoke to the coachman and the footman who greeted him.

She watched as he came into the room, noticing the unconscious wariness of his steps. Godwin's manner was always controlled; he prided himself on the calmness with which he responded to any crisis. But this evening her newly enlightened eye saw the apprehension that underlay his careful casualness.

He came across the room to where she stood and she turned to offer her lips to him as she always did, noting with a twinge of wry feeling the flash of surprise in his eyes. He responded at once, taking her in his arms.

Releasing her, he took the glass the footman offered him and then dismissed the man. Then he asked, "You have seen Leonie?"

"Yes."

He waited for her to go on and when she did not, he asked," Did you — ?"

"I expect you have heard what she has to say already."

He looked at her sharply. "I did not stop at the Villa Margherita." When she did not comment, he went on, "I have to be careful about my visits — because of de Brieux. I have to have a reason for seeing him. Did you talk to her about our plan?"

Our plan? thought Amantha. She said, "Yes, I told Leonie that I will do what you want me to do, I will take her baby, that she need not worry any more."

She did not look at him but knew that he was eyeing her in apprehension, but relieved. He said, "Is she — is she pleased?"

Amantha returned his look coolly. "She is relieved, naturally. She can't be pleased by any of this, can she?"

He did not answer. Amantha plucked a small paté from the tray and sat down on a nearby chair to eat it. Between bites, she asked, "Godwin, how are you going to manage about hiding the baby's birth? Leonie did not tell me. She only said that she was going soon to visit an old aunt."

She saw Godwin relax at the practical tone of her voice. He took a small sandwich from the tray. "That is what she will do while she is waiting. At the end of her term she will go to a clinic in Geneva, which she will enter as my wife. When the child is delivered you will come with me to fetch it. When Leonie leaves the clinic she will return to Philippe and nobody need know anything about it."

Amantha mulled over what he said. Glancing at him, she realized that in his absorption with the details of his carefully arranged plan, he took no thought of what her reaction might be. After a moment she said, "Godwin, I don't know anything about such things, but it seems to me that what you are doing must be dangerous."

He was quick to reply. "Of course it is outside the law. But money is a great help in cases like this. The main requirement is to keep the matter secret. I could lose my reputation, even be subject to prosecution. But I must protect her. There is no other way out."

Amantha thought for a moment. "There's something else. When is the baby due?"

"Five months from now. We can't wait much longer because Leonie thinks she will not be able to conceal her condition."

"Godwin, we've been married two and a half months. If the baby is born in five months' time — "

He looked at her in surprise. Obviously she had raised a point he had not considered. He said slowly, "We don't have to announce the baby's birth to your relatives till the time is right. I shall postpone our going to Baltimore on the basis of your being pregnant and my not wanting you to travel. We shall stay in Paris. We must hope that the people we see do not notice. We must take a chance on that. I don't believe this will make much difference to your aunt, will it? She will suppose you're just absorbed in your new life."

Amantha did not answer. It was true. She felt very distant from the circle of aunts and uncles and cousins, as if a great deal more time than two and a half months had passed since she had left Baltimore. She felt a pang of loneliness, of being cut off from familiar and trustworthy friends. But then, she reflected, this sense of lost support was mistaken. Kind and generous though they were, none of her kin had formed very close bonds with her. Godwin was really the closest and most reliable friend she had.

Godwin went on talking. "Tomorrow I am going to Paris. I promised Philippe I would take care of some business for him."

He got up abruptly and left the room. When she went up to dress she heard him moving about in his dressing room, which adjoined her boudoir.

"Godwin," she called, "how long will you be gone?"

He answered by opening the door and putting his head around it. "I don't know. Philippe has a thousand and one instructions. I have arrangements to make and I don't know how long it will take. Perhaps a week."

He came into the room, fully dressed, and surveyed her from head to foot. "You're very handsome this evening." He stepped over to her and put his arm around her waist. "You will have a larger scope for wearing your new wardrobe when we travel."

"Where are we going?"

"We'll begin with Italy. You should know Rome and Milan and Florence and Venice. We'll return to Paris after that." His arm tightened about her and she turned her head to look into his eyes and saw that desire for her dwelt there. She felt a compelling warmth rising in herself. But it was not Godwin who roused this feeling. Instead, the image of Leonie returned — Leonie, remote and yet vibrantly near.

Godwin was aware of her sudden stiffening and relaxed his embrace to look at her. She willed herself to soften her bodily response. It is part of the bargain, she told herself. I am Godwin's wife. It is a bargain I did not make but which I must accept. He came closer to her and she passed her hand to the back of his head and held it there while he kissed her.

73

* * *

The carriage rolled away down the drive, the bright morning sunlight flickering on Godwin's straw hat through the branches of the oleanders. He would be gone for a week and then they would prepare to leave the Villa Delfina for Rome.

Amantha watched the carriage disappear around the curve of the drive and then turned away to stroll around the shaded terrace. Morning sounds came over the mossy wall that closed off the kitchen quarters — the singing of a girl engaged in hanging clothes on a line, the cackle of hens, the sound of pounding as the cook prepared for the midday meal. Amantha enjoyed these noises that spoke of the stir of life and people. Without them, she thought, there would be a deadly stillness in this bright world. An odd sense of freedom took possession of her as she watched Godwin's departure.

Standing in the shade of an orange tree and listening to the full-throated song from over the kitchen wall, she wondered at herself. Actually, it seemed that the new light in which she saw Godwin had freed her. She had accepted him last night calmly without any of the ardor that had been hers before. In that, also, they were partners and their partnership would subsist only as long as they lived up to their bargain. She was no longer subordinate to Godwin, but his equal. He had placed in her hands a most powerful weapon. It seemed to her that he knew this and accepted it without question as an element in their relationship.

Breaking off her train of thought, on impulse she went into the house and fetched her parasol. She longed to be once more with Leonie.

She was still some distance away when she heard the piano. She recognized a Beethoven sonata. When she reached the steps of the loggia she stopped, waiting to see if Leonie had noticed her approach. But the music continued. After a moment she stepped quietly onto the loggia and sat down on a rattan seat covered with large cushions. The Beethoven sonata came to an end. Amantha, her enjoyment of the music lingering,

74

did not realize that Leonie had left the piano until she heard the slight swish of her skirt as she came out of the house. She gave a low gasp, the merest breath of a sound, when she saw Amantha.

"Mon dieu!" she exclaimed, "Why didn't you let me know you were here?"

"I was enjoying the music. I did not want you to stop." Amantha gazed up into her face as Leonie stood beside her. Slowly Leonie sank down onto the seat next to her. She reached out and placed her hand on Amantha's knee.

"Amanthe, I can scarcely believe that you are here — that you exist — that Godwin found you."

"Well, I do and he did find me. He wanted me to tell you that he and I have reached an understanding. In other words, I made peace with him."

Leonie scrutinized her face. "And with yourself?"

"Yes. I've never been bothered about myself."

A rare smile appeared on Leonie's face. "Ah, Amanthe. How honest you are."

Amantha ignored what she said. "What really bothers me —it is a terrible thing that you will lose your child. I know, you've said it does not seem real to you. But when it is born—?"

"Godwin says I need not see it. If I do not see it, it will have no reality —." She did not finish what she was going to say, stopped by the disbelief in Amantha's face.

Amantha said, "This is Godwin's idea. I don't think it is yours. He thinks that it is possible for a woman to feel this way, because he thinks that is the rational way to deal with it."

Leonie gazed at her for a long moment and then said, "You must not think of him as so coldhearted, Amanthe. I know that he is not."

Amantha looked away. She had heard the subtle reproof in Leonie's voice. Leonie went on in a different tone. "It is true. A man cannot really feel what a woman would in such a situation. But Godwin has worried a great deal about how to solve our problem. He said he would find someone to take the child, someone who would be trustworthy. He did not say how he was going to find her — someone honest and decent. I pointed out to him that he was seeking a paragon — someone who couldn't possibly exist. But he has found you. He has always been lucky, he says. When he first told me about you — that you were only eighteen and correctly brought up, innocent, and in love with him, I was aghast. I did not believe him when he said he was certain you would respond to the demand he would make. Now I know a miracle has happened."

"Oh, no, I'm no miracle!" Amantha blushed deeply.

Seeing the blush Leonie said, "Godwin knows he can never make this up to you. He knows that what he is doing is outrageous — that he is asking something of you that he can never repay."

Amantha said flatly, "I don't think Godwin sees it like that."

"He does! He must!"

Amantha shrugged and said pointedly, "You know him better than I do."

She had effectively silenced Leonie, who sat back in her chair, her hands limp in her lap.

Amantha watched her. She was almost prostrate now with despair and remorse, but even so there was a great sea of passionate feeling in Leonie that flowed just below the surface, never welling up — unless perhaps it had with Godwin. If so, it had once more sunk out of sight, yet it lay there, underlying the outward poise she presented to the world. Amantha's own fund of emotion seemed to herself, in contrast, to be meager, untapped. But she felt now reserves within herself that she had not been aware of before and that had not been reached by anyone, yet stirred now by Leonie's mere nearness. She knew then that she was jealous of Godwin, on whom these riches were lavished. She was hungry for a share of them.

Leonie looked at her, as if aware of the trend of her thoughts. "Cherie, do not let me make you unhappy. You must know that Godwin has not been my lover since I found that I had conceived — before he went to

76

Baltimore and found you."

Amantha dropped her eyes, "I have known that, though he has not told me."

"Then how did you know?"

"Because of yourself. You would not have made me your friend if it had been otherwise."

Leonie touched her hand. "Amanthe, how can you be so sure of me, of what I am?"

"I don't know. How can you be so sure of me?"

"Ah, you are crystal clear, ma petite. There is no shadow in your soul." Leonie stroked her arm gently.

Amantha was silent for a while, uneasy and yet not certain why. Finally she said, "What would you do if Godwin should fail to carry out his plan, if he does not succeed?"

A tremor went through Leonie's body, almost a shudder. "I would have to confess my sin openly and leave Philippe and bury myself somewhere, in a convent."

"What about your baby? Would you give it up to strangers?"

Leonie bit her lip. "What else could I do? I would bring disgrace on Philippe and his family and on my own."

Amantha said slowly, "I don't think Godwin would let you do that."

A flash of anger showed in Leonie's face. "He cannot prevent me from doing what my conscience requires!" All at once Leonie withdrew into herself.

Amantha got up, too restless to sit any longer. She strolled slowly down the loggia, absently admiring the masses of roses planted beyond the shrubs. When she strolled back she saw Leonie still seated on the sofa, her head buried in her arm resting along its back. For the first time in her life she was intimately involved in someone else's distress, someone else's fears. She leaned over Leonie and said, "Please don't grieve so much. We shall manage somehow."

Leonie raised her head and sat up. She threw her arm around

Amantha. "It is you, who have come to share my misfortune."

"And your happiness."

"Happiness! How can there be happiness?"

"There will be," said Amantha, confidently. She knew that she was not made to be an unhappy person. Even now she felt the spring of her own resilience bubbling to the surface. Cheerfulness would always return to her. She glanced up to see Leonie gazing at her as if half persuaded to believe her.

Each morning, while Godwin was away, Amantha walked over to the Villa Margherita and sat on the loggia while Leonie played the piano before coming to join her. One morning the count came out of the house in his wheelchair, pushed by a footman, and sat chatting with her until Leonie appeared. In the shaded brightness of the day he looked even more gaunt and hollow-cheeked than he had in the lamplight. Amantha could not imagine being married to him, in spite of the gentle courtesy with which he treated her. A sudden recollection of Godwin's vigorous, demanding body assailed her. She wondered, had Leonie ever experienced that sort of sexual pleasure with the count.

But on these mornings they were usually alone. They did not talk about Godwin nor of the future that lay just ahead for them. Sometimes they spoke in French but at times in English, which Leonie spoke easily and almost without accent. When she was in the convent school, she explained, one of the nuns had been an Englishwoman and Leonie had been her favorite pupil. Often Amantha brought a book to read while Leonie occupied herself with sewing or embroidering things for the baby, Amantha supposed. Watching over the edge of her page she dwelt on the angelic perfection of Leonie's blond beauty. She was like the image of the princess in the fairy tales, thought Amantha, and there was often a marked air of remoteness about her, as if she might float away from the loggia and disappear in the bright air. So strong was this fantasy that on one occasion Amantha put out her hand suddenly and placed it over Leonie's. Leonie, startled, drew back with a look of alarm, until, recall-

78

ing herself, she relaxed and caught Amantha's hand in her own.

"What is the matter?" she asked.

Amantha laughed. "I have a funny feeling sometimes that you will vanish into thin air."

Leonie's eyes widened in astonishment. "Vanish? But why?"

"Oh, I don't know. It is just a fancy."

The day that Godwin returned they were standing together at the top of the steps of the Villa Margherita. He was a day ahead of himself. They heard the carriage wheels on the drive and interrupted their parting conversation to see who was coming. Godwin, stepping from the open carriage, looked up at the two women standing between the stone lions' heads that guarded the stair top. He was still dressed as he had traveled from Paris, but hatless.

"Ah, there you are!" he exclaimed to Amantha, and after he had greeted Leonie, he added, "They told me you were over here."

"I was on my way home. I'm glad you have come. The day is getting hot and I did not want to walk."

"Oh, why didn't you say, then?" Leonie cried. "I would have sent you home in my carriage!"

Amantha made a little deprecating wave with her hand. "I hadn't thought of it till this moment." She noticed as she spoke that Leonie and Godwin were exchanging a long look, as if she was silently questioning him about what he had done and he was trying wordlessly to reassure her.

"Will you stay for a moment?" Leonie invited him.

But he shook his head. Glancing at Amantha he replied, "Not right now, thank you. I shall come later to tell Philippe about the actions I have taken on his behalf."

In the carriage together they were at first both silent, and Godwin said, "I'm told that you have made a habit of visiting Leonie every day."

The servants have told him, Amantha thought. She could not tell whether he was pleased or not. She said easily, "I felt lonesome and she is very good company."

Godwin looked at her alertly. "I trust she has enjoyed yours."

"Why, I suppose she has or she would not welcome me. Do you find it strange?" He is uneasy about us, she thought.

"No, not strange. I'm just surprised — at what you would find to talk about."

He wants to know what we have said to each other about him, thought Amantha. She shrugged and said, "Just women's chatter," and he made no further comment.

After lunch he left her and although he did not remind her, she knew he had gone to the Villa Margherita. It was early evening before he returned and he came directly to her dressing room where she was getting ready for dinner.

"Will you dismiss your maid for a few minutes?" he asked. "There is something I must talk to you about at once."

He seemed agitated and was frowning anxiously. She was surprised, but she told the maid in her newly acquired Italian that she would summon her again when she wanted her. When the door closed behind the woman, she turned to find Godwin standing by her dressing table absentmindedly fingering the jars and bottles. He looked up at once.

"I have had a long talk with Leonie," he said. "She has made a proposal that astonishes me. In fact, she demands that I do what she wants, if you will agree."

He seemed mystified by whatever it was that was being required of him and his frown deepened as he gazed at her.

"Well, what is it?" Amantha inquired impatiently.

"She wants to make a change in the plans for the next four months, while she awaits her confinement. She proposes to go to her aunt's house, as arranged. But after perhaps a month she wants you to come to her, to stay with her for the rest of the time."

"Does she want you to be there with her?"

"No. I do not understand this, but she wishes you to be there with her. She says that this past week has decided her on this course. As a practical matter, it has advantages. You can pass for her cousin with the local people until it is time for her to go to the clinic in Geneva. She wants to know if you will agree to do this."

In her surprise Amantha was silent for several minutes. Godwin's return, it was borne in on her, meant that the daily sessions with Leonie had ended and a real sense of desolation assailed her at the thought. Leonie's companionship had become an integral part of her life.

"Of course," she said. "I'd love to be with her." She was aware of the mingled bewilderment and suspicion in Godwin's mind.

"I've no idea why she should want this," he said in a complaining voice. "Of course I've heard that pregnant women do get strange ideas. However, since you are willing to do what she wants, I think it will be best that we leave at once for Rome. After we've completed our tour, I will take you to her. I shall be in Paris. If you want me, you can let me know. There are matters that will need my attention. Then, it is settled?"

"As far as I am concerned, yes," said Amantha, feeling freer, and more cheerful.

He suddenly asked point blank, "Do you have any idea why she wants this?"

She met his eyes. He cannot grasp the fact, she thought, that we can be friends in spite of him. "I don't know why she wants it. She has said nothing about it to me. But I would guess that she is appalled at the idea of spending so much time at her aunt's house, alone, without companionship. From what I have heard, I should think that would be very depressing — especially under these circumstances. And as for wanting me with her — well, after all, I'm the only one besides you she can be open with, aren't I?"

He was silent, as if what she said cast a new light on the matter for him, and the frown lifted from his face as he left her to finish dressing.

* * *

Amantha had expected the weeks after they left the Villa Delfina to pass slowly, overshadowed by the ordeal of the waiting to come. But the time went swiftly in the crowded hours in the ancient Italian cities, where Godwin insisted that she see the famous churches and museums and palaces and provided a busy round of social evenings among the many people of consequence he knew there.

Finally, he took her back to Paris, to the spacious apartment he had acquired near the Luxembourg Gardens. She walked about the high ceilinged rooms, marveling at the luxuriousness of the furniture and appointments. After a few days Godwin announced that it was time for him to take her to Leonie.

In the time of Henri IV the house was a hunting lodge. In the seventeenth century it had been rebuilt in stone, a square house surrounded by stone terraces, lawns and gravel walks, beyond which were stands of oaks and beeches, the remnant of a once great hunting preserve. Its remoteness had preserved it through the vicissitudes of history, even the disturbances in the countryside during the Terror, while Paris was in the convulsions of the Revolution. A narrow road, not much more than a lane, connected it with the village, which lay beyond the wood, amidst farmland. The railroad was several miles away.

The old closed carriage, with the elderly coachman and the dappled grey horse, waited for them by the station platform. There was a half obliterated crest on its door. Godwin helped the coachman and the station master boost the trunks and boxes onto its roof. Amantha climbed into its musty interior. Godwin said nothing to her as he joined her.

She had got used to his periods of taciturnity. Throughout their travels in Italy he had been talkative only when he was showing her monuments and churches or explaining their history. Often he sat beside her in morose silence, his thoughts far away with Leonie, she guessed.

She did not mind his abstraction. Her own thoughts claimed her

82

attention. They tended to dwell on Leonie, on the role assigned to herself in the future. She found she could not visualize a child, and this made it impossible for her to imagine what the day to day nature of her life would be. Especially she found it difficult to imagine a future without Leonie. During the last few weeks, in the midst of the activities Godwin arranged, she had been constantly aware that she would before long be once more with Leonie. But after that, after the baby came, what then?

Leonie was in the big, low ceilinged, dark panelled central room of the house when they entered. She wore a dark dress that accentuated the whiteness of her skin and hair, startling in the dim light, as she came across the floor to embrace Amantha. For a moment then, still with her arm around Amantha's waist, she looked at Godwin and stood still while, taking his cue from her, he moved forward and accepted her cool kiss.

With the adroitness that she always displayed in social settings, Leonie steered them through the evening without awkwardness. Familiar with the places Amantha had visited in Italy and with many of the people she had met, Leonie prompted reminiscences and anecdotes and added some of her own. Thought Amantha, she is not nearly as nervous as I've always seen her, and in fact there was a calm assurance in Leonie's manner that revealed a different woman altogether from the harassed Leonie she had first met.

Godwin was silent unless Leonie spoke to him directly but his manner was not somber as it had been on the journey. His attention, Amantha saw, was fixed on Leonie, who gave no hint that she was aware of this.

He stayed the night, leaving early in the morning to catch the daily train that made a connection with the Paris express. Amantha, lingering in the high canopied bed, was roused by the sound of the door opening. A short, dumpy, elderly maid in a large apron entered with a big tray which she set down on a small table near the bed. It held a coffee pot and a plate of brioche and a pitcher of hot water, which she took over to the stand where the big porcelain basin sat. She merely murmured, "Madame," when Amantha greeted her, and left the room. How, Amantha suddenly thought, am I going to explain all this to Aunt Katherine? Because I'm going to have to keep writing to her.

She dressed and went carefully down the broad, shallow stepped stairs into the big room where they had sat the evening before. There was no one about and she was very conscious of the stillness. It was a dark house of panelled walls and windows set in bays; in utter contrast, she thought, to the brilliance and open spaciousness of the Villa Margherita. At dinner they had been served by an elderly manservant who had not spoken. The elderly maid who had brought the water for her to bathe, had, while they were still downstairs, opened her dressing case and placed her things on the boudoir table. Otherwise there seemed to be no servants.

She gazed out of the window at the park. There was a stable, she knew, and there must be quarters for the coachman, but they were not in sight from where she stood. There was no sign of a gardener and she then realized that there was a general air of neglect both inside and out, as if there were not enough people to maintain the house and garden in proper condition.

A sound behind her interrupted her thoughts. Leonie came into the room. This morning she wore a light colored robe loosely fastened by a sash.

"Amanthe," she said, holding out her hands, "you rise early, as I do."

"Yes," said Amantha. "I've always liked the morning, even when I've been up late. I like to hear the early sounds."

Leonie took her hands and drew her close to her, taking her into her arms. Amantha, surprised and delighted, responded eagerly to her kiss. Leonie did not release her at once. Instead she held her against herself. Amantha was aware of the delicate scent of her skin, the warmth of her body, the pulse that beat in her touch.

Slowly Leonie relaxed her hold and, keeping Amantha's hand in her own, drew her across the room to a large seat in one of the bay windows.

84

The still landscape outside seemed to combine with the stillness in the house.

Leonie said, "You are not wearing a corset."

"I did not see why I should have to here," said Amantha.

"You haven't a maid. It is awkward. Ernestine — the woman who brought you your breakfast — can help you when you need. But you must tell her. I sent her to you."

Amantha laughed, "Leonie, I never had a maid till I married Godwin. There was always somebody available to help fasten things up. Though I must say I never had such clothes as I have now, either. My Aunt Katherine would be amazed."

Leonie raised an eyebrow and then smiled. Obeying an impulse Amantha leaned over and put her arm around Leonie's shoulders, "I am so glad to be here," she said.

Leonie contemplated her. "Here, you are my cousin. You have come to keep me company while I wait for Tante Melisande to die. This is all comme il faut, you know. Tante Melisande is my godmother. I have always been her favorite. If anyone notices that you are different — not the typical French young woman — the explanation is easy. You're from another part of France so your accent is different. The servants will not see anything strange. They have never been away from here and they mistrust all strangers."

"But what about your aunt?"

"Her apartment is on the other side of the house. She never leaves it. She has a nurse to look after her — a peasant woman who has been with her a long time. Every so often the local doctor will come to see her. Her condition does not change."

"Will the doctor come to see you?"

"Mon dieu, no!"

"But you should have some medical attention."

"That I do not need," Leonie said firmly.

Amantha felt a quick misgiving at the determination in her voice.

But she realized that she was learning to know a Leonie new to her. She asked hesitantly, "Are you afraid?"

Leonie looked at her thoughtfully. "Yes, I am afraid. But not of dying. Not of pain. I am afraid of what I have done. It is not only I who must pay for what I have done. I shrink from the thought of the burden that I have placed on you — "

Amantha broke in. "You mean the baby. I will not let the baby be a burden."

"Ah, ma petite, how confident you are! But the child itself —" Leonie did not finish her statement.

"Presumably the child will never know that it is not mine." Amantha stopped, appalled at her own words. "That will be terrible, really, that it should not know you as its mother."

"No, no. It will be much better that the child should not know. It will be saved from any taint from me."

"Taint! Leonie, there is no taint! The poor baby — "

Gently Leonie took Amantha's face between her hands and covered it with soft kisses. "Mon coeur," she breathed.

There was a music room in the house with an old grand piano, which Leonie had had repaired and tuned. It was her aunt's, she said.

"When I was a child and came to stay with her here, she would make me practice on it. She was very severe. When she herself was very young her parents had realized that she had unusual talent for playing the piano. When she was a young married woman her family were friends and admirers of Franz Liszt. He recognized her gift and she was for a while his pupil. She was an ardent romantic. If she had not been a young woman of noble family, she might have been renowned as a concert pianist — not a thing possible then or even now." Leonie paused and then went on. "Perhaps that was the real reason for the sadness in my aunt's life. She was born to be an artist, a bohemian. She was stifled as the chatelaine of a great house. You see what has happened — she became eccentric, rebellious, refused to live with her husband, a man who thought of women only as ornaments of society. So you see her now, alone, deserted by everyone except me."

"Do you wish, too, that you could have been a professional musician?"

Leonie hesitated and then shrugged. "It does not seem important now."

After a few moments she asked, "Shall I play for you?"

"Oh, yes," said Amantha.

The walls of the music room were lined with bookshelves, filled with old volumes, many of them, Amantha discovered, in Latin, obviously the legacy of a scholarly ancestor. But in one corner she found a shelf of old French novels, including *La Princesse de Cleves*, Madame de Lafayette's masterpiece. Intrigued and conscious that her knowledge of French was now so much greater than it had been, she plucked it from the shelf and, while Leonie played music she had never heard before, she began to read.

Leonie, coming to a pause, came to see what she was reading. She exclaimed, " Cherie, what an antique! Have you nothing better?"

"Oh, I brought a box of books from Paris," said Amantha. "But I am enjoying this. I was supposed to read it in my French class in school but I never did."

They sat in the bay window again, when Leonie tired of playing, and Amantha watched the evening come noiselessly across the garden, formal and unpeopled, hemmed in by the great oaks and beeches. Faintly the sound of the bell of the little church in the village reached her. Leonie, watching her, said, "That is the angelus. We hear the bell when the air is still."

Amantha, always wary of any reference Leonie made to the practice of her religion, glanced at her before she asked, "When does the parish priest come to visit your aunt?"

"The cure never comes."

"Never?"

"Tante Melisande quarreled with the Church many years ago. She will not permit any religious person — not even the Pope himself — to set foot in her house. Her servants are careful not to let her know when they go to mass — which is not often."

"You mean, your parents let you come and stay with her when they knew she was that way?"

Leonie smiled at her. "It has always been accepted in the family that Tante Melisande lives in her own way. They did not fear that she would corrupt me."

The old manservant came to draw the curtains and light the lamps. He served their meal at a small table near the fireplace; Leonie said the dining room was not convenient for the two of them. Afterwards Amantha noticed that she seemed tired and listless, and suggested that she had better go to bed.

Leonie exclaimed, "My poor Amanthe! I am sacrificing you to my own weakness. There is nothing for you to do here, yet I must have you with me — yes, I must."

Amantha, unhappy at her distress, said briskly, "Of course I must be with you. I want to be. Come on, let me help you upstairs."

They went slowly up the wide, shallow steps together, Leonie leaning on her arm. When they reached the landing Leonie said, "Your room is next to mine. There is a door between. It was closed last night when Godwin was with you. I shall open it tonight." She drew Amantha to her and kissed her again on the lips." Goodnight. Sleep well."

Amantha stood where she was and watched Leonie go to the door of her own room and open it and pass through. When she entered the room where she had slept the night before, she found the bed turned down. Leonie must have sent Ernestine to do that — and, yes, there was a door open in the farther wall, a door she had not noticed in the uncertain light the night before. She stood for a while in the middle of the dark room lighted only by candles on the dressing table and by the bed, uncertain about Leonie's intent. Did she mean to reassure her, in case she was fearful, alone in a strange house, with no one within call? It would be like Leonie to think of that.

She had tucked the first volume of *La Princesse de Cleves* under her arm when they came upstairs. She debated now whether she would try to read it by candlelight. She noticed that the curtains had not been drawn at the windows; she could see out into the dim garden. The night was dark for the moon had not risen.

She looked again at the open door and then stepped softly across to it. She paused at the threshold and listened. She heard a low murmur, which puzzled her until she realized that it was Leonie's voice in prayer. She looked into the room. It was similar to her own, with the same sort of high, canopied bed dimly seen in the candlelight; there were fewer candles here. At first she could not find Leonie but then she saw her, kneeling before a prie dieu in a far corner. She moved away from the door. She undressed and got into bed. The relaxation of the quiet, un- eventful day still held her. She decided it was too difficult to try to read by candlelight. She put out the candles and sank back in the pillows.

She did not know whether she really went to sleep or simply lay in a half dream. She was roused by an indefinite sound. The room was lighter than it had been. The moon had risen and a big patch of moonlight lay on the floor. When she sat up she saw that Leonie stood beside the bed. She was in her nightgown and robe and her pale hair hung over her shoul- ders.

She said softly, "Amanthe, come to me. I cannot endure being alone any longer."

Amantha, astonished, got up at once and followed her through the door and across the room to the bed. In the downy mattress their bodies sank together. Amantha felt their mingled warmth, the welcoming soft- ness of Leonie's body. Leonie drew her into her arms, holding her head against her throat. Amantha suddenly realized that this was the reality of what she had vaguely yearned for, this immersion in Leonie's bodily presence. There was no coercion in Leonie's embrace; she simply held her in her arms and for Amantha reality gradually became dreaming. At some time later — she could not estimate the passage of time — she roused and was aware that her own cheeks and throat were wet with Leonie's tears. She strove to raise herself, anxious to comfort her, but Leonie's arms pulled her closer, her voice murmuring in Amantha's ear. Once more reality became dreaming.

When she woke in the morning the room was full of light. The curtains had not been drawn here either. Now Leonie lay further down in the bed, in an exhausted sleep. Amantha got out of bed carefully and went to look out of the window. It was a fair day and in spite of the chill in the room she stood for a while watching the scene. A small cart drawn by a donkey was coming down the road; it came from the village, she supposed, with fresh baked bread and other things for the kitchen.

"Amanthe," Leonie's voice came from the bed.

Amantha turned to see that she had raised herself on her elbow. Without waiting Amantha went back to the bed and climbed in beside her. Leonie's nightgown, of a filmy fabric like her own, was pulled off one shoulder and exposed the soft, white pendulant breast with its rosy nipple. Eagerly Amantha took it in her hand and kissed it. She felt Leonie's hands on her own body, as if to restrain her. Chagrined, she looked up into Leonie's face.

"Don't you want me?" she asked urgently.

Still Leonie held her quiet." Of course. I have wanted you for a long time. Last night I disciplined myself not to seek out your response."

"But why?"

"Mon coeur." Leonie's hands pulled her against her, as she kissed her. "I must know if you really want to come to me. Do you know what I wish to do? Do you understand what I long to arouse in you?"

Amantha gazed at her in half comprehension. "Leonie, it is you who stir me so that I cannot think of anything else. From the first moment I met you this feeling has been growing in me, though for a while I did not recognize it or understand it — this hunger for your touch, your kiss, the feel of your body. I have longed to be with you. Surely you must know this."

Leonie sank back into the pillow. Amantha hung over her, instinctively careful not to press against her swollen belly. They kissed, entering each other's mouth. Leonie held Amantha's head captive above her, murmuring endearments, until Amantha eased down beside her.

Amantha felt the slender, nervous fingers seeking over her body, expertly exploring the creases and valleys of her back and thighs, entering the soft moist center of her sentient being. Oh, let me, my love, float like a cloud in the sky above you, sail like a leaf on the autumn breeze, plunge into the depths of the sea, and rise again into the sun drenched air of your smile—.

Her mind, drugged by the waves of pleasure flowing through her from Leonie's fingers, dragged up from the depths of memory bits and pieces of love poetry she had discovered in schoolroom texts and mooned over in her burgeoning adolescence. Those amorphous feelings were real now; the beloved had entered into her far beyond the common physical joining.

At last, the ripples of satisfied desire fading away, Amantha rolled over on her back and looked up into Leonie's smiling face.

Leonie said, almost laughing, "Ma petite, how you respond to me!"

Amantha lay still, trembling. Leonie reached once more between her thighs, which Amantha clamped together to trap her fingers, raising herself at the same time to clasp Leonie in her arms. She was too full of happiness to speak.

* * *

It was an intimacy of body and mind that Amantha had never before experienced and only vaguely imagined. Awareness of Leonie filled her spirit and thoughts constantly. Her body tingled with the remembrance of Leonie's touch. She caught herself at every opportunity watching Leonie, her heart swelling as if it would burst with joy. She thought of

91

the fantasy that had come to her at the Villa Margherita — that Leonie might vanish and leave her longing without the hope of fulfillment.

She was troubled at first that in their nightly sessions it was Leonie who gave and she who received. But she very quickly learned that Leonie, in spite of the child growing within her, yearned for the comfort of physical love. Delicately, led by Leonie, she caressed her body, soothed the nervous tensions that gripped her by fondling her breasts, gently stroking the sensitive places of her body. Leonie melted under her touch into quiet content.

In the daytime they continued to explore each other's world. Amantha learned that Leonie's father was an administrative official in a remote part of the French colonial empire, in the Far East, that he had gone there when her mother died and lived now with a native woman and a family of children he did not want to bring back to France. She had a brother, an officer in the French army. She saw very little of him or his wife; their tastes were not congenial.

"And besides," said Leonie, "Philippe finds them boring. They have no intellectual interests and they don't agree with his political views."

One day Amantha asked if she knew anything about Godwin's mother. She knew who she had been, said Leonie; of course she was dead now. She knew who her family was but that was all, except that they were Huguenots — French Protestants — and therefore not intimate with families like Leonie's own, who were uncompromising Roman Catholics; the enmity of centuries, though now attenuated, still lived to cause a barrier. Amantha, thinking of the easy going Episcopalianism of her own upbringing, sought to grasp the significance of what Leonie said. Godwin never spoke of his French relatives. They lived elsewhere in France, not in Paris.

Amantha, striving to piece together the puzzle of Godwin's life before she knew him, tried to fit this information in with what she knew of his Baltimore background. Aunt Katherine had told her that Godwin's father had married his French wife on one of the trips he made to France in connection with the sale of the tobacco crop from Godwin's Chance. The Shenstones had raised tobacco at Godwin's Chance since early colonial times and for many years their crop had been exported to France. Godwin's father had been drowned at sea, in a shipwreck while crossing the Atlantic, when Godwin was still a boy, before the Civil War.

Leonie, understanding the trend of her thoughts, said, "Godwin does not tell anyone things about himself. You will learn this."

Sometimes, since her pregnancy was not easily borne, Leonie was hasty and irritable and Amantha was aware that her own healthy vigor provoked Leonie's vexation. Yet these moments were brief and were always brought to an abrupt end by Leonie herself, contrite.

"Cherie, I should not make you bear my bad temper. You need to get out and away from me sometimes. I know of something we can do. You are a horsewoman, aren't you?"

"Why, yes, I can ride."

"Well, then, there is a saddle horse here and I have a riding habit. At other times when I have visited Tante Melisande, I would ride for exercise. This is something you must do."

"That's a nice idea." Amantha smiled at her, and looked her up and down. "But, you know, I don't think I could wear your habit. You've always been slim, haven't you?"

But Leonie dismissed her objection. It would be possible to make the habit fit her. Ernestine was a seamstress. So on fine days, Amantha rode out through the wooded park, always followed by the old manservant, riding a donkey. It would not be comme il faut for her to ride alone; the neighborhood would be scandalized.

Amantha also discovered that Leonie, in spite of her concern for the social amenities, was not shocked by any situation, any human behavior. She found all sorts of scandalous incidents merely matters for comment, in private, intimate conversation. Amantha sometimes gasped with surprise at the things Leonie could discuss without embarrassment. Her mind reverted briefly to Aunt Katherine and her circle of friends. She knew

93

that, even out of earshot of their adolescent daughters, those matrons could not have brought themselves to mention such things. When she tried to speak of this, Leonie smiled in amusement.

"Cherie, a woman does not need to be stupid or ignorant. She must only not admit to what she knows when this would be inconvenient or frowned upon."

She also came to realize the influence Leonie could wield when she wished to. It seemed that even Godwin was not always aware that he made decisions and undertook actions that Leonie willed. And sometimes he seemed, in spite of himself, forced to obey her even when, had it been anyone else, he would have refused.

"You know," Amantha said in the middle of a quiet moment, "Godwin still does not understand why you wanted me to be here with you. I can't make him see that, after all, it is only natural that you should want me to be close to you, for the baby's sake. He mentions this in almost every letter I get from him."

Leonie said in sharp irritation, "Of course. He is a man. Why should you expect him to understand such a thing? He sees you, he sees me, only in relation to himself. And he does not see the child as a being with a potential character of its own. He sees it only as an inconvenience."

"And another thing," said Amantha, "he never says anything about coming to see me. I did really expect him to come occasionally. Do you know why?"

Leonie's grey eyes dwelt on her for a long, cool moment. "I have forbidden him to come," she said.

In his next letter Godwin said he was going away, to Russia, on a business trip. He would be gone for a number of weeks.

As the days and weeks passed, the burden of her pregnancy bore more and more heavily on Leonie. Amantha, helping her to undress and bathe, looked at the tightly stretched white skin of her belly covered with its network of fine blue veins.

"It can't be a very big baby," she said, remembering cousins of hers when they awaited the birth of a child. "Perhaps it is a girl."

"A girl?"

"Would you like it to be a girl?"

Leonie hesitated. "Life is not very easy for girls — and this one —." Leonie did not finish her sentence but asked, "Do you want it to be a girl?"

"Oh, yes! But I don't know about Godwin."

Leonie heard the apprehension in her voice. "Cherie, he does not want a child. It doesn't matter whether it's a girl or a boy."

The one thing they did not speak of, as the days and weeks went by, was what lay closest to their hearts: their coming separation. Inwardly Amantha fretted; she could not accept the idea that the time was coming when Leonie would no longer be in her life. But Leonie had made it very clear: for Amantha's own sake and for the baby's, there must not be any further communication between them after the birth. Though she raged, when Leonie first stated this, she could not budge her.

* * *

Geneva was mild and sunny in the early summer. The Clinique Saint Jacques was a sober building, originally the town house of a wealthy burgher, in a quiet, staid street. It did not take Amantha long to realize that it was luxuriously equipped and appointed for the benefit of wealthy patrons and that it exuded an atmosphere of discretion.

She had accompanied Leonie and Godwin in the train, giving what support she could to the exhausted Leonie, whose younger sister she was reputed to be. At first, it had been Godwin's idea that she should stay in the new Paris apartment to await the event, but Leonie had decreed otherwise. In the clinic she sat beside her, trying to comfort her through the throes of fear and depression that took possession of her at the end, while at the same time trying to conquer her own dismay at the sight of Leonie's suffering.

95

The birth took place several days after their arrival. Fortunately the baby, a girl, came easily, being small though perfect. The doctors said that, in spite of her exhaustion, Leonie would recover quickly.

But what now? Amantha wondered, sitting in an ante room waiting for the nurse to come and say that she could see the mother and baby.

Presently the door opened and Godwin came into the room.

"How is she?" Amantha demanded, jumping up.

"Getting on very well, the doctor says." He showed the relief he felt after the tension of the last weeks. "You can see her now."

She followed him into the room and he held the chair by the bed for her to sit down. Leonie lay with her eyes closed, the pale blond hair confined in a braid. At the sound of their entrance she opened her eyes and looked at Amantha. She reached out her hand.

"Mon coeur," she said in a faint voice.

"Have you seen the baby?" Amantha asked eagerly, taking her hand.

Leonie's head moved slightly to say Yes. She closed her eyes again. For a moment there was silence in the room and Amantha was aware of Godwin standing behind her chair. Presently Leonie opened her eyes and this time looked at Godwin. "I want to talk to Amanthe alone."

Godwin was startled but he said, "Of course," and left them.

Leonie watched him leave and then said, "Mon coeur, it is now that we must say goodbye."

"Oh, no!" the cry burst out before Amantha could stop it. She leaned over Leonie and gripped her shoulders.

Leonie's eyes were fixed on her. "Yes. We must."

"For a while, Leonie," Amantha pleaded. "Just for a while?"

Leonie raised her arms to put them around her. "We cannot know what the future holds. The baby is yours. Remember me in her. Kiss me once more, Amanthe, and go." Their lips met and then with a firm pressure she pushed Amantha away. "Mon âme, mon âme, go now," she said, in a half-stifled voice. "Go quickly!"

* * *

The next day Amantha sat in the formal parlor of the clinic, staring without interest at the expensive but austere chairs and carpet. Outside the tall window the green trees moved in the wind from the lake and the sun shone in a blue sky. Opposite her sat the nurse whom Godwin had hired to look after the baby on the trip to Paris, a taciturn, scrubbed-looking German-Swiss woman in a highly starched uniform, who betrayed no thought or feeling in her face. A clock ticking loudly on the mantel marked off the minutes of their silent waiting.

The door opened and a plainly dressed woman entered and beckoned to the nurse to accompany her. Amantha sat on alone until they returned, the nurse carrying a sleeping infant wrapped in blankets. The woman addressed Amantha in French.

"M. Shenstone has instructed us to turn the child over to you. He says you will look after her until Mme. Shenstone can leave us. She will require a few more days' rest before she can travel."

The woman paused but did not wait for Amantha's stumbled reply. "The nurse has been properly instructed about the child's care, how she is to be fed and when. M. Shenstone is waiting for you at the carriage."

In the dry efficiency of her manner Amantha sensed a desire to be finished with the responsibility for a case that had reached its normal conclusion but which perhaps was fraught with the threat of irregularity.

Amantha got up and looked into the bundle of blankets. The sleeping baby grimaced without waking. She gathered up her handbag and gloves and led the way out of the door the woman held open. They were escorted to the waiting carriage and then the tall street door of the clinic closed firmly behind them.

Once they had left Geneva, she supposed, and had hired a different nurse, no one would be aware that the woman who had borne the child was not the woman who would henceforth appear to the world as its mother.

Godwin was waiting to hand her into the carriage. Seated beside her, with the nurse and baby opposite, he was silent. When they reached the hotel where he had taken a suite, he told the nurse to take the baby into another room and then said to Amantha, without preamble, "Leonie will leave in a day or so. Philippe is expecting her to return to Rapallo by the end of the week. He has grown very restive at her long absence. Her aunt is still alive."

Amantha, overcome by a feeling of forlornness, asked, "How does Leonie feel now about the baby?"

He stiffened and replied with a frown, "As she always has, of course. How else would she feel? There is no change in the circumstances. Everything has gone very well. No one will suspect anything. When I tell you the time is ripe, you can write to your aunt in Baltimore and announce that the child has come. The date on the birth certificate isn't a matter anyone can notice."

When they arrived at the Paris apartment, there was a French nurse who took the baby from the Swiss woman and carried it off to the prepared nursery.

Slowly Amantha stripped off her gloves and took off her hat. Godwin seemed to feel some reproach in her silence and said, "I have told you that you need not trouble yourself with the child. She has the wet nurse now and there will be other suitable people to take care of her. She does not have to be a burden to you at all." There was a tone of exasperation in his voice, as if he was annoyed at having to repeat assurances he had made before.

"You misunderstand, Godwin," Amantha began and stopped. How impossible it was to convey to him what was going on in her heart. She was trembling with the rage and despair that filled her.

"I misunderstand what?" he demanded impatiently.

"I'm not worrying about the baby. What happens between the baby and me is my affair." It gave her a small sense of pleasure to see his surprise at her statement but she went on. "As you say, there is no reason

98

why anyone should doubt that she is mine, and in fact she now is, since Leonie has given her to me."

She turned away from him and after a few moments' indecision she went to the room where the nurse had taken the child. The nurse, sitting beside the crib, looked at her in curiosity. She was a buxom country girl, professionally trained for her job. To her it was not a strange or unusual thing for a lady like Mme. Shenstone to turn her baby over to a nurse. A young baby was an encumbrance to such a lady.

Amantha walked over to the crib. The baby still slept. She paced about the room, conscious of the nurse's unwinking stare. She returned to the crib and looked down at the baby. As if in response to her concentrated gaze, the child yawned and opened her eyes. Amantha said under her breath, with a sob, "They'll be grey like her mother's."

She looked up to see the nurse staring in astonishment at her tears.

That night they had their first open quarrel, the first in which they shouted at each other. In the looming darkness, Amantha, tossing sleeplessly, imagined she heard the baby cry. Carefully she began to get out of bed, intent on going to the nursery, which was placed well away from their bedroom. Godwin, who never slept heavily, roused at once and lit the lamp.

"What are you doing?" he demanded.

"I'm going to see about the baby. She is crying."

"You can't possibly hear her from here. Besides, the nurse is there to attend to her."

She did not answer but started towards the door. He said loudly, "Get back in bed! You're not going there!"

"I am," said Amantha.

Furious, he got out of bed. He was wearing his pajama top but not the pants. "Get back in bed! I won't have this disturbance! Get back there, I say!"

"I will not. I'm going to see if she's all right. You're not going to stop me!"

99

He stepped in front of her and shouted, "You do as I say!"

Enraged, she shouted back at him, "Get out of my way!"

Disconcerted at the anger that blazed in her eyes, he tried to temper his voice. "I tell you, it is not necessary. I won't have this!"

With all her strength, Amantha pushed him aside and went past him to the door. "I don't care what you say. I don't intend her to grow up without a mother!"

In the morning, when the fury of the night had left her, and Godwin, sullenly silent, had left for his business appointments, she realized that this was the first time she had seen him out of control of himself. It was a measure, she supposed, of the toll exacted by the tension of the past months, even on him. His iron will had met a check and he was having difficulty accepting the fact.

When he returned in the evening he had reverted to his usual manner, the only evidence of the conflict of the night before being the sharp glances he cast at her from time to time. He made no further attempt to prevent her when she sought to attend to the baby. Perhaps, she thought, his good sense told him that to preserve peace between them, he must not create of the baby's presence a cause for dissension. She recognized in this the source of the strength he displayed in overcoming obstacles. He could always bide his time.

And, the thought occurred to her, he probably remembered with chagrin the lack of dignity in his appearance and behavior when he had tried to prevent her from leaving their bedroom. This would sting him fiercely.

In the meantime, their new household was harmonious. They had returned to the measured calm that had come to be the character of their dealings with each other.

Part II

For Amantha the ordeal of adjusting to her new life in Paris went on, out of sight. The constant though unseen presence of Leonie underlay her thoughts and emotions. It became an element of her very being. As time went on the keenness of grief grew less, but she knew it lay there, ready to assault her at every vulnerable moment. Her only news of Leonie was through Godwin, who, when she questioned him, said, yes, he saw her whenever he visited the Villa Margherita. He was still the count's financial adviser. The count often asked after Amantha; he seemed to feel a real affection for the pretty, cheerful young woman Godwin had married.

He was, said Godwin, getting feebler, though he was still able to consult with other scientists in his field. In his youth he had made his mark in that science. Colleagues and aspiring young researchers now beat a path to his door, as they had been doing for some years, ever since his health had broken down and he had become unable and unwilling to travel to scientific meetings.

And Leonie? Amantha asked.

Godwin was at once wary. She seemed well, he said. Sometimes, as in the past, she came to Paris to spend a few days at the de Brieux mansion, usually to attend to family matters for Philippe. Otherwise, she seemed to be entirely immersed in the affairs of charitable organizations.

She never appeared at any social functions, though the count urged her to do so. He was troubled, said Godwin, by his awareness that she was still a young woman, with no children to occupy her. Said the count, he himself was not a great believer, but he was thankful that Leonie seemed able to find solace in her religion.

For Amantha there was anguish in the thought that, on occasions when she did not know it, Leonie might be a short distance away and yet unreachable.

The child was christened an Episcopalian in the American Cathedral in Paris. Godwin made no question about this, since it was close to his mother's religious affiliation. She was to be named Godwina, he said; when he announced this he waited to see what Amantha would say. She was surprised and somewhat dismayed. But she saw that this was something that had significance for him and that it was not something she could successfully combat. And he so seldom gave any affectionate notice of the child that she hesitated to object. It was bound up, she found out through discreet questions, with some deep instinct in him that she was sure few people — if anyone, now that his parents were dead — realized existed under his usual outward manner. In all the success of his financial career, Godwin never forgot for a moment that the basis and core of his fortune was the Shenstone tobacco crop. This attitude must be a legacy, she thought, from his father, who also had never neglected Godwin's Chance.

The first September after they were married Godwin did not take Amantha with him when he crossed the Atlantic to look after his tobacco crop at Godwin's Chance. The new baby was too young to travel, he explained to Amantha's Aunt Katherine. But the second September he took them both to Baltimore. They could stay with Aunt Katherine while he went to Godwin's Chance. They would take Amantha's maid and the baby's nurse. Marie, the maid exclaimed with delight at the prospect of travel. But the baby's nurse, Jeanne, the country girl who had been with them since their arrival in Paris from Geneva, was terrified at the idea of crossing the ocean.

Godwin said promptly, "We'll get another nurse."

"Oh, no!" exclaimed Amantha. "We can't have a new nurse for her when everything else will be strange. She'll be very upset."

Godwin stared at her for a moment. "Well, then, what do you propose to do?"

"I'll look after her myself."

He objected at once and vigorously, but in the end they sailed with Marie in an adjoining cabin with the baby. Amantha spent most of her time happily playing with the little girl, who struggled determinedly to walk, clinging to her skirts. Godwin came into the stateroom one afternoon, just as the child threw her woolly toy across the floor. It hit against his leg. He looked down at the white blond head. The child did not cry but said, "Mamma, mamma!"

Amantha smiled and said, "Well, fetch it, then," and the little girl tottered over to retrieve the toy and bring it to her. Amantha glanced at him with a meaningful smile. "She takes after you, doesn't she?"

He grunted in response but she knew that for once his attention had been captured without arousing the censure he usually displayed.

Aunt Katherine, who found her house overly full with an entourage that included Amantha's French maid, commented privately to her husband, "I would never have believed that Amantha would change so much. She was such a child when she married. Now she is so self-assured that she has me at a loss sometimes. She seems to take so much for granted — as if she had been born with a silver spoon in her mouth and had always been used to having every whim satisfied."

"Godwin is getting to be a very wealthy man," said Uncle Ralph. "He is getting richer every day, from what I hear. No wonder she is so high and mighty."

Not exactly high and mighty, thought Aunt Katherine. But she understood what her husband meant by that phrase. Aunt Katherine herself, used to the easy-going ways of her black servants, was somewhat intimidated by Amantha's French maid, tongued-tied in English but voluble in French with Amantha, but who seemed to her to be excitable and capricious. She marveled at the careless ease with which Amantha soothed the woman without losing her manner of command. It must be her European experience that had brought about this transformation in the naive, hesitant girl she had last seen.

"Amantha," she said, as they were together in the sunny sewing room after breakfast, "when you wrote and told me about the baby's christening and told me that she was to be called Godwina, I thought what an awful name to saddle a girl with."

Amantha, standing by the window and supporting the little girl who leaned against the glass, said, "There has always been a Godwin Shenstone."

"Couldn't he wait for a boy?"

"Godwin doesn't like children."

Aunt Katherine burst out indignantly, "Do you mean to say that you are not going to have another child?"

Amantha did not answer. She was smiling down at the blond little girl, playfully running her forefinger along the downy hairline of her forehead. The child's serious face broke into a crowing laugh and she held up her arms.

Aunt Katherine said, "She's such a solemn little thing."

"Sometimes she is," Amantha said, picking the child up and allowing her to pull gleefully at the masses of gold-brown hair piled on her head.

The French maid, thought Aunt Katherine, would probably be annoyed at this destruction of her handiwork. But Amantha seemed untroubled by the thought of any such consequence of her actions.

Aunt Katherine said, "She doesn't favor you at all, Amantha," her gaze dwelling on Amantha's dark-blue eyes and shining golden brown hair. "She must take after Godwin's mother. I never saw her. She never came to Baltimore — she was afraid of crossing the ocean, poor thing.

The only picture I've seen of her was a wedding photograph and you can't tell anything from that."

Amantha did not reply. Aunt Katherine, watching her play with the child, thought: marriage, of course, usually cured a woman of too-romantic ideas. And Godwin probably would not welcome a continuation of the effusive idolatry that Amantha had shown him during her engagement. But there was something about this even-tempered, poised, self-assured young woman that baffled her. It was only natural, she supposed, that it should be with the child that Amantha displayed spontaneous affection, not with Godwin, in public. Godwin was certainly much more demanding than he had been. Perhaps that was only because he now had an acquiescent wife who always sought to humor him, discreetly, efficiently. Aloud, she said, "I suppose you call her Winnie."

There was a flash of Amantha's dark-blue eyes. "Oh, I do, but not in front of Godwin. He does not like nicknames."

The peace of Aunt Katherine's house was also disturbed by a constant flow of aunts and girl cousins, eager to see Amantha's Paris gowns. To the aunts, Amantha, with a husband and baby, was a prime subject of interest. Aunt Katherine parried their curiosity, not voicing her own speculations.

In any case, she would be glad when he got back from Godwin's Chance and took his family abroad once more. But even as she thought this, a doubt niggled in the back of her mind. She wished she could understand more about Amantha, could really be assured that she had found happiness in her new life.

* * *

Godwin's business dealings had grown steadily in scope since she had married him. He was a coming man, everyone said; a man whose wealth and power were ever increasing. For her it meant a busy social life as the wife of such a man. Thanks to Leonie's instruction, she gained

105

the reputation of being preeminent in social grace and competence. Godwin's French friends marveled that such a young woman — and an American! — should have such ease and aplomb in dealing with Parisian society. His non-French friends relied upon her for guidance and advice in all matters of social consequence. She knew that this gratified Godwin. She wondered whether he realized that it had been the education Leonie had given her that had brought this about. From Leonie she had learned how to make an entrance into a drawing room with the maximum of elegance; how to be a gracious hostess at brilliant dinner parties; how to arrive at the Opera, sweeping past the admiring throngs gathered on the sidewalk, wearing the fine gowns and brilliant jewels that Godwin provided.

He was often away, usually for a few days at a time, on business trips. And when he came back to her she was aware of a mistrust in his manner. She was puzzled at first to   account for the short temper he displayed and the curtness with which he spoke to her, even when getting into bed with her.

One evening, when he was away unexpectedly, she found herself faced with carrying out a large after-dinner party without his presence. It was a test of her capabilities, and at one point, she took advantage of a quiet corner of the drawing room to drop down on a seat for a few moments' respite. The Chevalier de Montbrun at once came and sat beside her. He was a frequent guest of the Shenstones and he still carried on with her the sprightly flirtatiousness she remembered from the Villa Margherita.

He said, "Madame, you are pensive."

Amantha, rousing herself to respond cheerfully, replied, "I am a little tired. I have had a very busy week, and Godwin is not here to help me. It is hard for me to make up for his absence on an occasion like this."

The Chevalier contemplated her for a moment. Then he adopted the tone he sometimes used, of the old and privileged friend. "Amanthe, you are young, pretty, charming. You conquer everyone."

Amantha smiled and shook her head. She recognized that there was a special meaning in his manner. More than once he had gently set her right about some social situation that he saw she did not understand.

"What is wrong now, monsieur?"

He did not smile in response, but said in a serious voice, "Perhaps you should let Godwin know that you need him to stay home more."

Amantha looked at him sharply. "I think you had better tell me what you mean."

He met her eyes. "There are always those who like to find cause for gossip. One supposes that a beautiful woman like you must have admirers and perhaps when your husband is not here you find pleasure in encouraging them. People think of you as clever, intrigante. Forgive me for speaking plainly."

A hot flush rose in Amantha's face and her eyes flashed. She said stiffly, "Thank you." Before she could say anything further they were interrupted by another guest and the Chevalier left her side. When the evening was over and the last guest had departed, she sank into a straight chair in the middle of the empty drawing room and tried to gather her thoughts together. She did not doubt the Chevalier's good intentions; he had always been her friend. He would not say something like that merely to be malicious.

Godwin, when he returned, made no mention of the success she had made of the party. Instead, his air of suspicion was greater than ever. She discovered that he asked questions —carefully and astutely — about her of her maid and the baby's nurse. Her irritation reached a climax. Finally, impatient, she challenged him.

"Why are you doing this?"

"Doing what?" It was his usual response when she questioned him about his actions, throwing her questions back at her.

"What are you so suspicious of? Why are you asking Marie questions about me — what I am doing while you are away —where do I go — whom do I see?"

He did not answer at once, as if he was searching for the right words. "Everything you do is my business. Just remember that — especially when I am not here."

"Godwin, what on earth are you talking about? You know what I do when you're away. I don't go anywhere I can avoid. I don't have anybody here."

He was staring at her with suspicion. "That's out in the open. What's underneath? I hear things from other people. They speculate about you."

It suddenly struck her like a bolt of lightening. She should have thought of it before; she was well-acquainted with the sort of spiteful gossip that was rife in the social world they lived in. Godwin had been made suspicious by the remarks of the men he associated with. She burst into a peal of laughter. Of course he had no inkling of what it was that precluded any possibility of her interest in other men.

Godwin looked at her with a mixture of mistrust and chagrin. "You needn't get hysterical," he muttered.

But he knew there was no hysteria in her laughter. It was the pure, merry laugh that was Amantha's own, her response to anything that struck her as funny. And he could not stand ridicule. She saw the redness in his face deepen and his teeth clamp together. He turned on his heel and walked out of the room.

He never referred to the matter again. And he dropped all of his attempts at surveillance. He was not much affected by the opinions of others. He must have come to the conclusion that he had been unduly influenced by the innuendoes of his friends; that she was still the open, trustworthy girl he had picked out in Baltimore to be his wife. He was also disinclined to waste time and effort on anything he considered unprofitable. He chose to believe the truth: that when he was away she stayed home and played with the baby.

In this new life together, the relative importance of their sexual activity had changed. Godwin still expected acquiescence and acceptance from her whenever he was home, but he was not as exigent as he had been in the first days of their marriage. Perhaps one reason for this was his absorption in his financial affairs, which were more and more varied and demanding. And she was no longer the untutored girl he had enjoyed teaching. As he did with any challenge, once it had been met, he put it in its place in his scheme of things and turned his attention to the next.

She had learned to recognize the signs, when he had been away, that he had seen Leonie. She knew that he visited the Villa Margherita often. He made no secret of this; he went to see the count, he said. He never mentioned Leonie unless she questioned him about her. Usually when he returned from any absence his outward manner was the same judicious calm he always cultivated; he was no more demanding in bed than when he was at home. But when he had been to the Villa Margherita he returned keyed up, impatient, captious about any laxity in the household management or Godwina's progress in learning to read. This must mean, she thought, that being near Leonie aroused in him the passionate, ungovernable ardor that must have been the essence of their liaison before she had entered their lives. And Leonie now obviously continued to refuse him. When he did speak of her, unwillingly, it was with a suppressed, baffled rage.

* * *

One thing she did notice was that his demanding attitude toward the little girl was more marked whenever he returned home from an absence. It was he who had chosen the strict English nurse for her. He was critical of Godwina's manners, of her rate of progress in learning to talk, to walk, to control her bodily functions. When she was with him he tended to concentrate his attention on her shortcomings, or what appeared to him to be her shortcomings. Amantha, he said, was too lax.

Yet the little girl adored him and seemed to discount his criticism. When he picked her up on his return home and after kissing her briefly, inspected her appearance to see if it conformed with what he thought it should be, she beamed at him with wholehearted delight. If he reproved

109

her for having sticky fingers, she was crestfallen and looked unhappily at Amantha.

"Surely," he said, frowning, "she can learn not to smear herself when she eats."

"Don't be harsh with her. She's only a baby, Godwin."

He was angry at the admonition. "I am not harsh with her. But a child is never too young to learn how to behave. You are too lenient. You have no sense of discipline and without discipline nothing can be accomplished."

He intends to bring her up in his own image, thought Amantha. But she did not go on arguing. She had early realized that she gained nothing in trying to combat Godwin's fixed beliefs. He had an obstinacy in maintaining his own opinions that made him impervious to any dissent. It was true that he was rarely wrong about anything, but it was also impossible to convince him of his error on the few occasions when he was. He knew and understood very little about children, and she thought, it was in a way fortunate that he did not wish to father any more. She had ceased to try to correct his misconceptions about Godwina and instead soothed the little girl's feelings when he was not present.

But though he was maladroit with the child, he was also watchful of any action on Amantha's part that would indicate neglect or malice in her treatment of Godwina. Especially when he returned from an absence he seemed to spy on her when the child was with her. More than once she overheard him questioning the nurse about her attitude toward the child.

The nurse, whose disciplinarian instincts matched his own, was disapproving of Amantha in a circumspect way. "I'm sorry to say, sir," Amantha had heard her say on one occasion when they were both unaware that she was within earshot, "that Mrs. Shenstone sometimes undoes my efforts to correct Miss Godwina. She objects if I punish her by putting her to bed without her supper, for example, when she has been especially naughty."

"But Mrs. Shenstone is not severe with her?" Godwin had demanded,

110

impatiently brushing aside the nurse's indignation.

"Oh, no, indeed, Mr. Shenstone! Quite the contrary. She is far too indulgent. I think it will be better when Mrs. Shenstone has other children. Then she won't make such a pet of Miss Godwina."

Godwin had made a noncommittal response. But his air of dissatisfaction remained. He thinks, thought Amantha, that because she is Leonie's child, I may seek revenge on her or at least vent my resentment on her when he is not around. Poor baby. She looked down at the earnest little girl diligently studying her ABCs, for Godwin had decided that three was a suitable age for a child of any intelligence to begin to learn to read. Amantha, seeking to mitigate what she considered to be too harsh a regime, had undertaken to teach her herself, though Godwin had expressed doubts about the likelihood of her success.

Amantha had kept her temper. "Regardless of what you think, Godwin, the baby is very willing to obey me and learn from me."

"You spoil her, of course," Godwin objected. "I disapprove of getting children to obey you by bribing them. And furthermore, I wish you would stop calling her a baby. She has outgrown that stage."

Amantha, at a loss for a reply that would adequately express her feelings, was silent.

Gradually Godwin became less severe towards her and towards the child, as if he felt reassured. When he arrived home in good humor from a business trip he was patient with Godwina and let her hug and kiss him. He allowed her to play with his watch-chain and did not protest when, laughing with delight, she thrust her fingers into the pockets of his waistcoat. For a few minutes he restrained his impatience and then gently but firmly set her down on her feet, saying, "Go to your mother." Disappointed, she nevertheless always obeyed, clutching at Amantha's skirts until Amantha gathered her up onto her lap.

* * *

They never went back to Rapallo. Godwin sold the Villa Delfina. The part of the year they did not spend in Paris was spent in various resorts on the southern coasts of Italy and France; San Remo, not too far away from the Villa Margherita, was a favorite.

One thing they shared was a liking for strenuous physical activity. Their life at San Remo made this easy to indulge. There was tennis, riding, and within decorous limits against which Amantha chafed, sea bathing. Godwin seemed to approve of her urge to exercise her muscles and lungs in the open air, free as much as possible from the confinement of ample skirts and the conventions that hampered spontaneity of action in vigorous women. In the evenings they often went to the casino. Godwin liked to dance and she was gifted with a good sense of rhythm. They were much admired by onlookers when they were on the dance floor.

Amantha knew that they made a very good pair. When they entered a room together the hum of comment rose immediately. They were inquired about, identified, characterized. "He's an extremely able man, with pots of money." "She's so clever and energetic — an American, of course." She knew at once what sort of comment would be made, none of it without overtones of envy and curiosity. She dismissed it all with a mental shrug.

She found it interesting to watch Godwin on these evenings when they mingled with the fashionable, extravagant throng in the gaming rooms. Amantha herself had no special fondness for gambling. Godwin was a bold venturer in the   many business affairs in which he was constantly involved. But wagering money at cards or dice or on the spin of a wheel did not attract him at all, except as a means of studying other people. He would often put up modest amounts of money in order to participate in a game or a wager but, Amantha noticed, though he was an excellent card player and a good loser, his attention seemed always to be focused on his companions rather than on the stakes. It was not an accident, she decided, that he was so successful a judge of other peoples' motives and capabilities.

He was still a very attractive man. In the four years of their marriage he had begun to show a few first signs of middle age. He was in his forties and Amantha was aware that he no longer had the resilient exuberance he had shown when she first met him. But the change in him was in small details that only she could observe. He had been a bachelor for so long that there were many people whom he had known over the years — whom she now met as his wife — especially women, who continued to treat him as if he was still eligible. It seemed to give him particular pleasure to emphasize, on such occasions, the fact that he now had a wife and one of remarkable beauty and social grace.

The house at San Remo suited her well. She especially enjoyed it when Godwin was away. She frankly admitted to herself that it was a relief to have the entire management of the household to herself and to act as spontaneously as she wished with Godwina.

There was a path of small pebbles that led down among the massed oleanders, sweet carissa, and overhanging bougainvillea to a terrace with a low wall in a corner of the garden that overlooked the sea. It was a secluded spot never frequented by anyone else, with a shady place protected by the shrubbery both from the sun and the wind from the water. Amantha had discovered it early in their occupancy of the house, and its air of privacy had attracted her. She had had a long chair placed here and a little iron glass-topped table. When Godwin was away and she could relax her vigilance over the exact functioning of the household which he demanded, she liked to go there and spend an hour or so of the morning or afternoon, free from surveillance.

She often took Godwina with her, firmly dismissing Mrs. Dawson, the nurse, letting the little girl play happily in the gravel and among the shrubs while she read. She knew that Mrs. Dawson strongly objected, but, with Godwin away, it pleased her to exercise her authority.

One afternoon she went to the nursery to get Godwina. The little girl sat at the nursery table laboriously tracing out the letters of her own name. Mrs. Dawson sat sewing nearby.

"I want Godwina to come with me," Amantha declared.

The nurse's face at once showed obstinate disapproval. "It is almost time for her nap, Mrs. Shenstone. I am sure Mr. Shenstone would not approve of this disruption of routine. It is not really good for the child."

Amantha, controlling her annoyance, looked down into Godwina's face, where eagerness and delight were followed by apprehension of being denied a treat. "It is I who shall decide what is best for Godwina, Mrs. Dawson." As she spoke, she smiled down at the sudden beaming pleasure on Godwina's face, and reached out her hand for the little girl to take. The warm, moist little fingers clung tightly to hers as they walked from the house down the path to Amantha's private spot. Once there she sat down on the shady chair, stretching her legs out before her and opening her book, reveling in the sense of luxury that dwelt in these stolen moments. "Yes, yes, Winnie," she answered the little girl, "you may do anything you like."

Godwina ran to the wall and pulled herself up to look over its edge, down the steep slope to the roofs of the houses below. Soon she was in a world of her own, talking busily to herself about the imaginary people that as a solitary child she invented for companionship. Amantha watched her for a moment, listening to the busy babble; it was with a stab of pain that her eyes caught sight of the pale blond head bobbing against the brilliant blue sky. What a self-contained little person she was, Amantha thought, and was disconcerted when Godwina, apparently suddenly aware of her scrutiny, stopped her chatter and looked around at her. She held a bright red hibiscus blossom in her hand and now with a quick smile ran over to her and placed it in her lap. Amantha, pierced by the love shining in the grey eyes, leaned over and kissed her, submitting while Godwina held her head down to kiss her again and again. Even Mrs. Dawson and Godwin, thought Amantha, could not quench that unstinting warmth of

114

heart; she knew where it came from.

As Godwina left her to return to her imaginary world, Amantha picked up her novel. She was immersed in it when a sudden call "Mamma, look! Mamma, look!" interrupted her. She glanced up to see Godwina standing beside a thick carissa shrub, pointing excitedly to what appeared to be a moving twig.

"It is a chameleon, Winnie," she said, at last seeing the little green lizard that crawled over the branches of the shrub. "See, he turns the same color as the leaf he is on. That is so you won't know he isn't just another twig."

"But why does he do that, mamma?" Godwina looked earnestly up into her face.

"Because he wants to protect himself from anyone who might want to kill him."

"Oh." Godwina's face was sober at the idea of predators. She seemed then to be absorbed again in watching the chameleon and Amantha returned to her book. It was some moments later when she felt a tug at her sleeve and turned to find Godwina standing by her chair. The child's face was troubled and the grey eyes were fixed on her. "What is it, Winnie?"

"Mamma, why would somebody want to kill the chameleon?"

"Well, another creature might want to eat him," said Amantha. How, she wondered, do you convey to a small child the concept of a world made up of predators and their prey? "Chameleons eat things smaller than themselves also."

An expression of extreme distaste appeared on Godwina's face. It was so exactly that of a fastidious woman presented with something that displeased her that Amantha almost laughed aloud.

"I don't like that, mamma."

"Well, I'm afraid that's the way things are, Winnie," said Amantha, winding a lock of the little girl's hair around her finger. The grey eyes continued to gaze at her reproachfully. As so often happened, when

115

Winnie looked at her, a shaft of longing and despair shot through Amantha. "I can't help it, Winnie. You needn't think about it. Just enjoy the chameleon."

Godwina leaned against her and she stroked the silky blond head. The child was suddenly tired and sleepy and she lifted her onto her lap. The little girl responded docilely and was soon asleep, her head heavy on Amantha's shoulder. How ridiculous, thought Amantha, to make so much fuss about discipline with such a naturally willing and loving child. As a little later she carried her still sleeping back to the house she felt a real pleasure in the thought of having thwarted Mrs. Dawson. It was as if she had thwarted Godwin himself.

* * *

Even while they were at San Remo Godwin came and went to Paris on his business affairs. Amantha was quick to see when he arrived back in a bad humor. It could mean only one thing. She knew that he never allowed disappointments in his business dealings to affect his usual bland manner. On these occasions, when he kissed her perfunctorily and she asked him, "Did you have a bad trip?" he always answered shortly, "No more so than usual." He must have visited the Villa Margherita on his way home.

This time his irritability lasted through the evening. He lost his temper over trifles and even her most casual remarks seemed to rake across his nerves. His angry eyes looked into hers fixedly until she was forced to look away.

After dinner, obviously too restless for a quiet evening at home, he suggested that they go to the casino and she readily agreed, relieved at not having to spend a long tete-a-tete avoiding a quarrel. When they arrived there he settled her at a strategically placed table and went at once to the gaming rooms, as if anxious for an outlet for his restlessness. Amantha, pleased that he had found a way to work off his irritability in a way that would not involve herself, turned her attention to the throng of visitors. Several couples she knew strolled by and paused briefly for conversation.

All at once a man's voice exclaimed at her shoulder, in French, "Mme. Shenstone! How fortunate I am! As beautiful as ever!"

The tone of extravagant admiration told her at once that it was the Chevalier de Montbrun. He sat down in the chair next to her. "You do not object, madame, if I remain here?" he asked ceremoniously.

"Of course not," she replied, smiling.

"Where is Godwin?"

"He is trying his luck at the tables."

"I am sure he will be lucky. He always is. He must have been born under a most propitious sign, to be so successful in money affairs and in his choice of a wife. How can he tear himself away from you?"

Amantha laughed merrily at the extravagant flattery. "Perhaps he has grown so used to me that now he must seek diversion in gambling."

"Impossible, madame," the Chevalier retorted. "It would be impossible for anyone to tire of your charms. But if he is so careless as to neglect you, he may come to regret it."

Amantha laughed again. "I did not say he neglects me. I said merely that he may now want more variety in his life."

She smiled into his eyes, enjoying the game he so loved to play. He glanced around as if to make sure that there was an audience to note that he was privileged to chat intimately with the beautiful Mme. Shenstone.

Amantha looked up quickly, aware that someone had come to join them. It was Godwin and he greeted the Chevalier absentmindedly.

But the Chevalier greeted him warmly. "Mon cher ami! How agreeable to see you again so soon. Unfortunately our visits to the Villa Margherita seem seldom to coincide. However, this time they did."

"As you know, I go to report to the count about his affairs," Godwin said with an abruptness that was almost surly. Amantha, used to the unruffled affability that he invariably maintained even when someone annoyed him, was shocked.

The Chevalier, quickly aware that his presence was not welcome, bowed to Amantha and said, "I regret that I must take my leave. My wife is waiting. Au 'voir, my friends."

Godwin said peevishly to Amantha, "I don't know why you encourage every Tom, Dick and Harry to talk to you."

"Godwin! Don't be so bad tempered. You've driven him away. And I wouldn't call the Chevalier 'every Tom, Dick and Harry. '"

"You know what I mean!"

His voice rose as he spoke and Amantha noticed that one or two people nearby turned their heads to watch. She got up and gathered up her gloves and adjusted the wrap around her shoulders.

"If you're going to quarrel, Godwin, I think we'd better go home." Without waiting for him to reply she left the table and started through the throng towards the entrance. Godwin, with automatic punctiliousness, stepped to her side and gave her his arm. Ordinarily he would have moved through the press of people with a self-satisfied smile, aware of the glances that rested admiringly on Amantha's white shoulders and swelling bosom set off by the low cut of her gown and the sparkling jewels at her throat. Tonight he looked neither to the right nor the left but stalked forward glowering. They waited in silence for their carriage and when it came sat for the first few moments of the trip home without speaking.

Amantha's sense of outrage cooled. "But, Godwin, what is the matter? What are you so angry about? You've been quarrelsome ever since you got home. Have you had bad news about your business affairs? If so, why don't you tell me about it? It may help you get it off your mind."

Her attempt at reasonableness seemed to infuriate him more. "This is none of your business." He was almost shouting and she was glad that they had arrived home. His manner was brusque as he helped her down from the carriage and followed her into the house. In the brilliantly lit vestibule Amantha paused. A footman stood waiting to take Godwin's hat.

As she turned toward the curving stair with the iron railing, she heard

Godwina's voice, "Mamma! Papa!" and looked up to see the child's head poked between the railings of the balustrade at the upper landing.

Startled, Godwin exclaimed, "Godwina! What are you doing out of bed? Where is Mrs. Dawson?"

As if in response they heard the nurse's voice. "Miss Godwina! What a naughty child. Why aren't you asleep? You must not leave the nursery when I have put you to bed."

At the sound of the admonishing voice Amantha ran lightly up the stairs. She reached the landing as Mrs. Dawson appeared.

"I'm so sorry, Mrs. Shenstone," said the nurse. "Miss Godwina has been very disobedient today."

Amantha repressed her own irritation. "It is natural that she should be excited about her father's return home," she began, but she was interrupted by Godwin, who had followed on her heels.

"Mrs. Dawson is right," he declared. "Godwina, go back to bed at once."

The little girl hung her head as the nurse took firm hold of her arm. Amantha exploded. "Godwin, don't act so! The child just wants your attention. If you go on like this, you will teach her to fear you. You will destroy her love for you."

Godwin shouted, the rage he had barely controlled through the evening breaking frankly into the open, "Shut up! Don't tell me what to do! I say she goes back to bed immediately. Mrs. Dawson, take her away."

But before the nurse could act, Godwina broke free from her grasp. Alarmed at the violent, incomprehensible clash of wills among the three adults, she darted across the landing and clung to Amantha's skirts, burying her face in the satin cloth as if to shut out catastrophe.

"Are you pleased at what you have done, Godwin?" Amantha asked with carefully suppressed fury. "You've frightened the baby out of her wits. Now, for God's sake, pick her up and comfort her."

For reply he glared at her and then at the little figure in the long frilled white nightgown. "I'll do nothing of the sort," he stormed. "Get

119

her out of my sight!" And he turned on his heel and stalked off in the direction of his dressing room.

Mrs. Dawson, aghast at a view of Godwin she had never before seen, stood uncertainly in the middle of the landing. Amantha said sharply, "If you please, Mrs. Dawson, go and warm some milk for Godwina and bring it to me." As the nurse retreated, she leaned down and lifted the little girl onto her arm. Godwina, her hand on Amantha's bare shoulder, looked into her face, her grey eyes wide with fear. "Mamma?" she asked.

Amantha, understanding the unarticulated question, answered mildly, "Winnie, you know you should not get up after Mrs. Dawson has put you to bed. But come now, we'll have some warm milk and go to bed."

Godwina, reassured, sighed and her soft, warm body relaxed against Amantha's shoulder as she carried her into the nursery.

Sitting beside the sleeping child she tried to understand what had caused Godwin's rage. There must have been a crisis at the Villa Margherita; the Chevalier had corroborated her surmise that Godwin had visited there before coming home. She was sure, judging from Godwin's moods over the years since Godwina's birth, that Leonie had not gone back to her liaison with him. She was also sure that on every visit he had paid to her since then he had entreated her to take him once more into her bed. On this visit the clash of bare wills must finally have reached a climax. Godwin would never accept defeat; he had always been able to have his way in anything he wanted. With lordly command he had arranged the manner of the child's birth, had saved Leonie from disgrace. He expected to continue to chart the course of their lives — his own, Leonie's, hers, Godwina's.

But he had never learned — or never chose to acknowledge— the strength of Leonie's will. The memory came to Amantha of the iron quality of Leonie's power to say No. Godwin must at last have discovered it.

Later when Amantha was in bed, Godwin came to join her, getting carefully under the covers without turning on the light. He was naked and reached for her eagerly. While she lay passive he took her with urgent intensity, anxious only to achieve the tremendous climax that was overtaking him. When he slowly relaxed, still without speaking, she knew the reason for the storm that had possessed him: he was seeking to quench in her body the fire lit by Leonie.

* * *

When they were back in the Paris apartment, Mrs. Dawson announced that she was leaving them. She had been in France long enough, she said; she had had a good offer that would take her back to England.

"You will understand, Mrs. Shenstone, that it is all very well to broaden one's experience by going abroad, and certainly Mr. Shenstone has been very generous. But I feel it is time to go home."

"Of course," said Amantha, delighted at the prospect of being rid of Mrs. Dawson. "I know my husband will be unhappy at your leaving." She wondered privately what really moved Mrs. Dawson to depart. Disillusionment with Godwin, perhaps, since he no longer held in her eyes the image of the all-powerful husband and father.

When she told him of Mrs. Dawson's decision, Godwin did not answer at once. He knew the woman could not be dissatisfied with her wages; he paid her well above the average. But he quickly dismissed the question in his mind and said, "We can send Godwina to a day school. She's nearly five now."

Eagerly Amantha seized upon his suggestion. "Oh, yes, and she'll be with other children. She needs that, Godwin."

That idea had not occurred to him, but he nodded. He would look for a suitable establishment.

He decided upon a school that was not very far from their apartment and which was favored by Americans living in Paris.

Amantha was surprised. Knowing his preference for all things French, she had expected him to choose a school that his French friends would approve, a school with French traditions, French methods, French exclusivity, the sort of school Leonie might have attended at Godwina's age.

Such a school would welcome Godwin's daughter; his French connections were impeccable and accepted without question.

When she expressed her surprise, he looked at her for along moment. There was an ironical tone to his voice when he said, "I would prefer that, naturally. But there is an important reason why it won't do. Think for a minute. Perhaps you're so used to her that you don't notice."

Bewildered, Amantha asked, "I don't notice what?"

"I'm sure you realize that Godwina looks very much like Leonie. In fact, the resemblance is remarkable enough to be noticed by people who know Leonie."

Too astonished to speak, Amantha considered. Of course she was aware of how much like Leonie Godwina was — the same white-gold hair, the grey eyes, the transparent skin, the slender bones. But it had never occurred to her that this resemblance would be so striking to anyone else, except Godwin. She seldom met anyone who knew Leonie; only the Chevalier and his wife, and they had never made any remark about Godwina's appearance.

"But why should that matter in choosing a school for her?"

A look of impatience crossed Godwin's face. "There are many people in French society who would recognize the resemblance. Her family has always been preeminent. When she was a young girl she was celebrated for her beauty — that particular kind of beauty, which isn't common. There is something medieval about it." Godwin paused for a minute as if conscious of getting too close to fervor in his description. "There was a great deal of talk when she was married to de Brieux. They said her family was anxious to marry her off because her beauty was too dangerous. They considered de Brieux a safe husband."

Amantha thought she detected a trace of sarcasm in his voice. He went on, "Her family made her life so miserable with their surveillance that at one point she threatened to take her vows as a nun. They did not want that. As it turned out she might as well have done. De Brieux has never been a real husband, though he was able to consummate the marriage. But he has been a good caretaker. The family honor has been zealously guarded."

The bitterness in his voice was unmistakable. Amantha reminded herself that Godwin had a circle of French friends to whom he had never introduced her. She had assumed that these were people he no longer saw because of the difference his marriage had made in his way of life. But now she wondered: were they the friends and connections of Leonie's family?

He did not say anything further and Amantha was left with her own surmises. She had suspected, even when Godwina was a tiny baby, that her resemblance to her mother disconcerted and repelled him. She understood it now more clearly: he had lost Leonie and the constant reminder of her in the child grated on his nerves. She supposed that his efforts, in the beginning, to keep Godwina at a distance, to hand the child over to servants, had been an attempt to put her out of sight and out of mind.

And now there was another worry. Godwina was growing into a more positive image of Leonie. This was undoubtedly the case, because Amantha could recognize little ways of talking, little gestures, a habit of tossing her head — as if Leonie herself had taught her. To Godwin this meant danger. Amantha wondered whether, under his cool, untroubled demeanor, Godwin harbored an abiding fear of disclosure, of the possibility that the deceptive arrangements he had made to disguise the facts of Godwina's birth would somehow be revealed.

So Godwina became a pupil at the nearby day school, and to Amantha's relief, they did not get another nurse for her. Now, as a rule, she took Godwina to school in the morning herself; it was within walking distance. At noon her maid Marie fetched her home. Godwin questioned this arrangement but Amantha pointed out that Marie would welcome extra pay for extra duty; she had a fiance, who was a cook in a popular restaurant and they intended to marry as soon as they had saved enough money to open their own patisserie. Godwin accepted the situation with a shrug. Marie had been the unobtrusive witness of so much of their marital life that he had come to discount her presence.

She wrote to Aunt Katherine to tell her the news that now the little girl had taken her first step into the world as a day pupil at a school where she would have the companionship of other children.

Aunt Katherine wrote back to say that she thought it a very good thing. No child should grow up isolated from others her own age. She added, at the end of her letter, "I have been quite ill this past summer since I last wrote to you. I am better now though weak. Do you intend to come across the water again? It seems a very long time since your uncle and I have seen you and the little girl."

Amantha, realizing that her letters to her aunt had grown fewer and at longer intervals, pondered the tone of her aunt's remarks. Of course her aunt and uncle were elderly and probably, in the aftermath of illness, her aunt was sensitive to her neglect.

When Amantha mentioned this to Godwin, he said at once, "Then when I go over to see about the tobacco crop, you and Godwina will come with me." He was always punctilious in honoring family obligations.

They stayed in a hotel in Baltimore; Amantha remembered the disruption of Aunt Katherine's household caused by their earlier visit. She did not take her maid Marie with her. Marie was a poor sailer and Amantha, who was never seasick, had had to nurse her on their first crossing. She sent her instead on an unscheduled holiday to her relatives in the small French town she came from. Aunt Katherine, relieved and yet displeased at Amantha's decision to stay at a hotel, said, "I could have managed very well."

"Oh, of course," said Amantha, "but I can see that you are not yourself yet."

They were sitting as always in the sewing room. It was Aunt Katherine's favorite spot. She eyed Godwina, who was dressed in the French style for little girls, in a very short, very frilly skirt with a sash around her waist. She sat quietly on a footstool close to Amantha's leg, turning her head from one to the other as they spoke. Amantha knew that her aunt noticed Godwina's quick little mannerisms, the curtsey she always made to an adult, her habit of addressing her as "madame".

Aunt Katherine said, "That child is more French even than Godwin. Doesn't she have any American children to play with?"

"Oh, yes," Amantha replied. "There are a lot of American children in the school she is going to now."

"Well, you certainly wouldn't mistake her for an American child. Is that the way Godwin wants her to be? I notice he's very strict with her. You'd think she was ten years older than she is."

"Godwin is strict about everything, Aunt Katherine. He doesn't like anything done in a slipshod way."

"That's the way he is with you, too, isn't it?" Aunt Katherine was thinking back to the cheerful, affectionate, carefree child who had spent most of her growing up summers and Christmas holidays at home with the Leggetts. "I'm sure I wouldn't put up with that sort of thing from Ralph."

Amantha laughed. "I can't imagine Uncle Ralph requiring anybody to do things his way."

"Oh, Ralph doesn't see anything wrong with it." Aunt Katherine contemplated her. Amantha was perfection itself, she thought. There was no disarray of any sort, in the well-kept beauty of her hair and face, in her clothes, in her manner, in her social ease, in her tact. "Godwin certainly knew what he was doing when he picked you for his wife. The Shenstones have always been known for getting value for money."

Amantha bowed her head to avoid meeting her aunt's gaze. The remark had hit a sensitive spot but she could not let her aunt know how painful it was. Yes, she thought, I do live in a gilded cage — and I can't even sing.

Aunt Katherine had gone on speaking. "He must be a difficult man to live with."

125

Amantha roused herself to say, "I've learned what he expects me to be and do. He gives me everything I want."

Aunt Katherine did not reply but Amantha could see that she was not satisfied.

Uncle Ralph, on the other hand, could find no flaw in Godwin. He enjoyed Godwin's visits to Baltimore, because Godwin always brought a breath of new beginnings with him. He talked about the new inventions that would within a decade, he said, transform the world — automobiles, wireless communication, airplanes — all things of great industrial and commercial value that would make fortunes for men alert and bold enough to venture money in developing them. Uncle Ralph, secure in his own predictable, humdrum business as a dealer in farm machinery, was enthralled by this vision. A man like Godwin, capable of imagining these things and grasping the opportunities they provided, had his unstinted admiration. And then he was a first-rate husband and father. "She's a very lucky girl," he declared to his wife.

Aunt Katherine replied, "She's a loyal wife." But she saw that he did not understand the implicit criticism in her remark. After all, wives were expected to be loyal and not reveal their husbands' weaknesses.

The next day Godwin took them down to Godwin's Chance. The house stood on a rise on a point of land surrounded by water. A branch of the St. Mary's River flowed at the foot of the slope of grass before it. Behind it was a creek that provided the water that had driven the old grist mill.

The house itself was a long, one-story wooden building with a gallery raised a foot or two above the grassy bank, onto which several doors opened. Godwin said that in the eighteenth century there had been a great storm that had devastated the dwelling then standing. The present house was built upon the stone foundations of the older one. The Shenstones had lived in Baltimore throughout the nineteenth century. They came to Godwin's Chance only for holidays in the warmer weather, to hunt or fish. The overseer of the tobacco plantation lived in the house now. The

126

overseer's wife would see that things were prepared for them to spend a few days.

On the trip down from Baltimore Amantha watched the landscape attentively, especially when they reached the tobacco fields. The tobacco crop at Godwin's Chance was the only one of his financial enterprises that Godwin ever discussed with her. She remembered back to the days when she had first met him in Baltimore and he had told her about Godwin's Chance. She had had romantic fantasies about the original Godwin Shenstone, arriving with the other early colonists on small ships that had entered St. Mary's Bay to carve an estate out of the wilderness.

Godwin had been indulgent of her fancies. But then and whenever after he spoke of Godwin's Chance he had dwelt on the importance of the tobacco, on the methods of growing and curing it, of the traditions and modern developments in its marketing. Nevertheless, Amantha believed that Godwin's Chance held a special place with him. Why otherwise had he given Godwina his name?

Godwin did not devote much time to the consideration of the historical value of the place. He had come, as he did each year, to look over the condition of the tobacco plantation and to see for himself if it and the crop it produced were being managed as efficiently as he required. The morning after their arrival he left the house with the overseer to go to the tobacco warehouses. Mrs. Foster, the overseer's wife, would see to anything Amantha might require, he said.

Amantha, holding Godwina by the hand, began a tour of the house. It had been added to in the course of the years and there were various up and down passages that led unexpectedly to bedrooms and sitting rooms now no longer used. Mrs. Foster trailed along behind her. She was a youngish middle age, in awe of the owner's sophisticated wife. But under the influence of Amantha's adroit friendliness, she was induced to recount details of the house's history and anecdotes of Shenstones who had stayed there in the past. Presently she was called away to the kitchen and Amantha stepped out of a door to see what lay beyond the house.

Across the creek were the woods, dense and seemingly trackless. Godwina, clinging to her hand, asked anxiously, "Are there Indians in there, mamma,? Uncle Ralph was telling me about Indians."

Amantha, having a very good idea of the sort of stories her uncle had told the little girl, smiled down at her. "There are probably some Indians left around here, but they don't have tomahawks to scalp you with."

They ventured further away from the house, towards the remains of the old grist mill. "Ah," said Amantha, "that's where that noise comes from." Since the evening before she had been aware of a murmuring that had been a backdrop to everything else all through the night.

The mill stood, a gaunt wreck, by the creek. The water, passing through the millrace, provided a steady undertone of sound. The current was swift but there were no obstacles in its way to create turbulence until it reached the weir and poured over the low stone wall into the pool beyond. The old mill itself was derelict, its walls rent by great holes where the boards had fallen away. Inside she could see the remnants of the big wheel, motionless but creaking as the wind traversed its ruined panels.

Amantha stepped closer to the edge of the steep bank to look down into the creek. She checked herself as Mrs. Foster, coming out of the house, cried out behind her," Oh, Mrs. Shenstone, don't go so close!" The woman hurried towards her. "That's a dangerous place. I'm sure Mr. Shenstone wouldn't want you to go near there. Don't let go of the little girl."

Amantha pressed Godwina closer to her side. "Godwina won't run away from me, Mrs. Foster."

"Well, the ground can be slippery and when we have a storm you can lose your footing on the stones. There's been people lost."

When Godwin returned in the evening and they were sitting on the porch having aperitifs she told him about Mrs. Foster's concern.

"She was right to warn you," said Godwin. There was a tradition of someone, on a wild night of wind and rain, being swept away beyond the possibility of rescue. "There is a small island down below there where the creek widens out. That's the first place where you could get out of the water and you'd probably be drowned by then."

"It looks quiet enough now," said Amantha.

"But deceptive. I've sometimes thought that I should have the rest of the mill taken down. It's apt to attract curious people. But it is the only one remaining around here that dates from so far back."

When they returned to Baltimore they did not linger. Godwin seemed anxious to get back to Paris.

Aunt Katherine, still irritable from her illness, protested that their visit had been too short. Surely, she said, if Godwin had to get back to his business affairs, he could leave them to return later. But Amantha said he would never agree to that.

Aunt Katherine studied her for a moment. There seemed to be nothing deceitful or unloving about Amantha but it seemed impossible to get close to her, to understand what her real thoughts and feelings were. The only thing that seemed entirely free and spontaneous about her was the love she showed for the little girl.

* * *

Her life in Paris became even busier than it had been before. As Godwin's wife she was expected to serve on the boards of charities, as hostess for ceremonial affairs, to attend the Opera and other cultural events, besides presiding at the dinner parties that Godwin gave. He frequently had guests from the States and from other parts of the world. Her American friends demanded that she join their card parties, though she was an indifferent player, and their other get-togethers. This schedule left her little time for herself. But one thing she insisted upon, even in face of Godwin's indifference, was to spend a couple of hours of the afternoon with Godwina. On fine days, after Godwina's nap, they walked to the Luxembourg Gardens and she sat among the nursemaids while Godwina played with the other children. She took a book along and thus salvaged a little time for herself. The directors of the school Godwina attended told her that the child should be encouraged to practice on the piano; she showed a real aptitude for music. When Amantha mentioned this to Godwin, he cast her a sharp glance but said nothing. So, each afternoon, while she wrote letters and social notes, Godwina practiced on the small piano in her sitting room.

What began to worry her was the feeling that she was growing more and more out of touch with Godwin's life. He was more and more occupied with his business affairs. As Uncle Ralph had pointed out, the variety of his interests made him much sought after as a leader in the development of new companies and products. He had very little time for anything not essential to his business interests. Often he arrived home late in the evening and, after their guests had gone, did not come to bed with her but disappeared into the room he used as an office, where he had a cot to sleep on when he worked very late. Sometimes he went out late and did not return till the afternoon or evening of the following day. He never explained these absences. She supposed it could be that he had found some other woman who gave him greater sexual satisfaction; in bed with her he was perfunctory and seemed to expect little from her. She was thankful for his lack of interest; she found it harder and harder to accept him. But, though this was something she could not explain, she did not believe that he went elsewhere for physical solace. It seemed more likely that his sexual drive was being absorbed by — or at least diverted into — the tremendous energy he put into the other aspects of his life.

Her social life was filled with the people he chose to associate with for business reasons and the Americans — Embassy people, wealthy visitors and semipermanent residents, students — who found in her a focus for their lives away from home. She seldom saw the Chevalier; he and his wife were not included in the lists of guests Godwin gave her who were to be invited to their dinner parties and musical evenings. She did enjoy the musical evenings. Godwin had always been a patron of artists and musicians; he did not neglect this aspect of his life. Often the big double drawing rooms of their apartment were filled with people invited to hear a singer, a pianist, a violinist, or some chamber music.

One afternoon when she had brought Godwina back from the Luxembourg Gardens, her maid Marie informed her that a young man was waiting to see her. Amantha looked at his visiting card: Antoine Reynaud, it said, master of the piano and music teacher. When Marie brought him in she saw a slight, dark-haired man with a mustache and bright curious eyes that ranged around the room. It was obvious that he was eager to take in all he could of the menage of the fabulous M. Shenstone.

"Madame," he said, "perhaps you will remember me."

Amantha smiled at him. "Of course. You are the pianist in the trio that played here in our house on the evening before last. It was a lovely performance."

He looked delighted. He had heard that the beautiful Mme. Shenstone spoke the most pure and elegant French and it was true! "Oh, thank you! I have come to speak to you about your little girl. Sometimes I teach at the school she goes to— I teach as a substitute for the regular piano teacher. We musicians must earn money as we can."

"Yes," said Amantha, and waited for him to go on.

"The little one is quite unusual. She has a great sense of music. She learns very quickly. It would be a pity not to cultivate that gift."

"I know she absorbs music readily. Sometimes when I practice with her, she corrects me," Amantha said, laughing.

He joined in her laughter, enchanted.

Amantha then asked, "What is it you wish to talk to me about?"

"I should feel greatly honored if I could be her teacher— it would be wonderful to help a child with such a gift."

"Ah." Amantha was thoughtful for a moment and then said, "M. Reynaud, you must approach my husband about this. If you will wait a moment, I will write a note for you to take to him at his office."

She got up and went to the little desk in the corner of the room by the window. She sat down and wrote quickly: "Godwin, this young man is

131

the pianist who was with us the other evening. He is a music teacher at Godwina's school and says that she shows unusual talent. He would like to teach her."

She folded the note and handed it to him. Quick to understand that the interview was over, he bowed himself out.   Amantha thought about him for a few minutes. He was personable and seemed to have a degree of breeding not usual in the many people who came to her in search of financial help. She often received people who came to her because she was Godwin's wife, who came to her for help of various kinds. She had followed her usual procedure by sending him to Godwin for Godwin's decision. Sometimes Godwin reported to her what he had done. If he did not, she did not question him. This time her mind dwelt on the young music teacher for a few minutes. She was concerned that Godwina should receive special teaching in playing the piano. But she had not resolved the matter enough in her own mind to raise it with Godwin. These days he paid no attention to the child. He saw her seldom; she had been put to bed by the time he came home in the evening.

The young man had appeared to her to be a gentleman, of their own social class. Because of Godwina, he had captured her interest. But when Godwin came home that evening their guests were already arriving. She was briefly aware that, under his usual suave manner as host, he was disturbed and angry. He left the house before the last guest had departed. Marie reported to her that he had left a message that he would be away for a day or two. He did not have a valet; he had always seemed to prefer a household of women servants. Perhaps also he preferred the freedom of making instant decisions about his comings and goings, without consideration of anyone else. His clothes were looked after by the housemaid.

When he came into her sitting room in the late afternoon on his arrival home — an unusual time for him to be home —she saw at once that he was about to vent the anger that must have been seething in him since she had last seen him. He said at once, "The young man you sent to me

— the pianist — Antoine Reynaud — he is the grandson of one of de Brieux's oldest friends. His father is a well-known mathematician. They are not well off but they are a very good family, well connected —. Do you see what that means?"

Amantha gazed at him nonplussed. "No, I don't."

He turned away from her in exasperation. "It means that he knows de Brieux, he knows Leonie — as a child he has been to her family gatherings. He has seen Godwina at her school. I am sure that is why he presented himself here."

"Godwin, I don't understand. He came because he wants to teach Godwina. He says she has unusual talent."

"That, of course, is an excuse to gain your interest. But it is another bit of evidence. Everyone in his family circle knows the reputation Leonie has as a pianist."

"But what is the point of all this?"

Godwin stared at her in angry disbelief. "You don't understand now? Of course he has noticed the child's resemblance to Leonie. It is unmistakable to someone like him. He sees an advantage for himself."

"How?"

"Are you purposely being stupid? He has blackmail in mind."

"Godwin! You are obsessed with this idea! There was nothing about him that made me think he wasn't sincere."

There was an unpleasant smile on Godwin's face. "He is no doubt clever with women. I sent him away with an excuse. I did not want to let him know I had any suspicions. If I had, he would have known that I understood what he intended. In other words, I would have acknow—ledged that I realized Godwina's resemblance to Leonie and what that implies."

Still Amantha protested. "Godwin, this is not necessarily the case. Please think about it. There is no reason for anyone to believe that Godwina is not my child, and she certainly is yours."

He came across the room to stand over her. She was frightened in spite of herself; something further was coming and she did not know what it was.

"There is every reason to think that someone may be able to uncover what happened in Geneva, someone who has seen Godwina and Leonie and who is led to investigate. Especially someone who knows that Leonie is married to an impotent old man — a vital woman who has never found in marriage the satisfaction she craves." He leaned down and put his hands on the arms of her chair, bringing his face close to hers. "And you — if you ever take part in any scheme to betray me, remember that you cannot escape your share in what was done. I'll see that you suffer the consequences."

She looked up at him and pleaded, "Godwin, why are you talking to me like this?"

Her plea had some effect on him. He straightened up and walked away again to the window, where he stood staring out at the darkening view. She waited. It was obvious to her that he was overwrought, that in the period he had been away he had been overcome by fears of disaster. As a wealthy man he had probably been threatened before with blackmail in other situations and was therefore quick to suspect other peoples' motives.

He turned away from the window. "I have decided to make a change. I am not going to tolerate this situation any longer. I am not going to continue to live under this sort of threat."

Alert, Amantha demanded, "What do you mean to do?"

"I am going to send Godwina to a convent school in Switzerland. It is what I should have done in the beginning."

Amantha jumped to her feet. "Godwin, you can't do this! She is my child!"

He ignored what she said. "I know of a well-recommended place where the nuns take little girls of her age. If anyone there should notice anything, the nuns will be discreet. She can go there as soon as she finishes this term in her present school."

"Godwin! Listen to me! She is my child! You cannot take her away from me!"

He looked at her with a dark frown. "This is sentimentality. You have been a very good substitute mother to her. You've done all that you should be required to do. There is no need for you to be burdened with her any longer. You have a very full life. You will be free to live it without the encumbrance of looking after her."

A wave of blinding, searing anger swept over Amantha. "You devil! I will not let you take her away from me! I will let the world know what happened at the clinic in Geneva."

He came very close to her and looked down into her eyes. He said through his teeth. "You will do nothing of the kind. How can you? If you destroy me, you destroy Leonie, you will destroy the child — supposing anyone believed you. The records there are in order. You will not find anyone to support your claim."

She saw the bitter mockery in his eyes and felt the chill of despair. "Does Leonie know what you intend to do? Surely she does not agree."

He drew back. "I have been to the Villa Margherita. I have talked to her. She agrees that it is a sensible thing to do. She agrees that you should not be expected to go on looking after the child. That you should be allowed to live your life without this burden."

In the midst of the turmoil in her heart and mind she was aware of a subtle calculation in his words. But this glimpse into his hidden intent was swallowed up by the upheaval in her feelings. She sat down again and dropped her head in her hands. She heard his voice saying, "I am going to Milan on the morning train. I'll be away several days. There is an important transaction I must deal with. I'll make the arrangements for Godwina when I come back."

He took advantage of her continued silence to walk out of the room.

She sat for a long time sunk in a swamp of despair, unable to think clearly, to weigh the situation, even to believe that what he intended to do was something that could really take place. There must be something that she could do to stop him. But she had never been able to confront him on any matter of real importance. She had been able to sway him sometimes in things that made life bearable. But Godwin owned her; he knew he ruled her completely. She had never had an independent life, a life outside his control.

At the bottom of her despair lay the thought of Leonie. Gradually her mind came back to what he had said: Leonie approved of what he intended to do. She could not believe this. Vividly the memory came back to her of the last time she had seen Leonie — Leonie in the hospital bed —"I give her to you"— how could it be now that she would consent to Godwin depriving her of the baby?

And then forlornly she realized her isolation. Once before, at the Villa Delfina when Godwin had first told her that Leonie was pregnant with his child, she had had this sense of isolation, of having no haven to which she could retreat, of having no ally to appeal to for help. Then she had been very young and ignorant; now she had learned only too well what the cost was of the life she must lead.

Marie came to find her sitting in the dark. Turning on the light and seeing her, she exclaimed, "Madame, I did not know you were here! I thought you must have gone out with Monsieur. I have put the little one to bed. She was unhappy because you were not there to kiss her goodnight."

Amantha raised her head but was unable to speak. Marie looked at her and cried, "Oh, madame, are you ill?" She came over to Amantha and touched her forehead.

Amantha, white to the lips, managed to shake her head. Marie continued to fuss over her. Amantha was seldom indisposed and had never been really ill, so the maid, disconcerted, strove to rouse her from her lethargy. M. Shenstone she said, had told the housemaid to pack his bag; he was going away in the morning again. Marie said fortunately there was no engagement this evening that she must keep; perhaps she was just tired; tomorrow she would feel better, if she went to bed early for a good night's rest.

Her words flowed over Amantha. She could not eat the light supper Marie insisted on bringing her. She consented to Marie's proposal that she go to bed. But first she went into the nursery and stood for a long while gazing down at the sleeping child, eager to take her in her arms but unwilling to wake her.

She did not see Godwin again that night. He must have returned late and slept in his study. He was gone when, waking from the fitful doze into which she dropped as dawn broke, she once more took up the battle against despair as recollection came to her.

Throughout the day and the next night she struggled with the emotions that clashed in her, her mind against her body, her body against her soul. Rational thought seemed to escape her; only the elements of her situation, warring in her, were clear to her. She must prevent him from taking Godwina away from her; she could not endure her life without the solace of the little girl's presence in it. Yet, what could she do and how? Leonie was the key. But to reach Leonie seemed impossible to her. The Villa Margherita was very far away; much further than its geographical distance. The fact of the count's existence, the weight of the de Brieux tradition, the cloud of social convention that enveloped Leonie also stood between them. It had been so long since she had last seen Leonie, felt her kiss, her embrace, that she sometimes wondered if in fact the house in Auvergne had been a dream. But the next instant the reality of Leonie came back to her, excruciating in its vividness.

In the morning she took Godwina to school. Godwina, with her usual sensitivity to Amantha's moods, held tightly to her hand as they walked along the familiar street, past the little shops, where the proprietors, setting out their wares at their doors, said Bonjour as they cast admiring glances at the child's blond beauty. Godwina did not ask questions but Amantha was aware that every so often she turned her head up to look at Amantha's face.

When she returned to the apartment Marie reminded her of her day's engagements. She shook her head. She must send regrets. As to any visitors who might come she was not at home.

Marie studied her face with concern. Pehaps madame had had an unpleasant surprise? If so, there were steps that could be taken — Amantha looked at her at first in blank incomprehension, until at last it occurred to her that Marie believed that she had discovered herself to be pregnant. Over the years it must have become plain to Marie that the Shenstones did not want another child. So this would explain monsieur's bad humor.

For a few minutes Amantha's mind wandered fitfully over this hypothetical problem but the misery in which she was sunk once more claimed her. Marie, not receiving any response to her gentle hints, desisted. When she returned with Godwina from school she found Amantha still sunk in dejection in the chair in her sitting room. Even Godwina's bright chatter about the morning events in her schoolroom did not rouse her.- Absently Amantha stroked the little girl's head. Godwina, eyeing her for a moment, decided that whatever was the matter was not within her power to cure and turned her attention to her imaginary companions; it was her habit of recounting to these figments of her imagination her view of the things that had happened to her.

Mechanically Amantha went through the motions of her daily life. She sat with Godwina while the child ate her lunch; Marie noticed with distress that she ate nothing herself. Afterwards she took Godwina to the Luxembourg Gardens. Automatically she went to the spot where she usually sat, giving only as much attention to her surroundings as was necessary to watch over Godwina. When they returned to the apartment she listened as usual while Godwina practiced at the piano. Then she put her to bed, giving her her bath. Wrapping the towel around her she was suddenly overcome by the sight of the delicate little body and covered it with desperate kisses until, realizing that she alarmed Godwina, she held her close before tucking her into bed. The housemaid who had brought the warm water and took away the tub stared at her in wonderment. Godwina's bath was usually a happy, frolicsome event.

Tonight it seemed fraught with tension.

The early dark came, closing out the world beyond the window of her sitting room. Slowly through the hours shrouded by her painful contemplation, she had been reaching a resolve: she would not, could not, give up Godwina. Desperately she had been seeking an avenue, a course of action possible for her to carry out this resolve. Wherever she sought, wherever her mind ranged, the way seemed closed. There seemed no means by which she could thwart Godwin. If she simply went away with the -child, he would pursue her. She had no money to use for shelter, food. If she took the child and left the apartment, he would fetch her back at once; there was nowhere she could hide. And she realized that such an action would place her even more firmly within his control: he could point to it as evidence that she was not fit to be entrusted with the child.

She did not hear Marie come into the room. "Madame," the maid's voice behind her caused her to turn and see Marie's outstretched hand holding a square white envelope. "Madame, a footman has just brought this. He refused to wait."

Amantha took the envelope out of her hand and looked at what was written on it: Madame Godwin Shenstone. For a long moment she simply stared at the angular writing. Leonie. It was Leonie's handwriting. There was no mistaking it. That fact filled her mind to the exclusion of everything else. From the envelope in her hand she felt a surge of passionate emotion flow through her body.

"Madame!" There was alarm in Marie's voice. "Are you faint?"

She shook her head and roused herself to walk across the room closer to the lamp, turning the envelope in her hand. The de Brieux crest was on the seal. With frantic haste she ripped the envelope open and unfolded the sheet inside. She read in French: Amanthe, my servant will come to seek you in the Luxembourg Gardens at nine o'clock tomorrow morning at the place where you take the little one every day. Come to me. Leonie.

Suddenly her control gave way altogether. She began to laugh like a madwoman. For a while she could not stop, could not govern herself. Finally, gasping, she found herself being held by Marie, who was saying, "Madame, calm yourself! Calm yourself!" She collapsed into the chair by the lamp, while Marie fetched a glass of mineral water and held it to her lips.

She said, breathing fast, "It's all right, Marie. I'm sorry to have alarmed you. I've never felt like that before. It is passing." She leaned back in the chair and closed her eyes, her mind racing around in circles: Leonie; the Luxembourg Gardens; Leonie knew where she took Godwina; had seen her sitting there watching the little girl.

After a while she reached for the envelope which Marie had picked up from the floor and placed on the table by the lamp. It was real. It was not a chimera. She felt the heavy linen paper in her hand and read the message again. Come to me, Leonie.

* * *

She sat as quietly as she could on the seat in the Luxembourg Gardens where on fine afternoons she always took Godwina. She had taken the little girl to school. She had told Marie that she had an engagement that would keep her out for several hours, perhaps into the afternoon. Marie was to fetch Godwina home at noon, see that she had her lunch and nap and remind her to practice on the piano. She realized that Marie must wonder at this unusual program. She rarely went out alone even to visit the nearby shops. Where would she be going that she could reach on foot and be away for so long a time? But though she gave a passing thought to Marie's speculations she could not possibly fail to do what Leonie required, no matter what suspicions she might arouse.

It was a cloudy, damp morning and at this hour there were not many people about. She wanted to get up and pace up and down the graveled space but restrained herself, unwilling to call the attention of any idle onlooker. Her mind ranged back to Geneva, to the house in the Auvergne,

140

to the Villa Margherita, in a jumble of images. Little incidents that had lain dormant in her memory came up before her eyes. The effort of the last six years to repress what so easily brought pain was nullified in the last few hours.

A male voice spoke at her elbow, "Madame?"

Startled, she looked round to see a footman in old-fashioned livery standing near her. He said, "Will you come with me, please, madame." She followed him out of the Gardens to the side street where a carriage was waiting. The coachman standing beside the horses touched the brim of his hat as she reached it. She saw the de Brieux crest on the panel of the door as the footman opened it and helped her in. Was it, she wondered, the same carriage that had taken her and Leonie to the coutourier in what seemed that long ago time when she had first come to Paris with Godwin?

The carriage traversed the Pont Neuf across the Seine and sought the old section of the city where the de Brieux hotel de ville stood in its grounds, a survivor among other old dwellings that had not so well withstood the upheavals of Parisian history. The gate in the tall iron fence was open and the carriage rolled up to the porte-cochere through the shrubbery that grew densely around the house. She recognized the air of age and mystery that had struck her so forcibly as a young visitor from a newer world. Once inside the eighteenth century closed out what lay outside.

A middle-aged woman servant wearing an apron greeted her at the door and led her up the flight of stairs to the sitting room paneled in white painted, gold trimmed woodwork and chinoiserie wallpaper. The woman left her at once, closing the tall door behind her. Amantha, mesmerized by her own memory, stood still in the middle of the room; as she remembered it, the heavy foliage of the trees and shrubs growing close to the windows shaded the light within. The recollections which assaulted her clashed with the tumult of emotions within her. In the course of the years since Godwina's birth her fantasy had returned often to the events

141

of her life in the time when she had first known Leonie. Now she was helpless in the grip of the reality of this scene.

Suddenly she was aware that Leonie was in the room with her. A door at the back had opened; beyond there was a glimpse of another gold and white room furnished as in the eighteenth century, with a satin-covered low bed in an alcove.

Leonie stood just within the open door. In the shadowed light Amantha saw that she wore a high-collared grey dress that clung like a robe to her slim figure; a gold cross lay on her breast, hanging from a chain around her neck. She came forward to just beyond an arm's reach of Amantha. Amantha looked into the grey eyes; she felt herself drowning in the pool of their clear light.

Leonie said, "Amanthe." Her voice was soft. Amantha recognized the steely quality under its softness. She tried to speak but could not.

Leonie, seeing her struggle, said, "I have come to Paris to see you. Godwin says he wants to send the little one to a convent school in Switzerland. I know the place. The nuns there would take good care of her." There was a neutral tone to her voice.

Amantha burst through the paralysis that gripped her. "He cannot do this! He must not do this! She is my child! He cannot take her away from me!"

Leonie's eyes suddenly widened. "He has been to see me, to tell me this. He says that you wish to be free of the burden of looking after her — that you are young and eager for a carefree life, that he thinks you should not be forced to continue to have the responsibility of her."

Amantha's eyes blazed as she stepped forward, her hands clenched and raised in front of her. She was shaking with anger as she stared into Leonie's eyes. "Did you believe him?"

"No."

Amantha gasped and caught hold of a chair back to steady herself. Her head dropped forward. In the midst of the turmoil that possessed her she felt Leonie remove her feathered hat and take hold of her arms.

"Amanthe, I could not believe him but I had to know from you yourself that what he said was not true. Ma petite, you have been made use of. Why should you not want to be free? Why should you continue to pay for my transgression?"

Amantha raised her head. "Free?" The bitterness rang in her voice. "I cannot be free. I am not paying for your transgression. Winnie is my child. It is devilish of Godwin to try and take her away from me. I am not just a — a nursemaid — a servant hired to look after her. Is that what you think I am?" In her rage she seized hold of Leonie's arm. "Do you really think of me as that?"

"No, no." Leonie made no effort to disengage herself. She had dropped her hands and now lifted them to her head.

Amantha let go of her arm. The fury that boiled in her began to subside. "Leonie, Winnie has always been the symbol of my love for you, for what you always meant to me. But she is herself, too, and I love her as I have never loved anyone else but you. You must understand that."

Leonie looked up. "Mon coeur, I cannot find words to tell you what I feel for you. That is why I have come to Paris to see you." She made a little gesture as if to reach out to Amantha and then checked herself.

Amantha saw it and waited for her to say something further but Leonie seemed to give up the attempt. Amantha said, "Godwin thinks I can be paid off. I've done the job he wanted me to do. Now he'll reward me by taking Winnie away from me, turning her over to strangers." Terror took possession of her. "Leonie, I cannot stop him from doing this! I have no means of stopping him. I do not have a penny. Godwin pays for everything. He gives me no money."

She was panting. Leonie, who had looked down while the words poured from her, now raised her head and said gently," Amanthe, you must understand that he will never abandon you. He knows he owes you something he cannot repay."

Amantha exclaimed contemptuously, "In other words, I've earned a life of luxury, which he undertakes to continue to give me. Abandon me! Do you think that matters to me? It is Winnie who matters to me." Driven by anger and fear she cried out, "If he takes Winnie away from me, I will not stay with him! I will leave him, even if I don't have anywhere to go, and I'll tell everyone why I have done so! I will! I will!"

Leonie looked at her in alarm. "Amanthe! You cannot!"

"You think I won't do that? You're mistaken. I will go to the Embassy and demand help. I'll tell them that he has taken my child away without my consent." She clenched and unclenched her hands, flinging her head up desperately.

Leonie reached over and covered her hands with one of her own. She said firmly, "He will not take the child away."

Amantha, breathing with difficulty, gazed into her eyes. Her own were full of tears as she threw herself with a sob into Leonie's waiting arms.

Leonie led her to a small settee covered in chinoiserie silk and drew her down beside her. For a while she said nothing, waiting while Amantha wept on her shoulder. Finally Amantha wiped her eyes and raised her head.

Leonie said, "Mon coeur, it is dreadful that you have had to suffer this. When Godwin came to tell me what he intended to do, I was stricken. We have not been together for so long, ma petite, but I could not believe that you had changed so much. No matter how long our separation would be, I did not believe you would be anything but yourself. He talked to me for a long time, telling me that he had been unjust to you and that he should make amends by relieving you of the responsibility of the child, so that you could enjoy your life as his wife without the necessity of taking care of her. I said nothing to him. I did not want him to know that I intended to come and see you, to find out from you what you really wanted. He told me he was going to be in Milan for a week and that he would return to see me at Rapallo when his business was finished. You know that it is only a step from Milan to Genoa and Rapallo." She stroked

Amantha's head, and then she asked, "Do you have any idea why he came to this decision so suddenly?"

Trying to gather her thoughts together, Amantha said hesitantly, "He is upset because Winnie is growing to be so much like you. He seems to be obsessed by the idea that some people — people who are friends of your family — will suspect that she is really your child, because she is so like you."

"Ah," said Leonie. "He has spoken about this to me. He says the resemblance is uncanny. What a malign joke of fate! It can undo all his precautions." She dwelt silently on this thought, her impatience showing in the disdainful drawing in of her nostrils. Amantha felt the nervous movement of her fingers as she held her.

Amantha said, "There was a young man who came to see me— he is a musician. He wanted to teach Winnie the piano. She has your gift. The people at her school have noticed it. He said she should have special instruction. Godwin was very angry about it. He said the young man might try to blackmail him."

"What is his name?"

"Antoine Reynaud. His grandfather is a friend of your husband."

Leonie's eyebrows lifted as she looked at Amantha. "Yes, I know him. Godwin did not mention this. But there is no reason for him to be alarmed. At least, not because of blackmail." She got up and walked away a few steps as if compelled to action. She came back and sat down again, turning to face Amantha. "Amanthe, there is reason for Godwin to be upset. His whole life could be destroyed if anyone should discover what he did to protect me."

"He has pointed that out to me. But Winnie's life shouldn't be made miserable just so he can feel safe. She is not to blame."

Leonie took her hand and held it. "She will stay with you. I know that she is a happy little girl. I have watched you with her in the Gardens."

Amantha, her heart overflowing, caught her arm. "Leonie, it is a dreadful thing that she does not know you as her mother."

Leonie put her hands on Amantha's shoulders. "Oh, no! She has a much better mother in you. Mon coeur — " she faltered, taking her hands away and once more standing up.

Amantha looked up at her. "There is something else I must tell you."

Leonie stood still, gazing down at her.

"Godwin does not love her. Sometimes he is unkind to her and yet she adores him. I cannot make him see what a dear little thing she is. He resents her existence. Quite often he tells me to send her out of the room, out of his sight." Amantha paused for a moment not looking up. "Leonie, he blames her for being the cause of your rejection of him. The poor baby. That is the real reason why he wants to send her away. He doesn't want to be reminded of you, of what you mean to him. As she gets older she seems to — offend him more and more."

Having finished she looked up at Leonie. She was heartsick at what she saw in Leonie's face. She got up and put her hand on Leonie's arm; she felt her trembling.

Leonie murmured, "Mon dieu! Must I be punished even more for what I have done?" She dropped her face in her hands. "I am the prisoner of my sin and Godwin is my jailer."

Amantha asked, "Has he ever spoken to you about her, except to complain that she looks so like you?"

Leonie shook her head. "I do not ask him about her. I know that he does not want to talk about her."

"Once when he was angry he said he had made a mistake in taking her as his child, as my child. He ought to have sent her away as soon as she was born, to be brought up by someone else."

Leonie took her hands away from her face. She was very pale as she muttered, "He is very wrong. How can he say that? He knows I would never consent to that." She frowned at Amantha. "Of course that was why he went to look for someone to marry, to take the child, so that, if it could not be mine, it would be his." She was angry as she turned away, angry and agitated. Then she said more calmly, "He says this because he is frightened. He could not admit to anyone that he is frightened, perhaps not even to me." She was silent again for a moment and then turned back to Amantha. "Ma petite, do not worry about this any more. The child will not be taken away from you, ever. It would be monstrous to do such a thing. He knows it would be. He should not have subjected you to this horrible threat. I will make him see that."

As she spoke her agitation slowly left her. She returned to the air of calm assurance that, to Amantha, was her natural state. Impulsively Amantha reached out to her and stopped, suddenly abashed. Leonie stood still before her, her inch or so of greater height seeming to increase. The grey eyes looked at her with their old clear invitation. There hung between them their joint memory, pristine, untarnished, alive. They looked at each other and saw themselves stripped of all disguises, all decorous trappings, of everything outside themselves.

Suddenly Leonie turned away and walked across the room to the tall gold and white door that led into the corridor. There was a bolt on it and she shot it into its socket and came back to Amantha. With deliberate competence she undid the buttons down the front of Amantha's dress and pulled it open over her breasts. Her long, slender fingers passed softly over Amantha's throat till they joined behind her head. She drew it towards her to kiss Amantha's eager lips, thrusting her tongue between them. There was not a sound in the room.

* * *

The low bed in the alcove had once been that of an eighteenth century lady who received her visitors there before she rose to dress. Now its satin cover was thrown back. Leonie lay on her back, naked. Amantha, resting on her elbow, contemplated the white body, the outline of the slender bones, the transparent skin, the bush of blond hair, a little darker than that on her head, that covered her pubis. She remembered the bed-

147

room in the house in the Auvergne, the soft downy mattress into which they had sunk together, the growing bulge of Leonie's belly. Now there was no impediment. Leonie lay before her unencumbered. She could seize the invitation laid before her without thought of the child within Leonie's body. In an instant she flung herself on Leonie and began to search out the treasures of her body. Her hungry, vigorous fingers sought the moist tender crevices between her legs. Her tongue searched her mouth, her hands roved over the soft, yielding breasts, the smooth rounded back. She demanded these pleasures, which in the house in the Auvergne and in recollection since then she had savored circumspectly, tentatively, in shadow form, till she was panting for breath.

Leonie lay beneath her quiet yet vibrant, passive yet absorbent, her eyes closed, her breath coming in little gasps. Suddenly she came to her climax, crushing Amantha in her arms, rolling over her, demanding her share of the erotic excitement that flowed between them. Her hands gripped and caressed Amantha's body, remembering the delight of its strong, firm muscles, the healthy energy with which it abounded. They lay wrapped together, slowly drifting into a calmer eddy, waiting for each other's energy to revive, for another passionate wave to envelop them. It came quickly, abundant, deep-plunging, sweeping them beyond all awareness of anything outside their joined consciousness.

At last they lay spent, for a while motionless and silent, dreamily happy in the warmth of their mutual bodily satisfaction.

Then Leonie said, "We have both yearned for that, haven't we? It was left unfinished before. Oh, mon coeur!" She turned on her side to face Amantha and stroked her cheek.

Amantha raised herself to look down into the clear grey eyes, those pools of light the image of which had always risen up in her mind in the solitary moments of her life. "Then I was half-afraid to touch you though you led me to where you wanted me. My darling —" She sank down beside her, overcome by memory.

Leonie stroked her head. "Ma petite, how I wanted you! You were irresistible to me. I could not do without you. It is part of my penance now that I can only dream of you. When Godwin brought you to me, when we met in the restaurant, I was undone the moment I saw you. How could this be? I asked myself. That night was a nightmare for me. I felt as if the Devil himself had arranged my life — had contrived events in order to mock me."

She broke off. Amantha thought back to that first meeting. She remembered the marvelous aplomb of the beautiful countess Godwin had produced to be her mentor. And she also remembered Leonie's nervousness, the reason for which she later understood when her pregnancy was disclosed. She raised her head to look into Leonie's face.

Leonie's eyes were closed and her mouth set. "Mon coeur, you could not then — and perhaps not now — understand what my life had been up till then. For a woman, to be beautiful can sometimes be a curse. I grew up being told I was beautiful beyond the usual. I knew it gained me privileges. I was pampered as a child. But when I reached puberty it became a burden. I was watched. I was surrounded by people who were to see that I was not seduced. No one ever thought that I myself would be able to protect myself from men who craved the use of my body."

She stopped and lay silent. Amantha felt her fingers searching gently over her body. She went on, "Ma petite, I did not want a man. I felt no hunger for a man's body. But I had strong desires and such desires were not comme il faut for a jeune fille such as I. I could not admit to having them. I was not foolish enough to think they were unnatural. I have always understood that there are demands of one's body that are normal if inconvenient. No one needed to instruct me about that."

"Leonie, I know. You were born wise. It's incredible. You were a magnet for me from the beginning. At the Villa Margherita — "

"Wise? No, not wise. But disenchanted perhaps. At the Villa, yes. I should have tried to avoid seeing you as much as possible. But I could not. And you were so innocent — more innocent than I ever was."

Again Leonie lapsed into silence. Amantha lay still beside her, her face buried in Leonie's neck, luxuriating in the scented warmth of her body.

Her soft voice began again, "You know, of course, that I did not choose my husband — I did not choose to marry. That was done for me. And it did not matter to me, because I knew by then that what I wanted was beyond my reach, would never be within my reach. And at least, if I had a husband, I would be free of intrusion into my private life. Philippe is a kind man. He was under no illusion about why he was chosen to be my husband. I have always suffered remorse because I have deceived him with Godwin. I was content to be his wife. I knew I would never find the love I wanted. There had never been in all my life any hint of someone who would fulfill my desire. But the Devil found a way to betray me. That was what threw me into such despair when I saw you for the first time. Oh, mon coeur —"

Leonie raised herself and caught Amantha in her arms. "Mon âme —" She was unable to go on. She buried her face in Amantha's shoulder.

Amantha, feeling the strong tremors that went through her body, was mute with the compound of pity and love that tore at her heart.

Leonie stirred in her arms, once more lying on her back, looking up into her eyes. "Godwin began to press me from the first moment we met. I had not been tempted before to forget I was Philippe's wife. Godwin always seizes what he wants. He knew from the beginning that I had desires that burned in me unsatisfied, and he wanted to be the one who conquered me, who brought down the defense I had created around myself. When he came inside that defense, I found him tender, passionate, faithful. I could not deny him."

In the silence that followed her words, she lay still in Amantha's arms. "And then I knew that I had conceived. It seemed such a natural thing to have happened. In the first few moments of my discovery that I had a child beginning to form in me, I was not alarmed. I did not think of the consequences. I did not reject it. But of course then reason returned and I knew that in some way I had to find a means of providing for it that

150

would not disrupt the life to which I was bound as Philippe's wife. Godwin found the means."

Again she was silent for several minutes. She buried her face between Amantha's firm breasts. Amantha felt the agitation in her breathing. She said, "My darling, don't grieve so. I will always look after the baby, if she is not taken away from me."

Leonie raised herself on her elbow. "She will not be. But you see what a price I have made you pay. Even Godwin —he cannot accept the fact that I can no longer be his lover. I could not be once I knew I had conceived. My conceiving was a sign to me that from then on I must expiate my sin. And then to have come upon you —! Oh, mon âme!"

She sat up all the way and covered her face with her hands. Amantha gathered her into her arms again and shushed her, crooning into her hair as it hung about her shoulders. Gradually they sank down into the bed again together, seeking once more the solace of each other's bodily response.

* * *

Leonie's carriage took her to the apartment house door. She would have been incapable otherwise of getting home safely. Leonie had judged that the danger of being observed arriving thus was less than that of allowing her to try to find her own way. Amantha sat in the carriage in a daze. When they had finally risen from the bed, Leonie had said that they must return at once to the worlds in which they lived. Amantha had pleaded, stormed, demanded, but Leonie had been adamant. The situation had not changed. She had dared the danger of their meeting, overborne by her own longing as well as by the outrage that threatened Amantha.

"You must obey me. We cannot do anything else." She had taken Amantha once more in her arms. "Mon coeur, mon âme." Amantha could feel the trembling in her body and the turmoil in her own answered. In

151

the end she gave up her protest. Leonie had dressed her and put up her hair, fastening the feathered hat to it. She had taken her to the carriage and put her in it.

Arriving at the apartment Amantha made a valiant effort to rally herself. It was late in the afternoon, almost time to put Godwina to bed. She knew that Marie would know at once that her clothes had been removed and put back on since she had left that morning.

It was Marie who opened the door of the apartment to her. Obviously she had been hovering anxiously near the door awaiting her arrival. She exclaimed as she saw her, "Madame, it is you!" The thin dark-haired, sharp-eyed little woman took in every detail of Amantha's appearance. Noticing Amantha's disorientation she seized hold of her arm and led her quickly back into her bedroom. Following her into the room Amantha took off her hat, flinging it down on the floor, and sank into a chair. Marie, talking rapidly all the while, stripped off her outer clothes and put a dressing gown on her, and pulling the pins from her hair, braided it quickly into a single plait. "Now, madame," she said, "come into the nursery and give the little one her supper. She has been asking for you all afternoon."

Vaguely Amantha understood Marie's stratagem: if the other servants saw her like this they would assume that she had spent the last two or three hours in her bedroom. They knew she had not been her usual self for several days. Obediently she went to the nursery, where Godwina, already in her nightgown, ran to her, saying, "Mamma, mamma!" Querulous at her absence, she soon became content. An hour or so later Amantha was in bed, the little girl beside her. Her last clear image was of Marie picking up her clothes and examining them with care.

When morning came she made no effort to get up. Marie brought her a croissant and coffee; reluctantly she ate and drank while Godwina sat on the bed with her own breakfast. She was aware that Marie dressed the little girl and took her to school. Otherwise she was held by an unshakable sense of detachment. In the night her mind roamed ceaselessly over the hours with Leonie. In the end the truth was borne in on her: the gate of paradise had opened for a brief moment; now it was doubly locked and barred. She could not face the bleakness of the future, at least not for a while. She sank back into the bed when Godwina left for school and lay in a blank stupor.

Marie, alarmed, tried to rouse her. "Madame, you must have the doctor. Let me send for him."

She looked at the maid without replying.

Gradually she began to take hold of herself, to come back to the world she must confront. Godwin would return and she would have to deal with him; she was thankful that he had not returned already. When he did, he found her still convalescent, sitting in an armchair in her bedroom in her dressing gown. He came in quietly and stood beside her.

"Marie tells me you've been ill." It was the first time he had ever seen her in less than blooming health and he was clearly disconcerted.

She made no effort to reply. He leaned over her and took her hand. "I have decided that I will not send Godwina away to the Swiss school. She can stay where she is."

Amantha's eyes filled with tears and she rested her head on the chair back. She saw that this was the closest that he could come to an apology. How dreadful, she thought, if she had not been with Leonie and had instead spent the days of his absence sunk in despair at the expectation that Winnie would be taken from her! He could have no concept of the torture he would have inflicted on her. She saw that he was contrite but uncomprehending. She lifted her head and saw that he had moved away to stand brooding a little distance off. But she must not let him suspect that she already knew. She closed her eyes and drifted into a dreamlike state. When she again revived he had gone. What, she wondered, had Leonie said to him? Had she told him that she had come to Paris and they had met? She knew that he would never tell her. The puzzle was too much for her and she drifted off again.

Godwin insisted on sending for the doctor who had come several times to see Godwina when she developed childhood ailments. Mme. Shenstone, the doctor told him, was suffering from fatigue. She obviously had been doing too much. The pace of her life was too fast.She must rest and be relieved of all duties for a while; otherwise she would become really ill.Her nerves would give way. As he must know, as a husband, women's nerves were delicate; they were subject to hysteria. This was part of their physical nature; the functioning of their reproductive organs made them unfit for playing the sort of roles that were natural to men.

Godwin listened attentively but impassively to what he said. When the doctor left he went to Amantha's sitting room where she was seated by the window, gazing out at the street scene below. She turned her head when she heard him come in.

"My dear," he said in a gentle but firm voice, "Doctor Duval says you must take a rest from everything. You've been overdoing it.If you don't take a rest now, you'll make yourself ill. I propose to send you to Nice for a week or so or however long you need. You will be comfortable there and there will be enough activity to entertain you. Marie will go with you, of course. She can let me know how you go on. And I can come down for a day or so. I shall cancel all our engagements for the time being."

It struck her that this was very like the Godwin she had first encountered, the authoritarian but considerate, the forceful but compassionate man whom she had married.

She looked up at him. "Godwin, I do not like to take Godwina away from her school and I certainly shan't go away without her."

A spasm of annoyance passed over his face, but he spoke mildly. "I don't think it will do her much harm. I hear she is considerably ahead of the other children in her class."

Amantha lowered her head. She still found it hard to think logically, to rouse herself to coherent speech. Godwin waited patiently. At last she said, summoning up all her determination, "Godwin, I don't want to go

154

away. I don't need to. I want to stay here at home." Irrationally perhaps, she feared that going to Nice or anywhere would put a greater distance between her and Leonie, though geographically they might be closer. Nothing, really, could bring Leonie closer.

Godwin was saying, "But Doctor Duval says you need to get away and rest completely."

Through Amantha's mind went the thought, Doctor Duval doesn't know what caused my fatigue. She said, "It would be less restful for me to go away. I'll be all right in a few days." The tone in her voice was uncompromising. She looked directly at Godwin as she spoke and saw that he was surprised. He expected that the crisis over Godwina being over, she would revert to her usual acceptance of any proposal of his without question. But he yielded and did not urge her further.

In a week's time her social schedule was back to normal. Godwina reverted to her usual imaginative chattering; she had been fearful while Amantha lay in bed, inattentive, and tearful if she was not at hand when she arrived back from school, or when she had her meals or practiced the piano. Marie once more cheerfully scolded if Amantha was late in coming back to the apartment after an afternoon engagement, with an evening affair in prospect. Sometimes Amantha was aware that Marie's sharp eyes dwelt upon her speculatively. She wondered what explanation Marie had imagined for her absence on that strange day. She wondered if Marie had recognized the de Brieux crest on Leonie's notepaper or the livery the footman had worn who brought it, or whether she had caught a glimpse of Leonie's carriage when it had brought her home. Marie had been in service in the households of several wealthy families before she had become Amantha's maid. It would not have been strange if she had suspected Amantha of carrying on an affair. But with whom? Obviously she had every intention of saving Amantha from Godwin's wrath; Amantha remembered how she had contrived to keep the other servants from knowing how long she had been gone before she returned home exhausted and disoriented.

She also wondered how much Marie had overheard of Godwin's announcement that he was sending Godwina to a convent school. She knew Marie must on occasion have been aware of angry scenes between them. But now Marie seemed restored to her usual voluble cheerfulness. She was always somewhat wary when Godwin was with Amantha. She knew when he spent the night with her and when he was absent. Now she was watchful but no longer apprehensive. She must have decided, thought Amantha, that whatever the crisis had been, it was now past.

It was Godwin himself who surprised her. He seemed to have changed his mind about the routine of his day. Typically, when Godwin came to a conclusion about the conduct of his affairs, he was prompt in making alterations to suit the circumstances. He made a practice now of being home fairly early in the evening. Sometimes early enough to see Godwina before she was put to bed. The little girl was ecstatic at the attention he gave her. The only difference in his manner toward her was that he watched her as if looking for some new development in her behavior — some further resemblance to Leonie, no doubt, thought Amantha.

Within the week he came into her bedroom as she was preparing for bed. Amantha was seated at her dressing table. She gestured to Marie who discreetly left them. She waited for him to speak.

He said, "I have engaged Madame Maillol to teach Godwina. She is well known as a piano teacher for young children. I know that you are anxious for her to have good instruction."

Amantha exclaimed, "Oh, Godwin! That is wonderful! Playing the piano is the one thing she likes to do beyond everything else."

It was the first time in a great while that she had looked at him with her old cheerful enthusiasm. She did not realize this herself until she saw the pleased surprise in his face. He smiled, gratified, and said, "Also, I'm going to make a change in how we arrange our entertaining. I am hiring a social secretary for you, someone who can do some of the drudgery for you."

156

"Thank you, Godwin."

He stood where he was as if there was something further he wanted to say. Amantha recognized this hesitation. Godwin rarely hesitated about anything. Presently he moved closer to her and put his hand on her shoulder.

"Shall I come back after you're in bed?" he asked.

After a moment she said, "Yes." She knew he saw the reluctance that she could not quite hide. But he seemed satisfied. He leaned down to kiss her but paused before his lips touched hers. Obediently she kissed him.

* * *

The Comte de Brieux died the following January. As he was one of the glories of French science there was a public funeral at the Madeleine in Paris, attended by a throng of scientists and intellectuals, important men in industry and politics, members of the diplomatic corps, members of the French Legislature, the President of the Republic. Amantha standing with Godwin to one side, watched as those who had come to pay their respects filed past the nun seated by the coffin, while the organ boomed. Her only glimpse of Leonie was of her leaning on the arm of a male relative, surrounded by a group of the women of the family. She was dressed in deepest black with a veil that reached almost to her feet and was so thick that it was impossible to catch sight of her face.

Godwin, as one of the count's personal advisers, was busy for several days with his affairs but he said nothing to Amantha about what would now take place at the Villa Margherita. When she asked him about Leonie he replied curtly that he had not seen her and had no information about her plans for the future.

It was the Chevalier who came to tell her about Leonie several weeks after the funeral. He was ushered into the drawing room by Marie, who took his hat and cane. Amantha had not seen him for more than a year and she was struck by the change in his manner. His sprightliness was gone. And he was grave as he came forward to kiss her hand.

"Ah, Amanthe, as beautiful as ever," he said, with automatic curtesy. "My wife and I regret that we have not had the pleasure of seeing you for some time. I have seen Godwin sometimes at the Villa Margherita, but you have been missing from our circle."

"Well, I have missed you too," said Amantha, uneasy because she was not certain why it was that Godwin had not included them in the invitations to their parties.

They chatted for a while, Amantha waiting patiently for the purpose of his visit to emerge. At last after a slight pause, the Chevalier said, "We mourn the loss of our old friend Philippe de Brieux. He died quite peacefully, in the end. It is very disruptive of one's life to lose an old comrade like that. There are so many habits that one must break. There will be no more Villa Margherita for us — no more pleasant evenings there with old friends."

Amantha, whose nerves began to thrill at the mention of the Villa Margherita, asked quickly, "Why not? Of course it will not be the same without the count."

"The Villa is to be sold. Philippe's will said it was to be Leonie's, but she does not want it. In fact, she has renounced almost all the property that she inherited. Most of it will go to Philippe's nieces and nephews. She has retained only the property that she brought to Philippe as her dowry."

At the sound of the Chevalier's voice saying Leonie's name a tremor went through Amantha. "But what will she do? Will she come to Paris to live?"

"No, no." The Chevalier was silent for a few moments. "Amanthe, I have come to tell you something that I have learned that has made me very unhappy and which I fear will make you also unhappy." He paused again while Amantha's anxiety grew. Then he asked, "Have you been in touch with Leonie? Has she told you anything about herself lately?"

"No. I know nothing about her."

"Godwin has not told you anything?"

"He says he has not seen her since the count died and that he knows nothing about her situation."

The Chevalier's dark eyes looked at her directly. She could not tell whether there was skepticism in them or some other meaning. He murmured, as if as much to himself as to her, "It is what I feared. She has consulted no one." More loudly he said, "She has decided to withdraw from society. You realize, Amanthe, that there has always been something of the devoté about Leonie. I have heard that even as a girl she threatened to take vows, to enter a convent –"

Beside herself, Amantha cried out, "That's not what she has done now, is it?"

He raised his eyebrows at her vehemence but said immediately, "No, no. It is not as bad as that. But as far as her friends are concerned, she is inaccessible. Do you remember that she had an aunt, somewhat deranged, who lived as a recluse in an old place in the Auvergne?"

"Yes, yes. I remember that." Amantha felt her heart beating fast, "She must be dead by now."

"She is. Leonie was her heir and inherited the house. Leonie has declared that she is withdrawing from the world and that is where she has gone to live. She will spend her life in prayer and meditation. She says she cannot take religious vows because she is too unworthy." He paused and then said in a confidential tone, "I believe it must be because there are things she does not wish to disclose. She does not trust the secrecy of the confessional. She will communicate with no one. Her affairs will be managed by a lawyer. He will report to her in writing once a year. She will not write letters. If she receives any she will return them unanswered. She will not permit anyone to go to see her; if anyone tries, she will have her servants send them away."

Amantha dropped her head on her hand. The Chevalier sat silent until she roused and asked, "Do you really think she will do this?"

"Undoubtedly. Leonie is immovable."

"Did she tell you this herself or –"

"Yes, yes. I would not have believed it if I had not heard it from her own lips."

"Did she – did she send you to tell me?"

The forlorn note in her voice brought an immediate response from him. "Ah, Amanthe, she would not forget you. She said that she would like me to come and tell you, in case you would not hear of it from anyone else."

From Godwin, thought Amantha. He means Godwin. "But Godwin knows this."

"He must. I do not know whether she took him into her confidence earlier. So there it is, Amanthe. We have lost two friends."

When he had left, she sat and pondered for a while. At least she knew where Leonie was. But she had a feeling of remoteness from Leonie, more than the physical isolation of the house in the Auvergne. And Godwin. He certainly had no intention of sharing his sense of loss with her, as the Chevalier had done.

She was melancholy and had trouble disguising the fact. If Godwin noticed, he made no comment. He did not speak of Leonie nor of the count.

Like the Chevalier, she grieved over the disappearance from her life of the Villa Margherita. Like him, she was aware now of the importance it had had for her, as it had had for him. It had embodied a range of emotions. It had been the site of her emotional entanglement with Leonie. It had been the place to which Godwin had always returned to Leonie. It brooded in the background of her mind and heart as the abode of Leonie. She would always recall the mornings when she sat on the loggia and listened to Leonie playing the piano; the evenings of the dinner parties over which Leonie had presided. The scents of its shrubs and flowering trees, the moonlight splendor in which she had so often seen it lit, the impress of Leonie on it, were engraved in her memory and senses. Now it was as if the villa had vanished from the earth. It was inhabited by strangers whose presence must certainly have annihilated the character, it had had when the count had lived there.

It was as if the inner part of her life had dropped away into an abyss, an abyss as deep as that in which Leonie herself seemed to have been swallowed up.

* * *

At the end of a year as her pupil, Mme.Maillol insisted that Godwina should give a recital -- not as one child among several but a recital of her own.

"It can be in your drawing room, Mme.Shenstone, as one of the evenings you and M.Shenstone devote to music. The little one is extraordinary. I have been teaching children for twenty years and never have I encountered such a gift in so young a child."

Twenty years, thought Amantha, suddenly apprehensive. Then in relief she realized that twenty years ago Leonie would have been seventeen, too old to have been a pupil of Mme.Maillol. The music teacher ran on. She was voluble, used to elaborating on the success she achieved with the children of wealthy parents. She was a stocky woman with a head of highly frizzed hair and quick, intelligent eyes and a fussy manner. But Godwina seemed content to be taught by her, seemed to respect the strictness she displayed as a teacher.

"Dear Mme.Maillol," said Amantha, seeking the most tactful way in which to quash the suggestion, "I don't think we should require our guests to listen to a child, no matter how gifted, simply because we wish to show her off."

"Ah, no, no, no! That is not the way to look at it. Godwina plays well enough to reward anyone who looks for pleasure in music. If she was not your child and I asked you to give her such an opportunity, I am sure you would be willing to consider it, would you not? You open the way for many young musicians."

"Seven years old is rather young," said Amantha mildly. She was aware that giving a recital for one of her pupils in the Shenstones' drawing room would be very good for Mme.Maillol's reputation as a teacher.

She finally convinced Mme.Maillol that she would not consent to a recital for Godwina. Then she considered whether she should tell Godwin of the proposal. She shuddered inwardly at the recollection of what had happened when Antoine Reynaud had proposed himself as Godwina's teacher. She knew that the situation would not repeat itself. Godwin was much more accessible to her now than he had been then. His fears about disclosure seemed to have become far less pressing, but she really did not know what lay beneath the surface. And there was no Leonie now to rescue her, no Leonie to take her in her arms. She turned her mind resolutely away from Leonie. She must concentrate on whether to inform Godwin.

In the evening when they had a quiet moment together, she described Mme.Maillol's proposal. He frowned at once and she hurried to add, "I don't think it would be good for Godwina. I don't like the idea of putting such pressure on a child, especially one so sensitive. Perhaps when she is older –"

"On no account, at any time." Godwin's tone was adamant. "I won't have her made a show of."

In his vehemence Amantha recognized at once the basis for his rejection of the idea: he did not want Godwina brought into the world of their social circle, where attention would be called to her distinctive beauty. They said no more about the matter. But Amantha, observing him when he was not aware of her scrutiny, noted that he seemed to brood. Some time went by, however, before he made his announcement.

He came into her sitting room in the afternoon at an hour when he was never expected at home. She sat at her desk writing letters. Godwina was having her lesson on the grand piano in the drawing room, as was usual when Mme.Maillol came to teach her. The sound of the music came faintly into the sitting room. Godwin sat down in the arm chair and seemed in no hurry to interrupt her. She finished her letter and turned in her chair

162

to look at him. He was smoking one of his small cigars.

He said, "We are going to move."

Surprised, she asked, "Where to?"

"To London."

"To London? Why Godwin, what do you mean?"

"That we are moving to London. I shall keep my office here, of course. It will really remain my headquarters. But London will be a very useful base. A great deal of my business goes through London and in some ways it will be easier to coordinate with my New York agent from there. Since I expect to be there the preponderance of my time, we shall live in London. I have bought a house in Eaton Square. I will take you over there in a few days so that you can see it and decide how you will want it decorated and furnished. We can stay at the Grosvenor while that is being done."

How typically Godwin, thought Amantha, to have everything in order before making an announcement. She said, "I have just been writing to Trudy Starratt. Ted is stationed in London now -- what do they call it, home assignment? They've been in Persia for five years. It will be nice to see her again. I must add a postscript to my letter."

She remembered Aunt Katherine writing to her soon after she had left Baltimore that Trudy had married a young Englishman from the British Embassy in Washington who was the son of a baronet, so that Trudy would eventually be Lady Starratt.

Godwin said, "Starratt?"

"Trudy is a girl I went to school with.She was Trudy Howard then. She married Ted just after we were married. He was a third secrtary of embassy then."

Godwin was pondering. "Starratt. I believe I know his father. He was at the embassy here some time back."

"They have three children. One of them, at least, should be the right age for Godwina to play with."

Godwin nodded and made no further comment.

The prospect of the move did not bother her very much. There was little in the routine of her life that would be disrupted by a change of locale. In essence her life in London would be the same as her life in Paris. Of course she would miss Paris. She had got used to French ways and French ideas about food, dress, theater, what constituted the proper things in social behavior. She would quickly learn what she must substitute for these in London. These demands would give a certain fillip to life for a while.

She was aware that Godwin watched her occasionally as if he wondered about the readiness with which she set about uprooting herself from Paris, from the spacious apartment, her French servants. Briefly there was trouble about Marie, who was torn between the desire to go with her and despair at leaving Paris. Amantha quickly divined the problem: Marie and her fiance were getting within sight of their goal of setting up a patisserie, withdrawing from their lives as the employees of others. Amantha, choosing carefully the moment to raise the question with Godwin, solved it within a few minutes. Godwin would provide the remaining cash necessary for them to establish their business.

When the settlement was made and Marie had wept tears of gratitude and remorse in Amantha's arms, Godwin eyed Amantha speculatively. He said, "You realize that you have done yourself out of a good maid."

"Oh, I know I shall not find another Marie. I shall just have to make do with substitutes."

Her equanimity seemed to intrigue him. "I'd have thought that you would be more unhappy about making this change. I gave some thought to that before I decided upon it."

"Thank you, Godwin, but it will not be such a terrible thing. It will be better for Godwina to live in an English-speaking country and learn other ways."

The moment she mentioned Godwina he was alert. "Yes. It will be better all round."

164

He did not elaborate but at once Amantha saw the real reason for his decision, beyond the business considerations he had discussed. Godwina was growing up. In London there would not be as concentrated a spotlight on her as there would be in Paris when she must finally take her place in adult society. In London there was not the memory of Leonie to be contended with. Visitors from France might comment on her appearance but they would be visitors, seeing her in an alien setting.

He was still watching her with speculation in his eyes when she turned away into the abstraction that often claimed her.

After all, she thought, Leonie is just as far away from me here in Paris as she will be in London.

Part III

Amantha was relieved to find that the new house was not as large as she feared it might be. But it had five storeys. She knew why Godwin had put the decorating and furnishing in her hands. He had confidence in her taste and knew that she would produce the result he wanted. They were able to move in within a few weeks of their arrival in London.

The transition from their circle of friends in Paris to their new circle in London was easily and smoothly made. Godwin was not a newcomer in the London financial world. He was well known and was welcomed into clubs and business groups. In fact, Amantha observed, there was little change in his affairs; his moving them to London made no difference in his business life except that he traveled less. Their musical evenings became an important feature of the Season; since the house did not have rooms as spacious as those of the Paris apartment, these were more intimate occasions for which invitations were much sought.

The Starratts had leased a house close by. Trudy quickly formed the habit of dropping in to chat in her sitting room. Amantha liked this sitting room better than the one in the Paris apartment. It overlooked a walled garden of trees and rose bushes, a quiet spot which caught the afternoon sun.

Trudy was frankly curious about Amantha's life since they had both left Baltimore. At the time of her marriage she had been a lively, handsome girl. Now with a fond husband and three children she was growing buxom.

"You've certainly kept your figure, Ammy." She used Amantha's schoolgirl nickname. "You know, you amaze me. Everybody is lost in admiration of your beauty and elegance. Well, we all knew you were pretty but I must say I'm surprised at your transformation. Your fame even got as far as Teheran. Everybody who saw you in Paris talked about what a wonderful hostess you were and what wonderful clothes you wore and what a model of grace and bearing you were, how well you danced. They described you as if you were a goddess. However did you manage it, Ammy?"

"I had a very good teacher."

"She must have been a French woman."

"Yes."

"And now you seem to have a musical prodigy for a daughter."

Amantha burst into laughter. Trudy joined her and said, "Ammy, you've always had the most wonderful laugh. Well, anyway. I can remember how everybody talked in Baltimore when you got engaged to Godwin. Of course, you were very pretty and as sweet as could be. But we were all flabbergasted. Why did he pick you? We thought he'd want somebody more worldly-wise. I suppose he thought he could provide that and wanted somebody fresh and innocent. I'm sure he got what he wanted. We were all envious, of course. The only thing that consoled us was that he was such an old man — forty years old. We pitied you there. Aren't girls silly?"

"Yes."

"How about children? You've got only the one chick. Don't you want any more?"

"Godwin doesn't."

"And his word is law. But that's strange. You would suppose he'd want a son and heir."

"He doesn't like children."

Trudy looked at her for a moment and asked with the candor of childhood acquaintance, "Well, do you and is he?"

"We do and he is." Amantha's tone was sharp and curt.

Trudy laughed. "Don't be so touchy. It's only natural for me to want to know how satisfactory your marriage is in bed. Now you can see mine is. I've got three."

Amantha did not reply.

Godwina was getting taller. She had always been small but now she was beginning to leave babyhood behind. She was slender and full of nervous energy, with the self-possession of an older child.

"Isn't she too thin?" Trudy asked. "Does she get enough to eat?"

Amantha glanced at her. "No. I starve her."

"Oh, Ammy! Perhaps if she played more outdoors and didn't spend so much time at the piano she'd fill out."

"Its her inheritance."

"You mean she gets it from Godwin. But that's not right. He was good at sports. And you were a whiz at tennis. Do you still play?"

"When I get an opportunity."

"We have tennis at Fairacres. Godwin certainly doesn't look his age."

"He plays racquets at a club. He says he gets more exercise in less time that way; he doesn't have much time for recreation. I've tried to tell him that it's too strenuous a game, especially since he plays with men younger than himself. But he doesn't like any reference to his age."

"Ah, vanity. That's what comes of marrying someone younger than yourself. But, Ammy, I do think you ought to bring Godwina down to Fairacres and let her play with my kids. She's around grown people too much. She should learn to play games with other children. What amazes me is that she is not spoiled rotten. Her father provides her with everything and she leads you round by the nose. But I've never met such a reasonable child. She makes you think you're dealing with an adult. She should have more of the carefreeness of her age. If she played some sport —"

"It's her nature, Trudy. I'm not going to force her to be an athlete if she does not want to be. You and I were tomboys. Winnie isn't."

"We certainly were. Do you remember how awful it was when we had to begin wearing corsets? I wonder if women will ever be able to dress to suit themselves and not the way men seem to think we should."

"I don't know."

"I have joined a suffrage society. Wouldn't you like to come to the rallies with me? It's really exciting to think that we could make a difference. I have big arguments with my father-in-law. He's against it all. I suppose you'll have to ask Godwin's permission."

She meant this as a sly dig and Amantha understood it as such. "Godwin thinks women ought to have the vote. He wouldn't care if I got involved with the suffragettes, as long as I didn't become notorious or got my name in the newspapers."

"Well I never. I should have thought that he'd be opposed to women having any sort of independence."

"Not women generally. Just me, his wife. But he has given me a bank account which he puts money into at regular intervals. I can do what I like with it."

"Amazing. In other words, he doesn't see women as a threat to him. But then he probably doesn't think most men are either. He's pretty autocratic, isn't he? He controls his own world."

They were interrupted by the maid, who brought Amantha a telegram. She tore open the envelope and read it. Then she said to the maid, "Tell Josephine that Mr. Shenstone will be home to dinner tonight."

When the maid had left the room Trudy asked, "Josephine is your cook, isn't she? Does she have to know when Godwin will be home to dinner?"

"She always takes special care when she cooks for him. She has been in love with him ever since he first hired her ten years ago."

Trudy stared at her. "Does he know this?"

"It's not the sort of thing Godwin would overlook."

* * *

169

Godwina took the music score off the rack and placed it neatly on the pile on the low stand beside the piano. She had been practicing for more than an hour, while Amantha sat in the armchair near the window with a book in her lap. She was almost ten years old now and after living in London for three years she knew she did not look the way she had in Paris. Her clothes were different. Her mother made a point of dressing her like Gwen Starratt. Gwen was her best friend. They were both day pupils in the fashionable girls' school just outside London. Most of the time they wore their school uniforms, ugly things but comfortable. When she was at Fairacres people sometimes thought she and Gwen were sisters, though that was silly because she did not look at all like big, boisterous Gwen, who had red hair like Aunt Trudy. When it came to getting other clothes she tried to persuade mamma to get the sort of dresses she liked. Mamma wore beautiful clothes herself and she knew mamma favored what she liked. But for some reason she did not; she said papa would not want that.

She had heard papa say to mamma that she did not look like a little French girl now and he seemed pleased about it. She was not so pleased herself. He did not like her to speak French either. But she always talked French with mamma when they were alone; mamma said she did not want her to forget. Everybody said mamma spoke the most beautiful French and she tried to imitate her. It was strange that papa was that way, because he was half-French and he preferred French things to any others.

She went across the room to Amantha and leaned against her chair. Mamma was not reading. Her book lay closed in her lap and she gazed out of the window but did not seem to be looking at anything in particular. Mamma was often this way when there wasn't anyone else present. She said, "Mamma."

Amantha turned her head and asked, "What is it, baby?"

Then she knew for certain that mamma was thinking sad thoughts;

170

she always called her baby then. "Mamma, I don't want to go to boarding school."

She loved to see mamma's dark blue eyes flash like that. It meant that she was angry. They never flashed like that at her, but she had seen them flash at papa.

"Who has said anything about boarding school?"

"I heard you and papa talking. He wants to send me to boarding school. He said I was big enough now so that it wouldn't hurt me." She saw mamma's face set.

"You are not going to boarding school. He knows that I won't let you go."

Godwina studied Amantha's face. Almost always she did what papa wanted, even if she didn't especially want to. But now and then she said No. Papa was always surprised when this happened but Godwina could have told him that he couldn't push mamma too far.

Mamma went on talking. "For one thing, it would disrupt your music schedule. You'd have to give up regular piano instruction. You wouldn't want that, would you?"

"Oh, no! I couldn't give that up."

Mamma reached out and stroked her head. "Don't worry about it, Winnie. I've told your father you can't possibly go to boarding school. You are not strong enough for one thing."

The school she and Gwen went to gave a lot of attention to playing outdoor games. Aunt Trudy approved of this. She thought girls' schools should be more like boys' schools and that girls should have a chance to excel in athletics. She hated having to play hockey — running around a field with a lot of other girls chasing a little ball. Gwen liked it. In fact, Gwen was captain of a team. But mamma had arranged with the school people that she would be excused from the games program so that she could use that time for music instruction with private teachers. Gwen did not know anything about music but she liked to listen to Godwina play and she was in awe of the way grown up people treated Godwina as a musician.

It was funny that papa did not seem to give much importance to her studying music. Yet he liked music. He knew a lot about music and he was always inviting musicians to come and play at their house. Sometimes some of these visiting musicians had wanted her to play with them; they knew she played well, better than a lot of grown people. But papa would never allow her to. He acted as if he was ashamed of her while she was playing and that stung her. He seemed to be the only person who didn't realize that she was an exceptional pianist. He didn't realize, either, how important music was to her. He thought it was just a pastime. Well, when she grew up and was famous, then he would see.

"Mamma, why does papa want me to go to boarding school?"

She saw mamma bite her lip before she answered. "He thinks you would get a better education if you lived at the school. He doesn't realize that it would upset your music training."

That wasn't true and mamma knew it wasn't. Papa didn't care about her music training. He didn't seem to want her to be a musician.

"Why doesn't he like me being a musician?"

Mamma did not answer right away. Then she said, "Winnie, you're still a little girl. When you get older he'll probably take your aptitude more seriously. He's a very busy man and he can't pay much attention to things outside of his affairs. Let's not worry about that now."

Mamma moved aside a bit in her chair so that Godwina could get in beside her. She liked to sit like this with mamma. She really did wish she could find out what made mamma sad sometimes. The funny thing was that nobody else seemed to notice. Most of the time mamma was busy arranging things, talking to people. She could laugh sometimes so that everybody in the room felt happy just hearing her.

She was supposed to be too big now to take naps in the afternoon but very often she did go to sleep for a while sitting like this while mamma read.

* * *

Amantha was surprised one day when Godwin handed her a list of guests he wanted her to invite for a dinner party and found that it included the Chevalier de Montbrun and his wife. It was several years since they had been guests of the Shenstones. She did not want to ask him why. Thinking it over, she came to the conclusion that here in this London setting, Godwin had grown out of his fears about the threat of exposure. In this more practical climate the past seemed further away and Leonie very distant. He never mentioned her.

In the course of the evening the Chevalier sought her out for a tete-a-tete.

"Madame, what a transformation," he said, looking about. "Godwin has become a London magnate. Do you miss Paris?"

"Of course. And our friends. We see many of them here but it is not the same."

He seemed to be in a grave mood and after they had chatted for a while he said, "You must want to hear of Leonie. Do you know, no one has heard anything of her since she retired to the Auvergne. I went so far as to get in touch with the lawyer who is in charge of her affairs. He tells me that he sends her periodic reports concerning her property but she never replies. The only way he knows that she is even alive is that the money he deposits for her is spent for her necessities. Her housekeeper dispenses it to the local shopkeepers. She has given him instructions about the regular payment of sums to certain charities, which he makes. Otherwise she might not be alive for all he would know."

After a few moments Amantha was able to ask, "What about her relatives?"

"They know nothing. I do not think they make any effort to find out anything. They seem to accept without question her decision to withdraw from the world. They do not expect to inherit from her. It is assumed that her property will go to the Church. So they do not have that interest."

Amantha did not reply and they sat in silence for awhile. Then the

Chevalier said, half angrily as if reflecting the tenor of his thoughts, "In fact, it is as if she was completely forgotten, as if there is no one to remember her. That wonderful beauty, that quick mind, that grace and illuminating presence — It is as if she had never existed. Of course, we know that people are fickle, that they do forget their friends — not you, my dear Amanthe. I know you do not forget your friends — but the general run of people — out of sight, out of mind."

Amantha said quietly, "Perhaps that is what she wants. Perhaps she decided to leave the world so that everyone would forget her."

"Then if that is what she wanted, she has succeeded very well. I have spoken to people who once knew all about her, who her family is, the story of her marriage to Philippe, and they ask me who it is I'm speaking of. It is unnerving. It makes me feel that I myself am losing my reality, that it is just a matter of time before I will be forgotten completely."

He sat and chewed over silently his sense of indignation. Amantha waited for him to go on, which presently he did. "We all know, of course, that the pace of life is increasing these days. All these inventions that Godwin talks about — people do not hold to the old ways so firmly. We give less importance to things that lie in the past. We don't have time to remember." He stopped and looked at her. His eyes were so full of unhappiness that Amantha put her hand over his to comfort him.

She said, "Dear friend, don't grieve so. If Leonie wishes it to be this way, we must accept it." She thought for a while and then said hesitantly, "If you should hear anything of her, you will let me know, won't you? There is no one else to tell me."

He bowed gravely. "You can depend upon me." He added, after a moment, "I do not think that Godwin can know anything about her. I have the impression that he does not concern himself with her any more."

After the last guest had left, Godwin suggested, as he often did, that they have a nightcap together. But Amantha said, "I'll have to go to bed at once. I have a raging headache."

174

She looked so white and drawn that he did not demur. She spent the night alone, lost in the vortex of memory the Chevalier had created.

* * *

They were strolling across the lawn at Fairacres, with parasols to keep off the sun. The wide meadows stretched out beyond the hedges, misty with the unusual warmth of an English summer day.

Trudy said, "Of course, I started it all myself. I have to admit that. Remember the play we put on to benefit the suffrage drive? There was a part in it for a schoolgirl and Gwen badgered me into letting her take it. Ever since she's been convinced that she is going to be an actress. You can imagine how her grandfather would take to that idea!"

"She'll probably outgrow it," said Amantha.

"I hope so, though I'm not so sure. She talks about nothing except acting and Ellen Terry and of course her part in those scenes from Shakespeare that the school puts on as part of their literature classes."

"Winnie has mentioned this. She thinks Gwen is first-rate, much better than any of the other girls."

"That's probably because they're best friends. But I see trouble ahead. If she really wants to make the stage her profession, I'm going to have to support her and that means family rows. Ted won't care. He likes the theater. But his father —"

Trudy did not finish her sentence. They reached the shade of the great oak tree and closing their parasols sat down on the chairs under it.

Trudy said, looking at Amantha, "You look like the latest fashion plate from Paris. But then you are. It seems to me you go to Paris pretty often."

"Godwin takes me there whenever he thinks I need new gowns. He

175

is very particular."

"And you couldn't be seen in the same dress very often, could you? There are dressmakers in London."

"I do go to them. But Godwin is prejudiced in favor of the French."

"He always has been. I remember how your Aunt Katherine used to talk about that. How is she by the way, since your Uncle Ralph died?"

"She's bearing up pretty well. Of course as you know Godwin took us with him the last time he went across, to visit her. She thinks Winnie is more like a normal child now — not a little stranger from Paris."

Trudy smiled at her, catching the edge in her voice. "You do have a time of it, don't you? I know that Winnie doesn't like the way you dress her. She complains to Gwen. She says it is her father who insists on it and you always do what he says. Which is strange, since he usually favors French things."

"He doesn't like her to look exotic in her present surroundings. Godwin thinks it is better if she looks like her schoolmates. He is probably right there, Trudy."

Trudy studied her face. "Is that what Godwin thinks or is that how you rationalize it?"

Amantha frowned. In her forthright way Trudy often came close to the mark. "When we go to Paris —" she began and stopped. Yes, when they went to Paris Winnie turned into a little French girl again. She refused to wear her jumpers and blouses and insisted on having dresses, not entirely the kind she liked but a good compromise. And she spoke only French to everyone. She insisted on visiting Marie, in the patisserie Marie owned with her husband in the rue Monge, and Marie always gratified her by exclaiming with pleasure at her appearance.

Trudy said, "Well, when you go to Paris —?"

"I let her get a dress or two of the kind she wants. Godwin doesn't like it. In fact he doesn't like having her with us then."

Trudy looked surprised. "Why not? Is he jealous of her, with you?"

"No, that is not it."

176

She looked unhappy and Trudy noticed. "Why don't you leave her with me, then?"

"Oh, no, I can't do that. She'd be very upset. She loves to go to Paris and — well — show off. People notice her, you know. She's not your usual eleven-year-old."

"No, she isn't." Trudy paused, as if considering something that she wished to say. Finally she asked, "Ammy, have you ever met any of Godwin's French relations? You've never mentioned them."

"No. His mother died when he was a young man."

"And of course he does not have brothers or sisters. At least, nobody in Baltimore has ever heard of any. But doesn't he have any other relations — uncles, aunts, cousins?"

"He has never spoken of any to me. If there are any living and he is in touch with them, he has never let me know."

"Then I suppose he hasn't any. He's never taken you to see wherever in France his mother came from?"

"No." Amantha thought for a moment. She remembered Leonie's reference to Godwin's mother's people. "I know they are Huguenots — French Protestants. I think they were country gentry. That is all I know. There was nobody at Godwina's christening. He let me have her christened, but as you know, Trudy, Godwin is against religion and church observance. He despises belief in the divine as a form of superstition. I think perhaps he is not interested in his French relations because they are old fashioned people with a provincial outlook. Baltimore is different because that is where the Shenstones belong and of course there is Godwin's Chance."

"I am just wondering where Winnie gets her looks. She is a beautiful child — like a child in an old religious painting, the Italian renaissance painters, for instance. I can understand why your Aunt Katherine doesn't feel altogether at home with her. And she is so ahead of her age intellectually. That's what the trouble is. She is so small — though I must say she is getting quite tall now — that people think of her as a child younger than she is. But she is very quick. She's much more mature than Gwen and there's only a couple of months' difference in their ages. She disconcerts me sometimes. I'm sure you are aware of this."

"Yes. Godwin has always treated her as if she was a grown woman, not a child."

"He is not very fatherly. Ted has his faults but at least he isn't a Grand Pasha."

"Godwin has only one wife and no harem."

Trudy laughed. "You know, it's funny. Ted tells me that Godwin has the reputation of being absolutely faithful to you. The men talk about him because he is so much admired — so successful in business and such a power otherwise, and therefore he could be expected to have a roving eye also — rather like the Prince of Wales. And of course everybody thinks you're the model of Caesar's wife. You're a strange couple in society these days, as I'm sure you know. Did you hear the latest about —"

Several hours later, as Amantha was dressing for dinner, she thought about her conversation with Trudy. Trudy had said that there was to be a special program for the prize-giving at the girls' school. There was to be a play and a concert — to show off the unusual variety of talents among the current crop of pupils, no doubt. Gwen would have the lead in the play; she could think of nothing else. And Winnie was to give a recital.

Amantha's mind dwelt on this prospect. Uneasily she felt she should mention it to Godwin. He had always refused to allow Godwina to play the piano before an audience, no matter how informal a one. The servants in the house respected her ability, though they had little appreciation of the sort of music she played. They often listened when she practiced in Amantha's sitting room, as they went about their duties. They recognized the seriousness with which Godwina treated her own gift. Godwina was not oblivious of this domestic audience.

If she spoke to him about the recital and he refused to permit it, she dreaded the thought of denying Godwina this coveted opportunity. She picked a moment to mention it when he was obviously much preoccupied with his business affairs; for several days he had paid very little attention to anything she said. Now when she talked about a program for the prize-giving at the school which would include Godwina playing the piano, he let it pass with only an absentminded nod. She sighed her relief and told the school's directress that Winnie could have her recital. There was not the remotest possibility, she knew, that Godwin would accompany her and join the other parents for the occasion.

There was then the question of a dress. Godwina refused to wear anything that made her look like a schoolgirl. For this occasion she had to have a dress that approximated what a woman pianist would wear before a real audience. She had often seen the women among the professional musicians who came to the Shenstone's musical evenings.

"But, Winnie, you're only a little girl. You can't dress like them."

"Not exactly," said Godwina, "but I can have a dress that looks something like that." In the end Godwina won. Amantha had already learned that she had an instinctive sense of style. The dress she finally accepted was very simple, a little longer than those she normally wore, a pale blue in color, silk, and with only a belt of the same material instead of a sash. Her hair she insisted must be held back from her face by a large barrette at the back of her neck; no bows.

Amantha realized that this was an event that in Winnie's eyes was a turning-point in her life. Being with her when she took her bath, which she often was, and drying her off with the big towel, an attention Godwina loved, Amantha saw the first signs of puberty in the thin little body — the soft fuzz beginning between her thighs, the softness growing about her nipples. Trudy had reported to her that Gwen was quite far along.

Trudy said, "I suppose you've told Winnie what she ought to know. You remember, we had to learn all that from the big girls at school."

"Yes," said Amantha, remembering. "I've told Winnie what to expect and what it means."

"I'm sure that those two have compared notes — and done a little

179

experimenting." Trudy looked meaningfully at Amantha as she spoke.

Amantha answered her gaze, "Winnie hasn't said anything about it to me. But suddenly she is getting shy about her body."

Trudy sighed. "We all have to go through it, don't we?"

The result of Winnie's preparations for her recital cost Amantha a sharp pang. When she saw Godwina dressed ready for the occasion she saw a miniature of Leonie. When Godwina appeared on the platform to play she could scarcely watch her and shut her eyes for a moment to regain her self-possession.

Godwina was very well satisfied by the small triumph of her first appearance before a real audience. Of course, she told Amantha, she realized that the group of parents and other relatives had no idea of what they were hearing, of the quality of the music or the excellence of her playing, but they clapped dutifully.

"I made some mistakes, mamma," she said complacently, "but you're probably the only person who noticed, except Mme. Vaux the music teacher."

Amantha, looking down into her upraised face, saw in it triumph, condescension, complete self-confidence. She caught her breath. This was Godwin's daughter.

Trudy also noticed. "I never saw such self-possession in a child that age — or several years older, for that matter," she said. "You'd expect stage fright. Gwen is so wrapped up in Ellen Terry that she thinks she is Ellen Terry. That's the only thing that kept her from forgetting her lines. Well, I'm glad this is over. You look a little fagged, Ammy. Will you come down to Fairacres for a day or two?"

Amantha nodded. She often visited at Fairacres with Godwina when Godwin was away for several days. He approved of the friendship between Godwina and Gwen. In fact, he urged her to leave Godwina with the Starratts; it would be better for her he said. Amantha ignored his suggestions. She recognized his purpose: he wanted Godwina out of the way. He did not openly banish her now, did not demand that Amantha

180

send her to the nursery when he was home, as he had done when she was younger. He made an effort to be attentive when she talked about her school or about things she had learned or seen; she was an observant child. When she played the piano he listened briefly and then walked out of the room.

Amantha saw that Godwina was becoming more and more aware that he was not genuinely affectionate nor even sympathetic toward her. When she was younger she had been delighted by any notice he paid her. Now she was becoming conscious of the fact that he did not want the affection she poured out to him. Amantha knew that there was a deep well of love in Godwina ready to rise to the surface at the least appeal. But she was also perceptive to an unusual degree, perceptive of the true character of the adults she encountered.

As she grew older there was bound to be a conflict between Godwin and his daughter. Like him, she held to whatever course she had decided upon. Like him, though she was loyal to her friends, she did not fail to see the flaws in them and did not allow herself to be led astray by their deficiencies.

Godwin, Amantha knew, did not realize this development in Godwina of traits so like his own. He saw her still as a child, one he wished to exclude from his inner life. It would be useless for Amantha to try to enlighten him. She had learned that he did not recognize in himself the qualities that were most distinctive of him.

That was how Godwina differed from him. That was how she was like Leonie. Godwina seemed to have, even at eleven years old, an understanding of herself. Perhaps, thought Amantha, I am attributing to her some of what I know is Leonie's unclouded insight into the clash of wills. I must not burden the little girl with emotional responsibilities that are not yet hers. But I must be watchful.

She was also watchful of Godwin. He had passed his fiftieth birthday — he forbade any notice to be taken of his birthday but she knew he was aware of this milestone in his life. He insisted on maintaining the same strenuous pace in his business and personal affairs as he always had. She tried to persuade him to seek some milder form of exercise than the game of racquets but he rebuffed her curtly. There was nothing the matter with him. He slept soundly at night. He had his usual good appetite. He had never abused his body with an excess of anything. He slept with her several times a week. He saw no need for concern.

Nevertheless, one day she noticed he looked seedy and he admitted that he felt as if he had picked up some common ailment. Several of his business associates had cancelled engagements because of illness. He seldom was under the weather and when he was it passed quickly. She suggested that he come home early and not go to his usual session at the racquet club. He did not answer her.

In the afternoon she went to a suffragist rally with Trudy. She had left Godwina at home and she was eager as she arrived back at the house to see if she was all right. As she stepped into the vestibule she listened as she always did on such occasions for the sound of the piano. She was reassured when she heard faint strains of music in the distance. Godwina must be practicing in her sitting room.

But the parlor maid, who had opened the door to her, burst out, "Oh, ma'am, the master is taken ill! He is in his study."

Before she had finished speaking, Amantha was going up the stairs, stripping off her gloves as she went. Godwin's study was on the first flight up, behind the drawing room. The door was open and she saw him lying on the leather couch, his arm over his eyes.

She sat down on the edge of the couch. "Godwin, what is the matter?"

He took his arm away and looked up at her. There was an expression in his eyes she had never seen before. She unfastened his cravat and opened the neck of his shirt; none of the servants had had the temerity to do this. She sent for some water and sponged his face.

He caught hold of her hand and said in a hoarse whisper, "She was in there — in the drawing room." He found the effort too great to speak further and gave it up. By degrees she coaxed him to get up and let her lead him to his bedroom, where she helped him undress and get into bed. She gave Ellen the parlor maid a message to send to their doctor. She sat beside him until he fell asleep without attempting to speak.

She went out into the corridor. Where was Winnie? There was no sound of the piano. She saw the maid, who had been hovering near the bedroom door, and asked her what had happened. The maid said that Miss Godwina had been playing the piano in the drawing room when the master came home. He had asked for Amantha and the maid had told him that she was out with Mrs. Starratt. He went into the drawing room and then suddenly came out, staggering, and went to his study. It was obvious he was not well. Miss Godwina? She was in the sitting room. She went there to play the piano after the master left the drawing room.

Amantha climbed the next flight of stairs and went to her sitting room. She opened the door and her heart turned over as she saw Godwina standing by the piano. Godwina was dressed as she had been for the school recital. When Amantha could speak, she said quietly, "Winnie, why were you playing the piano in the drawing room?"

The clear grey eyes looked directly at her. Godwina said, "Because I wanted to."

"You know you are not supposed to use that piano. This is yours here."

"That is a concert grand, mamma. I wanted to try it. Don't you remember, Mme. Maillol in Paris used to teach me on it. Why can't I play on it now?"

It was on the tip of Amantha's tongue to say, because your father says you're not to. But she checked herself. "You should have waited till you could ask permission."

Godwina tossed her head as she did when she was thwarted and turned away from her. Amantha said, "And take that dress off and put on your ordinary clothes. I got you that dress for the recital. You're not to use it for anything else." When Godwina did not move and did not answer, she said sharply, "Do as I say at once."

She walked across the room and taking Godwina's hand led her to the door and down the corridor to the room that was once the nursery and was now Godwina's bedroom, next to her own. Godwina went obediently with her and did not protest when she unbuttoned the dress and took it off her. She put on the clothes Amantha handed her and stood patiently while Amantha fastened the buttons.

They did not speak until at last Amantha asked, "Winnie, why did you do this?"

Godwina did not look up. "I wanted to feel the way I felt when I was playing in the recital — I wanted — " She suddenly burst into tears and ran into Amantha's arms.

Amantha, soothing her, listened with a heavy heart to her sobs. At last when she quieted and raised her head, so that Amantha could wipe away her tears, Amantha asked, "Winnie, what happened with your father?"

Godwina wiped her nose with Amantha's handkerchief and swallowed. "I don't know. I was playing Mozart's Sonata in A Major. I heard Ellen open the door and papa's voice, so I stopped. He must have heard me playing because he came to the drawing room right away. He saw me standing by the piano and I thought he was going to scold me but he stopped and all at once went out of the room. I heard Ellen ask him if he felt all right. I waited till they went away and then I came up here."

"He did not say anything to you?"

Godwina hesitated and then, looking at her in distress, said, "He thought I was someone else."

She whimpered as Amantha caught her closely in her arms. It was an involuntary movement and Amantha held her tightly, murmuring, "Oh, baby, baby!" When she finally released her Godwina saw that she was pale and downcast.

The doctor told Amantha that Godwin had been making too many demands on himself. He must learn to go more slowly, to reduce the number of hours he worked and take more time for mild recreation. Amantha, listening to this prescription, said she would pass on his suggestions when Godwin felt better.

Which he did in a few days. He was up and about the next day and back in his office on the third. He made no mention of what had happened. But he reiterated his prohibition about the drawing room piano. Godwina was not to play it; she had a perfectly good one to use in Amantha's sitting room. Amantha noticed that he also avoided looking at Godwina and gave short answers when she spoke to him.

Amantha saw that Godwina was badly affected by the episode. Except when alone with Amantha or when she was with Gwen, she was a quiet child. Now she was untalkative and sat studying her music scores, or at least, Amantha decided, holding them as if she were, to cover her brooding. Amantha realized that there was a growing rebellion mixed in with her unhappiness. She tried to rouse her, to coax her to shake off her moodiness but Godwina resisted her efforts.

Godwin announced that he was going away on a business trip to the Orient and he would be gone several weeks. After he made this announcement he was silent for a few minutes and then added, "My dear, I'd like you to come with me. I know you'd enjoy the trip. You can leave Godwina with the Starratts. They always seem willing to have her stay."

Amantha said promptly, "I can't, Godwin. She is not very happy just now. It would be unkind. Can't we take her with us?"

He was immediately angry. "No! I will not have her with us."

Anger rose in Amantha in response. It did not seem to occur to him to inquire what made Godwina unhappy. Did he really not know that it was his treatment of her? And did he not care? Or was he really unaware? She said, "Godwin, she is your child. She is also Leonie's child. She is a little girl. You should not act towards her this way."

She was not prepared for the fury that appeared in his eyes. He was standing over her and in his rage he seized hold of her arm in an iron grip. He had never used any physical force with her before and she was astonished as well as indignant. He declared furiously, "That passage in my life is closed. Finished. I want no reminders. I'll not tolerate any reference to it, any recollection of it. I forbid you ever to speak of it again to me."

Alarmed at the redness of his face and his heavy breathing, Amantha sat still and bore the pain of his grip without protest. Suddenly realizing that he held her with force he released her arm and moved away. There was no possibility of reasoning with him in this mood so she said nothing. After several minutes he turned back to her and said in a voice still filled with anger but under control, "I'm leaving at the end of the week. I'll keep you posted about my itinerary."

* * *

A certain tranquility settled over the house when he left. Godwina's spirits began to revive. She no longer brooded. Each night when Amantha went to bed she found her already under the covers, asleep. Amantha made no engagements for evening affairs. She joined Trudy at feminist meetings, more a spectator than an activist, since she knew she could not make commitments without Godwin's consent. Otherwise she let the days and nights slip by in peace.

Trudy, dropping in for a cup of tea one afternoon, said, "I do wonder about you, Ammy. When we were girls you were always enthusiastic about everything. You were fun to be with because you were excited about something all of the time. I know we were all as ignorant as could be about most things in those days and since then we've learned a lot that has sobered us up. But nothing seems to matter much to you now — except Winnie. If you have a row with Godwin, it's bound to have something to do with her. You did have a row with him before he left, didn't you?"

"Not really a row. He wanted me to go with him but he wouldn't take Winnie. He was going to leave her with you."

"Well, I'd have been very glad to have her. She and Gwen like to be together. I suppose he just wants you to himself. That's rather flattering after more than ten years of marriage." She watched as Amantha walked with languid grace across the room to look out of the window.

At last Amantha said, "It's just the passage of time, Trudy. I was really a child when I married. I don't think I had as much common sense as you had."

"You mean you would not have married Godwin if you'd known better. I don't know about that. It was a pretty heady business, being pursued by a man like him, even if he was twenty years older."

"Perhaps I've just been spoiled. I can have anything I want from Godwin, you know."

Trudy looked at her skeptically. "All the dresses you want and theater tickets and that sort of thing, yes." She paused and then asked, "Is it really that bad, Ammy, putting up with Godwin?"

Amantha's smoothly coifed head turned abruptly around. "No, of course not. I don't complain of him."

"Well, you can't call your soul your own. You did really love him when you married him. From what I remember, you adored him. You were speechless about him. He has worn all that away, hasn't he?"

"He's not a sentimental man, Trudy. But without him I would not have Winnie."

"She was an accident, wasn't she?"

"Yes."

Godwin wrote regularly, whenever he moved from one place to another. He said he was acquiring Oriental antiquities which he was having shipped home. Amantha wondered what they would do with all these things in the house, which was already full of paintings and objets d'art that Godwin had gathered over the years.

"You can always get a bigger house," said Trudy.

Trudy had a penchant for visiting dealers in antiques. The Starratt houses were well supplied with china, paintings, carpets, objets d'art which several generations of Starratts had accumulated. But, said Trudy, she wanted her own collections of things for a house which some day she and Ted would have for their own. She took Amantha with her on many of these expeditions into odd corners of London to visit dark little shops filled chiefly with rubbish among which sometimes there was a treasure to be found.

Amantha wondered if this in fact ever happened. But Trudy's enthusiasm did not wane. While Trudy rummaged around in jumbled lots of chinaware and tarnished silver, Amantha's attention wandered to tables loaded with old prints and engravings and piles of dusty books.

In one such shop she noticed in a far corner a quantity of paintings in frames stacked against the wall. Idly she moved them so that she could look at them. She recognized them as being in the style of the French impressionists; there were canvasses by several of these painters hanging on the walls of the Shenstone house. Surely, she thought, none of these could be the work of such painters. If so, they would be on display in the windows of art dealers in Bond Street or other places where wealthy people would be expected to see them and buy them. Nevertheless, as Trudy would contend, it was in such out-of-the-way places that treasures might be found.

Examining some of the paintings, her own taste and knowledge told her that these were not the work of first-rate painters but that of imitators and even copyists. Some of them were pleasing enough and one or two she rather liked. They were obviously French, scenes of river banks and villages and country lanes. A few were interiors or portraits of men, women, or children. But none of them were, she knew, of a quality that Godwin would permit in his house.

She gave up the hunt through the stacked pile, rueful at the state of her gloves. She turned her attention to some books on a table; she sometimes found books in French which she bought for passing entertainment. The shopkeeper had noticed her interest in the paintings and he came to her side and said, "Madam, would you like to see more of the pictures? I can pull them out for you."

She was reluctant to say Yes, because she knew he hoped she would make a purchase. He did not wait for her reply and began to set aside the paintings she had seen and to draw out others. He propped them up against the clutter of objects surrounding them and tried to provide a little more light.

"Where do these come from?" she asked.

"These are from France, madam. They were sent to me by somebody who bought them at an estate sale — the property of a gentleman who collected them during the lifetime of the artists. You see, they are about twenty years old." He pointed to faded lettering on the frames.

"Some of them are not signed — unless there is some symbol hidden in the detail that identifies the painter."

"That may be, madam, that may be." He was getting near the end of the pile. He lifted up one more painting, a small frame perhaps two feet square, and placed it in front of her.

At first all she saw was that the palette of colors that the artist had used was lighter than those of the other paintings she had been looking at; there were no large black or dark patches and she thought of Mary Cassatt and Berthe Morisot. But then her heart stopped. This was the portrait of a young girl with pale blond hair seated at a piano with her eyes turned toward the viewer — clear grey eyes wonderfully painted. There was a small tag on the frame which read in French Girl at the Piano.

Trudy's voice sounded at her shoulder. "Good lord! That's Winnie!"

Amantha murmured, "No, not Winnie."

"It's just like her!"

The shopkeeper, alert to the interest aroused in the two women by the painting, said, "The painting is twenty years old."

"Where did it come from?" Trudy demanded.

"From the sale of the property of a deceased French gentleman, madam. I've had it here for some time. I think perhaps these paintings are valuable."

"But you have not had them appraised?"

"I cannot afford that."

"But then you might be selling them at a much lower price than you could obtain otherwise."

"That is true. Does madam believe that this painting is valuable?"

He addressed his question to Amantha, who did not seem to hear him. Trudy, noticing this, asked, "Ammy, do you want the picture?"

Amantha turned to look at her. "Yes," she murmured.

It was Trudy who bargained with the shopkeeper. "You haven't any idea who the painter was? Can the person you bought it from find out?"

The shopkeeper said No.

Finally they left the shop with the painting wrapped in newspaper.

Trudy said, "Ammy, you must take it to Sotheby's or somewhere to have it appraised. You can probably find out who the painter and the subject were that way." She glanced at Amantha, who did not answer. "Are you all right? You look pale."

"It was very close in that shop."

She arrived home before Godwina returned from school. The parlor maid took the package from her and carried it up to her sitting room.

"Just put it down there," she said, pointing to a chair. "I'll undo it."

She took off her gloves and unwrapped the painting and stood it so that the light from the window fell on it. It was a painting whose colors though muted held within them a limpid glow. If this was the work of a minor artist, he or she had been inspired when creating it. The girl could not be anyone but Leonie at fifteen or sixteen, virginal, angelic, ethereal. The clear grey eyes gazed out of a pale dewy-fresh face, surrounded by disheveled pale blond hair. Whoever had painted it had caught a glimpse of the essence of Leonie. The expression in the eyes was both appealing and withdrawn. She wore a white dress only lightly outlined. In fact, it looked as if this might be a sketch, done from life and never finished; the piano was indicated only by a few strokes of the brush.

Amantha leaned her chin on her hands gripping the top of the tall chair back, her eyes closed. For four years now Leonie had inhabited her inmost being, as alive as she had been in that last meeting in the de Brieux mansion. Nothing had faded and now this sketch, these few strokes of paint on canvas had brought Leonie out of the shadows where she had hid her image away from any searching eyes.

After a while she roused herself to pick up the painting and carry it to the wardrobe in her dressing room, where she hid it, the face turned away, behind her gowns.

The next time they met Trudy wanted to know what she intended to do about identifying the painting.

"Nothing," she said.

"Well, what are you going to do with it?" Trudy looked briefly around the sitting room to see if it was in sight.

"Really nothing, Trudy. It's not a painting Godwin would approve of. It's just something I like."

Trudy studied her face for a while. She had grown used to Amantha's lack of spirit but now she detected something more. It seemed sometimes that Amantha was actually grieving. But over what?

She was surprised when Amantha said, with urgency, "Trudy, please don't say anything about the painting to anyone."

"Well, of course I won't, if that is what you want. But why, Ammy? It seems to make you unhappy. And it's such an amazing likeness of Winnie. Or what Winnie will be in two or three years' time."

"No, no," Amantha protested distractedly. "No. She won't be just like that. Winnie won't be so vulnerable. She is too like Godwin."

Trudy gazed at her, puzzled. "You're talking in riddles, Ammy. I do sometimes think that when she gets older, Godwin will meet his match in her. But where will you be then — in the middle?"

Amantha simply gazed at her. "Godwin must never see this painting, Trudy. For my sake, he must never see it or know about it."

Amantha's head was lowered. She looked so dejected that Trudy got

191

up and went over to put her arm around her shoulders. "What is it, Ammy? Can't you tell me?"

Amantha did not respond but raised her hand to cover Trudy's.

Trudy tried again. "Ammy, are you in love with somebody?"

Amantha raised her head. "If I am in love with somebody, who would it be?"

Her tone was so bitter and her expression so disdainful that Trudy was nonplussed. "I have no idea. But you do act as if you are in love. I hope you're not getting yourself in hot water. You have a hard enough time with Godwin without that."

Amantha sat back in her chair and looked up at her "Don't worry, Trudy. There's not a man on this earth that could tempt me." Her tone was so utterly dismissive that Trudy sighed in relief.

* * *

Godwin came back earlier than he had planned. He cabled ahead. His ship would dock in Liverpool and he expected to be met there.

Amantha and Godwina were there to meet him. He kissed Amantha and then, with a little hesitation, kissed Godwina on the forehead. He seemed to realize as he did so that she was taller. She was no longer the little girl he was used to.

Godwin came back from his trip to the East in unusually good spirits. He came back early, he said, because he was able to finish up his business successfully and quickly and he had missed her. He looked well; he seemed to have shed years in his vigor and outlook. He was amorous in bed. He was eager to plunge into the whirl of London life.

There was a subtle change in his attitude towards Godwina. She joined her parents at dinner now when they did not have guests. She sat in the middle of the long side of the dining room table and turned from one to the other of them as they spoke, alert and eager. She was no longer frightened into silence by her father's presence. If he talked about something

192

within her ken, she spoke up. Amantha, watching Godwin, saw that at first he was disconcerted by this forwardness but then seemed to be resigned to it, as if he realized that she was approaching adolescence and could not be ignored as when she was younger. Perhaps, Amantha thought hopefully, he would eventually come to accept her as herself and not simply as the unwanted reminder of her mother.

Godwina's self-assurance was growing. She was no longer a child being taught music as an accomplishment. She studied now with young people older than herself. Her virtuosity was recognized and respected. It attracted the attention of professional musicians. She played in informal recitals with them. Very often she knew personally the musicians who came to perform at the Shenstones' musical evenings. She had no doubts about her own ability. She was acquiring a personal circle of friends who were charmed by her combination of musical talent, unusual beauty, and a natural grace of manner.

It was obvious to Amantha that the time was coming soon when it would be impossible to deny her the recognition of her gift. She did not know how much Godwin was aware of Godwina's burgeoning, whether he had learned from others of her growing reputation as a pianist.

Trudy, who was inclined to be critical of so much attention being paid to so young a child, admitted that Godwina did not seem to be spoiled by it. "But, Ammy, she does certainly seem to have a mind of her own. I'm afraid you're going to find yourself in the middle between two first class egoists."

"She is just a little girl still," said Amantha stubbornly. "I am glad she has Gwen. She needs someone her own age."

"Oh, they're devoted, though Gwen is out of her depth sometimes with Winnie's musician friends. Gwen is still certain she's going to be the next great actress on the London stage. I suppose they make a good pair. I've promised Gwen that sometime this year, perhaps around her birthday, we'll stage an Elizabethan masque at Fairacres. Queen Elizabeth stayed overnight at Fairacres on one of her royal progresses, so that will be appropriate. Winnie is to be one of the court musicians."

Amantha, stretched to the limit, occasionally found a quiet moment. It was then that she brought the painting out of its hiding place. It was otherwise undisturbed. Either her maid had not noticed that it was there or discreetly overlooked it. Gazing at it gave her the only surcease she had from the feeling of loss that underlay everything else in her life. There was no other thing or person to which she could turn for comfort.

* * *

A couple of months after Godwina's twelfth birthday, Godwin was notified that a great storm had devastated lands around the mouth of the Chesapeake Bay and caused havoc at Godwin's Chance. He would have to go across the Atlantic at once, he said, to assess the damage. Amantha could visit with Aunt Katherine. Apparently, he expected Godwina to accompany them. Amantha protested. "Godwin, will it do any good for you just to be there? Wouldn't it be better to wait till things clear up?" But he said that he had to go. He was suddenly so alarmed at what he had heard that he swept aside any attempt of hers to restrain him.

On the ship across the Atlantic he was restless and impatient, pacing the deck for hours even in bad weather, checking the weather reports received by the captain every few hours. These reports were not good. The storm was followed by heavy rains that, with only temporary breaks, were continuing. The lands surrounding the Bay were flooded; the rivers were out of their banks. Godwin seemed completely obsessed by the thought of the destruction at Godwin's Chance. The news he had received was piecemeal and incomplete. Nobody yet knew the extent of the damage. He had little to say to anyone except the ship's captain and the officer in charge of the weather reports. Amantha was aware that he had become remote, far out of her ken, wrapped up in a world to which she had no access.

Watching him drive himself to exhaustion in his frustration, Amantha

194

realized fully for the first time that Godwin's Chance was his talisman, the symbol of his financial power, the inner token of his life. He was a man who despised the sentimental; the bowing to tradition except in the most superficial, social matters; the cultivation of nostalgia; the reliance on fetishes. The Goddess of Reason was the only deity he acknowledged. Nevertheless, the very strength of his will hid an emotional basis of his character that he himself did not recognize. She knew that he was far from being the coldly rational man he believed himself to be.

Godwina was frightened by him now, as she had been when she was younger. The first steps to independence she had taken during the last year were lost as she was once more the little girl conscious of a rejection she did not understand. Amantha, noticing this, made a point of keeping her close by. Godwina's stateroom connected with that of her parents and in the night Amantha got up to go to her when she cried out. She was afraid of the violent motion of the ship in the stormy weather; this passage was rougher than any they had experienced before. The objects in the cabin, the bottles and jars on the dressing table flew about and crashed. The tables in the dining room were fitted with fiddles to hold the china and silverware. Walking along the corridors was difficult and perilous. Even then Godwin roamed about the more sheltered decks. His attention remained riveted on his intent to reach Godwin's Chance.

It was pouring rain when they arrived at Aunt Katherine's house in Baltimore. Godwin scarcely waited for their greetings to be exchanged and the luggage unloaded before he began to speak of making arrangements to travel down to Godwin's Chance. Aunt Katherine said it was impossible. No real news had been received since the storm because communication was so difficult. The whole region was flooded. The only means of transport was by boat. They had heard that the overseer's family, like many other people living in the vicinity, had had to be rescued. The tobacco fields were inundated but the damage there seemed less since that was higher ground.

Amantha saw Godwin's growing impatience as he listened to Aunt

Katherine's account. When she finished he left the house. He was going to see what he could do, at least to get down to St. Mary's City. From there he could make a better estimate of the possibility of reaching Godwin's Chance. He came back in the evening. He had heard more detailed news of the conditions down in the lower Bay. It had not reassured him. He would leave in the morning.

Amantha, listening quietly to his statement, suddenly spoke up. "Godwin, please don't go there now. There is nothing you or anyone else can do until the water goes down. You are just endangering yourself. Please don't go."

He turned his head to look at her, surprised by the firmness of her demand. "I've got to go. I must be there so that I can have things done as soon as it is possible. I can't sit here twiddling my thumbs. I can't take you with me because I think the conditions are pretty bad. But I have got to go."

For the first time in a good while he slept well that night. Amantha, lying awake listening to his breathing, fought the urge to awaken him and try to convince him that he should not go. Perhaps it was the nervous strain of the stormy ocean crossing and the constant sense of anxiety created by his driving intent, but she felt an inescapable need to restrain him. As he said, rationally, there was no real danger in his going to St. Mary's City. But what lay beyond that and how would he react to the situation he found there? She had a great mistrust of him, of what he would do, how foolhardy he might be. She had never had this strong feeling before that she should try to change his course of action.

He woke early — he was an early riser by habit, in any case — and dressed quickly. Amantha got out of bed and put on her dressing gown. He said, "Don't bother. I'll get some breakfast on the way." She followed him down to the parlor, in spite of his efforts to dissuade her. The weather was still rainy but at the moment there was a let up. He had ordered a cab and they waited for its arrival. He seemed very cheerful, exhilarated by the prospect of effective action, of being able to control the situation that lay before him. When the cab came he bent hurriedly to kiss her. Overcome by the strength of her own feelings she caught hold of him and exclaimed, "Godwin, don't go! Wait another day. They say there is water everywhere. You'll just be waiting in St. Mary's City. If you wait here —"

His patience seemed to give out. He pushed her away. "This is pointless. I tell you I am going to find out for myself. Stop hindering me." He took her hands away from his arm and turned to the door as the cabman came to fetch him and strode out of the house.

Amantha, still driven by her inner need, followed him to the door and stood helpless as he got into the cab and rode away into the grey dawn light, the cab horse's clip-clop the only sound in the empty street. It was then that she became aware that Aunt Katherine had also come down to the parlor in her dressing gown. She put her arm around Amantha.

"Don't distress yourself so, child," she said. "You can't stop him. We'll just have to hope for the best."

* * *

It was three days before word reached them that Godwin had been drowned. To the local people he died a hero. When he reached St. Mary's City he insisted on going down to Godwin's Chance, though the land was so flooded that common landmarks and fishermen's shelters and the small cabins of farm workers were swallowed up by the vast sheets of water. It would be weeks before any sort of normality returned to the area.

Portions of the house at Godwin's Chance had been unroofed by the storm. The remainder lay under several feet of water, the swift flowing waters of the river and creek that lay on either side of it. The small boats that tried to navigate it were frequently swept out of their courses. Godwin had insisted on taking one of these small boats out into the current to reach a bit of land that still rose above the flood. A woman and some children had been marooned there in a sharecropper's cabin. The boat

197

had capsized and there had been no chance of rescue. Amantha, listening to this account through the cloud of shock that held her captive, remembered the silently flowing yellow stream in the millrace, swift and unstoppable. The memory rose before her eyes; she could not banish it.

She was caught in mute protest against the reality of Godwin's death, held in the grip of a paralysis of will. Mechanically she went to bed at night to lie in a sleepless daze, conscious only of Godwina pressed against her. Godwina was half-terrified by a catastrophe she only partially understood, half unconvinced that it had happened. Throughout her short life Godwin had come and gone sometimes for days, sometimes for weeks. Perhaps this story of his drowning would turn out not to be true. She could get no reassurance from Amantha, who responded with a hug when she put her arms around her neck seeking comfort, but said nothing.

Aunt Katherine, in alarm at Amantha's complete withdrawal into herself, tried her best to rouse her to a consciousness of what was happening around her. Amantha shed no tears; it was as if the shock had dried up any spring of emotion in her. Aunt Katherine found herself more and more left to the company of Godwina. Such a curiously grown-up child, she thought.

Godwina, aware that Aunt Katherine felt excluded from Amantha's mind and emotions, made several careful attempts to excuse her mother. Mamma wasn't feeling well, she said. Aunt Katherine, recognizing these efforts and captivated by the quaint courtesy which prompted them, kissed her and said she knew that Amantha was very sad and that they would have to give her time to recover.

Godwina grew restless in the atmosphere of subdued distress in the house. Her one answer to such moments of unhappiness was to practice her music. She tried the piano in Aunt Katherine's parlor but it had not been tuned for years and she made a face at its sound. Realizing that Amantha could not help, she appealed directly to Aunt Katherine, who sent for the piano tuner that very day. After that she played softly at odd moments when there were no visitors.

Godwin's New York agent arrived with the New York, London, and Paris newspapers, filled with long accounts of Godwin's major successes in the financial world, his reputation as a patron of the arts, his humanitarian enterprises. Amantha responded with murmured phrases to the visitors who came with condolences; it was obvious to Aunt Katherine that her responses were automatic, unfelt. She tried as much as she could to shield Amantha from the flood of visitors and letters. Mechanically Amantha obeyed when she said it was time to come to dinner, time to go to bed, time to get up and dress.

Two weeks passed before the flood waters receded enough for Godwin's body to be found; it was identifiable only by his clothing. Foster, the overseer, badly shaved and in bedraggled clothes, came to tell them. Standing in Aunt Katherine's parlor, he said, "Mrs. Shenstone, ma'am, we tried all we could to keep him from going out in that boat. The water was so deep you couldn't tell where the current from the creek was. You know, Mrs. Shenstone, that nobody could stop Mr. Shenstone from doing something he'd made up his mind to. He was a brave man. There were two watermen lost with him."

He held out his hand to Amantha. In the palm was the signet ring Godwin always wore. Amantha gazed at it for a long moment, then suddenly turned on her heel and walked quickly out of the room. Foster stared after her and then put the ring carefully down on a nearby table.

"That poor lady," he said to Aunt Katherine. "This is a terrible business, Mrs. Leggett. He was a wonderful man."

Aunt Katherine, eager for him to leave so that she could see to Amantha, replied, "I'm sure he will be greatly missed by many people, Mr. Foster."

Godwin was buried in the corner of the graveyard filled with Shenstones. Amantha, wearing a high-collared black dress and a hat with a black veil, refused to allow Godwina to be dressed in black. A dove grey was enough, she said. Aunt Katherine, looking at the pale child with the two pale blond braids hanging down her back, agreed.

The letter from London arrived. Aunt Katherine gave it to Amantha, who tore open the envelope and read it, holding it in her hand for several moments before she said in a stony voice, "Mr. Weatherbee says Godwina and I must come back to London immediately. There can't be any more delay in settling Godwin's affairs."

"Who is he?" Aunt Katherine inquired.

"Godwin's solicitor — his firm is in charge of Godwin's affairs. Mr. Weatherbee is the senior partner."

Godwin's New York agent came to escort Amantha and Godwina to the ship in New York. Aunt Katherine had been anxious when they left her house. Amantha was surprisingly efficient when it came to packing and getting ready to leave but she wondered how she would manage during the sea voyage.

Their passage across the Atlantic this time was calm, with a number of days when Amantha could sit on a deck chair in a sheltered spot, with Godwina beside her. Godwina had got used to her profound withdrawal. She always responded when Godwina made an appeal, but it was always brief. They stayed in their stateroom most of the time; an arrangement had been made by the New York agent at the time he booked their passage to have their meals served there. Every morning when the weather permitted they walked up and down the promenade deck. Once Godwina persuaded Amantha to stroll through the public rooms. When they reached the midships lounge Godwina exclaimed, "Oh, mamma, look, there is a piano!"

Amantha glanced where she pointed but made no response.

One morning, as they approached the end of the voyage, they went out on deck even though the weather was misty and cool. Godwina stood beside Amantha by the rail, watching the water pass swiftly by the side of the ship. Every so often she looked up at Amantha's face. It was as if, she thought, there was a curtain drawn over it through which she could not see. For days now she had tried to pierce this cloud in which Amantha was wrapped but she had not succeeded in the least. She felt her mother's withdrawal as a burden on her heart. She did not have the solace of music and its inaccessibility irritated and saddened her. Then she remembered the piano in the lounge. She looked up again at Amantha but Amantha was far away. Quietly she left her side and walked quickly to a door into the ship and went through it.

There was no one in the lounge. It was not a place where many people sat, only an occasional person who sought a quiet moment alone. She had no music scores with her but there was a lot that she could play from memory. She sat down and began to play. Within a few minutes she became aware that several people had come to listen. Before long there was a fair-sized crowd standing next to the walls or sitting on the steps that led down to the well in which the piano was placed. They clapped when she came to a pause and asked for more music. She was exhilarated and happy, freed from the claustrophobic gloom of the past weeks.

Then glancing up, she saw Amantha standing in the entrance to the corridor. She stopped playing, holding her breath, staring at Amantha. But Amantha made no move and said nothing. She went on playing, finishing the piece she had begun, and then, faltering, excused herself to the people nearest her and ran over to Amantha, who took her hand. They walked down the corridor to their stateroom.

Apprehensive and defiant, she waited for Amantha's scolding. But Amantha sat down in the armchair without a word. She seemed to have forgotten Godwina, the lounge, the music, the listeners. With a cry of despair Godwina climbed onto her lap, beating her fists on Amantha's shoulders. Amantha caught her hands and held them while she sobbed in fright and frustration.

* * *

A younger partner in Mr. Weatherbee's firm was at the dockside to greet them when the ship reached Liverpool. He saw them ashore and sent their luggage on ahead. As many transatlantic passengers did, they spent the night in Chester in a hotel where Godwin was well known. In London the next day the Starratts with Gwen were on the station platform when the train arrived.

Trudy exclaimed, seeing Amantha in her black dress and veil, "Oh, Ammy!" and took her in her arms. Ted Starratt, a tall thin fair man, stood by sympathetically and then said he would fetch a cab. Gwen, unnaturally quiet, put her arm around Godwina. The two girls walked together silently behind their parents to the cab.

Trudy raised the question of their going to the Starratt house. "Come and stay with us for a day or so, Ammy. " But Amantha said no, she must be in her own house. Mrs. Heston, the housekeeper, was expecting them. The other servants were on leave but Mrs. Heston was there to look after the house.

The constraint of meeting was broken when they arrived. Gwen, bursting with the need to talk to Godwina, followed her up the stairs to Godwina's bedroom, where they fell into each other's arms and started to giggle. Ted, standing in the vestibule while Mrs. Heston greeted Amantha, said to Trudy that he would go along now and leave them to themselves. He would come back for her later. It was with obvious relief that he went out of the door.

In the sitting room Amantha took off her hat and veil and laid them aside. Trudy, kissing her, said, "Ammy, I haven't had a word from you. If it hadn't been for your Aunt Katherine, I'd not know anything at all. "

With an effort Amantha replied, "I haven't written to anybody. "

Trudy studied her face. After a moment she said, "You'll have to come back to earth sooner or later, you know. "

Slowly Amantha raised her head to look at her. She did not answer.

Trudy went on. "He was your lord and master so long you don't know what to do without him. "

Amantha put her hand up to her head. "He wouldn't listen to me. "

Trudy stared at her indignantly. "Ammy! Don't tell me you're feeling guilty! Aunt Katherine wrote and told me what happened, how he insisted on going down to Godwin's Chance. What on earth would make you think you could stop him from doing what he wanted to do? Ammy, you were married to him for twelve years. You surely had learned that. "

At first Amantha was silent and then she said, "Trudy, I can't think. I can't pull myself together. I — I —" She was unable to finish.

Trudy led her to a chair. "Sit down and let's talk about what you have to do now. You can't go on brooding this way. Come on and tell me. What is it about Godwin? Of course we are all sorry he was drowned. It seems a pity he wouldn't listen to you. He should have listened to you on a lot of occasions, I'm sure. "

The vigorous forthrightness of her voice broke over Amantha like a cold shower. She shivered and said, "Trudy, I can't tell even you what I feel about Godwin. "

Trudy pulled up a chair to sit close to her. "Well, you can try. Everybody thinks you are overcome by grief. Of course, under the surface, there is the unspeakable — that you miss his attentions to you in bed. Nobody can say this aloud because as respectable women we're not supposed to have sexual desire. In truth, we can live with a husband for years and get the habit of bodily satisfaction. Yet, when he dies, we're supposed to forget all that. But you can admit it to me, Ammy. "

"Yes, yes, " said Amantha, striving to be coherent. "Godwin always wanted me to be ready for him in bed. But not at the end. He was too preoccupied. "

Trudy scrutinized her face, in doubt about her meaning. "So? Aunt Katherine has misgivings. After all, she knew Godwin before you did and I know she wasn't ever really satisfied that she did right in letting him marry you and take you away the way he did. It seemed the thing to do at the time; you didn't have anything and he offered you everything. I think she had a real mistrust of him: why was he doing it? I suppose nobody thought that Godwin could be infatuated enough to do something uncalculated. "

Trudy paused and watched to see what effect her words had. Amantha did not raise her head. After a silence she said, "That wasn't true. He would never be infatuated — the way I was with him. But he could — he was — "

Her sentence trailed off and Trudy said, "You mean, he could be — really was in love with someone — in love so that he didn't calculate the odds. " When Amantha did not respond, she added, "But not with you. "

Amantha raised her head abruptly and stared at her, her dark blue eyes glowing for a moment. "Yes, " she said and looked down again.

Trudy sat back. "I should have guessed that some time ago. But I didn't. You found out about it at the very beginning? And you didn't know what to do?"

Amantha took a deep breath. "Trudy, you know that I was very ignorant when I first met Godwin. I loved him to distraction. But it wasn't Godwin I loved. It was someone that existed in my imagination. I didn't realize that then. "

"Why did you stay with him?"

Amantha did not answer and presently Trudy said, "Because of Winnie, of course. He would never have let you have Winnie. But, Ammy, he didn't love the child. He always wanted her out of the way. I suppose it would be just meanness, to deprive you of her out of revenge. "

Amantha spoke up. "No, it wasn't that. What would I have done, Trudy? Where would I go? I hadn't any money and he did want me for his wife. "

"Even if in second place. She was a married woman, I suppose or he would have married her."

Again Amantha did not answer. After a silence Trudy said, "Well, we had better look to the future. What are you going to do now?" She saw that Amantha once again had retreated into some distant cloud land. She put out her hand to touch Amantha's. "Wake up, old girl. "

Slowly Amantha came back to her. "Mr. Weatherbee expects me to be in his office tomorrow morning, with Winnie. He has apologized for not coming here to see me, but he is an old man and does not get about easily. Someone is coming to fetch us. "

"Well, then, I'll come over tomorrow and you can tell me about it. In the meantime, Ammy, will you be all right? Your servants are not here. Your house was not prepared for your return. They were apparently all waiting for orders from Godwin— from the other side of the grave, I suppose. "

"Mrs. Heston is here. She will see to anything that needs to be done. I don't want the servants back yet. Yes, yes, Trudy, I shall be all right. "

When Trudy left with Gwen she made a tremendous effort to keep her mind on the need to pay attention when Mrs. Heston asked her for instructions, when Winnie, clinging to her, wanted reassurance. Winnie had never been afraid of the dark, but now, when night came and they sat together at one corner of the dining room table eating the meal Mrs. Heston served, she was querulous, nervously glancing about the shadowy, only partially lit room.

"Mamma, are we going to stay here?"

"Why, yes, Winnie. For a while, anyway. "

"Gwen wants me to go and stay with her at Fairacres. They are getting ready for the Elizabethan masque. You remember that, don't you, mamma? I was going to be a court musician. "She looked anxiously at Amantha, fearful that this strange remoteness had obliterated all memory of so important an event.

Amantha gazed at her for a moment. An echo came to her of that forgotten life before they had sailed for Baltimore. "Yes. I remember. We'll have to see, Winnie. I don't know what Mr. Weatherbee is going to require me to do. "

Relieved, Godwina declared, "I don't see why he should have anything to say about things. "

"It depends on what arrangements your father has made. We'll find out tomorrow. "

* * *

Trudy was already at the house when they returned from Mr.

205

Weatherbee's chambers.

"Well, what did he say?" she demanded. They were in Amantha's dressing room.

Amantha, taking off her hat and veil, said, "Help me get this off, Trudy." She was struggling with the fastenings of her black dress. She gave a sigh of relief as Trudy pulled the dress off her.

"Of course he would have been horrified if you had come to see him dressed in any other way, " said Trudy, hanging the dress in the wardrobe. "What dreadful things women have to wear. "

"I was very careful," said Amantha, sitting down at the dressing table with her back to the looking glass. "I did not want to offend him in any way. But I could not bear to have Winnie in black. I knew he did not like that. It was the first thing he noticed — that she had on a grey dress."

Trudy looked at her intently. Amantha seemed sensible enough and talked as if she was her normal self. But there was something odd, nevertheless, as if her attention had wandered elsewhere. Trudy asked again, "What did he have to say?"

"He said that Winnie is Godwin's heir. She inherits everything except for some bequests he has made to various people and institutions — some of these are large amounts but his estate is very large and Winnie inherits a great fortune. She is to have some control of her property when she is eighteen and when she is thirty she will be completely in charge. He says he did not approve of this arrangement and told Godwin so. He thinks Godwin should have kept some restraint on Winnie, for her lifetime, because after all she will soon be a woman and women cannot be trusted to take care of money. He warned Godwin that there will be adventurers who will want to marry her for her money — or seduce her for it. But Godwin refused to follow his advice."

"And what about you?"

"I have an ample trust fund for my lifetime; I'll be very well off. " Amantha paused for a moment and then said, "None of this is new to me, Trudy. Godwin told me about these arrangements quite a while ago. I did not pay much attention then. It all seemed so far off. He had always said he would look after me. "

Her manner was so casual that Trudy said, "And you never doubted him?"

Amantha looked at her in surprise. "Why should I have? No, I never doubted him in that way. " She was silent for a while, gazing unseeingly at the floor.

Trudy prompted her. "Who is Winnie's guardian?"

Amantha's eyes suddenly flashed at her. "I am. I am her personal guardian. There are trustees to look after her property. I am to say where she will live, where and how she is to be educated. I have the same authority where she is concerned as he had, until she is eighteen, when she will have some say. Do you see, Trudy, this is very important, because I can now make sure that she will have the sort of musical life she wants. Nobody can deny her that now."

"Why do you think he did this, Ammy? On her account or yours?"

But Amantha simply shook her head and did not answer.

After a while she said, "Mr. Weatherbee had a great deal to say about what a serious responsibility I have, that I must be careful never to talk to newspaper reporters and I must be beware of kidnapping and blackmail threats —"

"Blackmail!" Trudy exclaimed.

"Godwin sometimes worried about blackmail, " Amantha said mildly.

"What on earth could be the basis for that? Of course, Godwin had a past before he married you. "

"I think Mr. Weatherbee meant to warn me that I had better avoid any indiscretions that might lead to blackmail. "

"The old stinker! Well, at any rate, you're in control now. "

Amantha shook her head, "There's a joker, Trudy. "

"A joker?" There was alarm in Trudy's voice.

"If I marry again, I forfeit everything. Oh, course, I'll have an income for the rest of my life — a third of what I have now — enough to buy gowns in Paris, if I want to. " She gave Trudy a wan smile. "Godwin would not leave me penniless under any circumstances. But I would have nothing more to do with Winnie. She would be in the hands of strangers. "

"Of all the —" Trudy began indignantly.

Amantha smiled at her. "Oh, no. But don't you see? Godwin would not risk leaving his property to the mercy of a stranger, especially a man I betrayed him with. I might be the one who was seduced by an adventurer."

"He thought he owned you even beyond the grave. "

"Mr. Weatherbee approves of this arrangement. Why should someone else profit from Godwin's genius, perhaps wreck what he had spent his life building up?"

Trudy's indignation knew no bounds. "Don't be so reasonable, Ammy! You're only just thirty years old!"

Amantha went on smiling, as much to herself as at Trudy. "In the first place, Godwin did not expect to die so soon. And then — Trudy, I haven't the slightest intention of marrying again. "

"That is what you say now —"

"And always will. " Amantha got up from the dressing table and crossed to her wardrobe. Halfway there she turned to look at Trudy. "You should know how I feel. You're the only one who knows anything of my intimate life. "

Trudy persisted. "Yes, but, Ammy, you must not let bitterness govern your life from now on. As time goes on you must allow yourself to look for happiness. "

Amantha shook her head. "It's not bitterness. "

"What is it then?"

"Memory. Memory will prevent me from ever wanting another man." She turned away from Trudy's bewilderment and sought in the wardrobe for a dress, a fawn-colored light wool which she knew fitted her figure like a glove; something Leonie would approve. As she drew it out her eye lit on the painting in the bottom of the wardrobe. On impulse she reached for it and brought it out into the light. She propped it up against a chair back.

"Oh!" said Trudy. "You've still got it. So that's where you kept it. " She went over to look at the painting more closely. "It's unnerving, Ammy, how it resembles Winnie. " She turned away from the painting to help Amantha into the fawn-colored dress, eyeing the painting over her shoulder.

Amantha made no response. Trudy finished the last buttons up the back of the dress and then asked, with deliberate audacity, "Ammy, is Winnie your child?"

She was astonished as Amantha switched around to face her, white to the lips, with blazing eyes. "Yes!" It was almost a shout.

Catching her breath, Trudy said, "You needn't bite my head off!"

But Amantha stood with her face in her hands, shaking. Trudy, contrite, put her arms around her. "I'm sorry, Ammy. It was a rotten question to ask. But perhaps sometime you'll tell me the rest of the story. "

Amantha stood passive while Trudy tried to soothe her. Presently she raised her head as if she was listening.

"Where is Winnie?" she asked.

Before Trudy could answer she went to the door and stepped out onto the landing. The door of the drawing room on the flight below was ajar and there was the intermittent sound of the piano interspersed by the girls' laughter.

Amantha stood holding on to the balustrade. She was flooded by the memory of the afternoon she had returned home to find Godwin prostrate in his study and Godwina in her recital dress. She said, "I can't live in this house." She frowned at Trudy standing beside her.

"You can get another one — a smaller one, I hope — something more manageable for you and Winnie. You certainly are not going to be entertaining as you did as Godwin's wife. There now, don't be so upset.

We'll find something. Come on now, let's go and talk quietly for a bit."

She led her down the corridor to her sitting room. She sat and watched as Amantha wandered about the room. She thought, You're in no shape to make any sort of decisions. He dominated you so completely that you're like a child looking for its mother—and you never had one. Aloud she said, "Ammy, you must give yourself some time to find your feet."

Amantha came to stand close to her. "I've told Mrs.Heston that I'm not at home to anyone. So many people come and leave cards. I must hire someone to take charge of them. Trudy, my mind is so full of things I can't control—I think I'm going mad—" She held her head in her hands.

Trudy got up to go to her. "What you need is rest and quiet. This has been a dreadful ordeal. Aunt Katherine has written and told me the details, about the funeral, about the hordes of personages and newspaper people. It must have been torment."

"Trudy, I am bad for Winnie. She has been so upset because I cannot pay attention to her as she is used to. She is so nervous. She is having nightmares. But I cannot help myself. I must not let her suffer because of me."

"She's happy now with Gwen. Ammy, why don't you bring her down to Fairacres? You probably haven't thought of it but we are having the Elizabethan masque I promised Gwen. Gwen is most unhappy that Winnie will not be in it and so is Winnie. I don't see why the child should be punished like that in the name of mourning."

Amantha stared unseeing out of the window. At last she said, "I cannot, Trudy. I cannot stand to be so surrounded by people."

"You needn't take part in anything. I'll see that you are left alone."

Amantha shook her head. "Trudy, you know that you will have your hands full. I should not create another problem for you."

Trudy was thoughtful. Then she said, tentatively, "Suppose I take Winnie with me. Gwen can look after her. She will be so caught up in the excitement that she won't have time to miss you."

"She's never been away from me."

"Perhaps it's time to loosen the apron strings."

Amantha raised her head to answer her gaze.Trudy saw in her eyes a wistful yearning that surprised her. Amantha said, "If I could have just a little while to think things out — "

Having made her suggestion, Trudy had second thoughts. "I'm concerned about leaving you here alone."

"Mrs.Heston is here. I shan't be alone in the house."

"Are you sure, Ammy, that you can manage?"

"Yes."

"Ted is staying in town. If you find you can't stand it, you can let him know and he will bring you down."

Amantha nodded.

Trudy said, "I'll come and get Winnie in the morning."

* * *

Trudy came down the stairs and entered the quiet drawing room. The two girls were seated on the piano bench, earnestly talking. I suppose, thought Trudy, they have to make some sense of the situation in their own way. As was often the case, it was Gwen who was listening intently while Winnie talked, her soft, quick voice flowing along. They both looked up when she came in.

Trudy said, "Winnie, your mother says you are to come down to Fairacres tomorrow with Gwen, to get ready for the masque."

Gwen gave a whoop of joy and grabbed Winnie around the waist. Winnie, sensing something strange, extricated herself and said, "What about mamma?"

"Your mother is going to stay here for a few days. There are things she must attend to and she doesn't feel like being with a lot of people."

Godwina stared at her. "I don't think I ought to leave mamma."

"She wants you to come to Fairacres, Winnie. She knows you need to be in a normal atmosphere. Don't you want to take part in the masque?

211

You were very eager to when we talked about it before and you won't want to disappoint Gwen, will you?"

Gwen interrupted. "Oh, Winnie! If your mother says you can come, why not?"

Godwina frowned at her. "Yes, I know. But, Gwen, I've been telling you how things were in Baltimore and on the ship. Mamma is very unhappy."

Trudy said sharply, "Winnie, you'll make her even more unhappy if you don't do what she wants you to."

Godwina looked up at her, uncertainty in her eyes. "Mamma doesn't always say what she really wants, Aunt Trudy. Sometimes she pretends she wants something because she thinks it is something I want."

Taken aback but quick to cover it up, Trudy said, "I think this time she really does want you to come and stay with Gwen. You are not a baby any more, Winnie. I think you're big enough now to do things for her because she needs you to."

Godwina's dismayed surprise was apparent. "You mean, Aunt Trudy, she doesn't want me to stay with her?" The enormity of this possibility gave a quaver to her voice.

Oh, lord! thought Trudy. Now I've put my foot in it. "No, that's not what I meant. Your mother is very tired. She can't come for the masque because she would not get any rest. But it makes her unhappy that you should miss the fun you and Gwen were looking forward to. And there's no need for that. She just needs a few days of quiet. She knows you will be safe and happy and she can be at ease. She must try to get used to your father's not being here."

Godwina's eager protest vanished. Her head drooped and she accepted Gwen's efforts to comfort her.

Trudy went on. "Then you'll get ready, won't you? Your mother says you are to go up to her dressing room and she will help you pack your clothes. We'll come for you tomorrow at ten." She leaned down and kissed her. Godwina responded obediently and answered Gwen's kiss more heartily.

When the front door closed on them, Godwina stood by the piano in deep thought. Her long talk with Gwen had cleared her mind of a lot of things. It was true that for weeks now she had not been able to communicate with mamma as she always had done, freely rattling on about whatever troubled her, worried her, mystified her. Mamma had been wrapped in a fog of preoccupation that made her inaccessible. Her responses had been automatic, sometimes inappropriate.

She had told Gwen this and Gwen had said, "Don't you remember, there have always been times when Aunt Ammy seemed not to take in what you said to her? You've told me that."

It was much worse now. And she had begun to notice that whenever mamma was inattentive, it had something to do with papa. Talking to Gwen had brought a lot of things out in her mind. She had told Gwen how everybody said what a brave man papa was to go out into that dangerous water to rescue those people. Gwen had told her that Aunt Trudy, when she had heard about it, said he should have thought more about his wife and child. Then there was Mr.Weatherbee. Godwina had realized, when mamma took her to see him, that mamma was very nervous but she got over it quickly when he explained papa's will. Mamma said later that she knew all about the details; papa had told her. But she had been afraid that something had been changed that she did not know about.

Godwina decided she did not like Mr.Weatherbee. He talked to mamma as if she did not know much, when as a matter of fact mamma knew a lot about all kinds of things. Papa always talked to her as if she was his equal. But she had to do just what he said. Mr.Weatherbee, like papa, did not give much importance to her studying music, though now she was a full-fledged student at the Royal College and everybody realized she could have a real career as a pianist ahead of her. Mr.Weatherbee did not think women had any sense and that they were foolish—like the business of being careful not to marry some man who would spend all her money.

213

He had said to her, "My dear young lady, you must always remember that your father has left you a very large fortune and that he is no longer here to protect you. He was a remarkable man, Godwina, and you must always be thankful that you are his daughter." Mamma had not objected to anything he said. But then mamma often did not say what she thought. Godwina heard her murmur at one point, "She is only twelve years old, Mr.Weatherbee," but he had ignored her.

When they left his office she had told mamma that she was unhappy about Mr.Weatherbee. Was he going to make it difficult for her to go on with her music? But mamma had been very certain. No, he could not; papa had seen to that. She need not worry about that. Then she had asked what he meant about mamma getting married again and mamma had been angry for a few minutes and said that would never happen.

It was very quiet in the house. Mrs.Heston was somewhere below stairs and there was not a sound. The furniture was shrouded in dust covers. She felt a little shiver go through her. She touched the gleaming surface of the concert grand. She and Gwen had pulled the cover off it. She could play it now whenever she wanted to. Mamma would not even notice when she did.

That was the trouble. Mamma seemed to notice so little. She did not even tell Mrs.Heston what to serve for their meals; she left it entirely to Mrs.Heston. Papa would not have allowed that. And mamma did not dress as well as she used to and her pretty gold-brown hair was put up anyhow.

Papa. Ever since they heard that he was drowned, she had been trying to understand how she felt about him. Before he died—for instance, on the sea voyage to Baltimore—she knew he had dismissed her from his mind. She had become afraid of him as she used to be when she was a little girl.But there had been a short period before that when she had felt a certain exhilaration in pitting herself against him. And he seemed to know it. Gwen did not always understand when she tried to explain things to her but Gwen always understood her feelings, as if by instinct. She could talk to Gwen about papa—about her ambivalence when she tried to clarify in her own mind what she felt about him. Of course she was proud of the fact that people called him a hero, a financial genius, a man ahead of his time, and she was proud she was his daughter. She really did feel she was truly his daughter because she could feel all this. On the other hand, she knew he rejected her—not as his daughter—she never had the feeling that he denied that she was his daughter—but because she was—inconvenient? When she talked about this to Gwen, Gwen said that she had heard Aunt Trudy say that he could not abide interference of any sort with anything that he wanted to do and that was why he did not want children.

It was the same when it came to the way he treated mamma. He was very careful with mamma, as if she was his prize possession—Gwen said this was what Aunt Trudy had said once. He took very good care of her. But he also made her unhappy, though mamma denied this when anybody said so. Mamma would never let her criticize him; she said she would understand things better when she got older.

Being older. Being older meant a lot of things. For one thing, knowing what men and women did in bed together. Mamma had explained to her about that, and she had told mamma that she did not like the idea of a man invading her body like that; in fact, she thought it was horrible. Mamma had said that it was perfectly natural for a girl to feel that way and not to worry about it. She wondered whether that was what papa did to mamma but she did not ask her that. Mamma was waiting for her to ask that and when she didn't, she saw that mamma was relieved. Well, she was older now since papa had died. It was up to her to look after mamma, who was altogether too kind to people.

Miss Godwina Shenstone. She liked the sound of that. Some day people would have to reckon with Miss Godwina Shenstone.

Godwina touched the gleaming black piano again, affectionately. She must be self-reliant now, not the anxious little girl who clung to mamma because mamma was the only certainty in her life. She must go upstairs and find mamma. She had to find out if what Aunt Trudy had said was true.

The door of the dressing room was still open as Aunt Trudy had left it. Godwina stopped in the doorway and looked around. There was no sign of mamma. But there was a small painting in a frame propped on a chair. It was by a French Impressionist painter. She knew that because there were several paintings by French Impressionist painters around the house; mamma was fond of that sort of painting.

She stepped closer to the painting. Its pale colors glowed at her. Jeune fille au piano, said the tag on it. Nonplussed, she scrutinized it.Then she glanced over at the reflection of herself in mamma's looking glass. Yes, the girl did look like her. But she was different. She was older. Where had the painting come from? Where had mamma found it? And why was it here now, propped up on the chair?

Godwina went in search of her. Mamma was in her sittingroom, standing by the window, leaning on the tall back of a chair. She did not move until Godwina came up behind her and put her arm around her waist. Then she smiled down at her.

"Mamma, where did the painting come from?"

Mamma did not reply but there was the strangest look on her face. She did not say what painting? She simply gazed down into her eyes until Godwina put her face against her shoulder. When she looked up mamma was still looking down at her and stroking her head.

"I've never seen it before, mamma. When did you get it?"

Mamma finally spoke. "A little while ago. I found it in a junk dealer's shop when I was out with Trudy."

"It looks awfully like me. And she has a piano."

"That's why I bought it."

"But you haven't hung it up anywhere."

Mamma seemed to struggle with a reply. What she finally said was, "There was nowhere to put it."

Godwina relaxed her hold on mamma's waist. Mamma kissed her.It was a spontaneous move and Godwina realized that such a kiss was almost the only spontaneous gesture mamma made these days.

She moved away so that she could face her. "Mamma, Aunt Trudy says you said I was to go down to Fairacres with Gwen tomorrow."

"Yes."

"But, mamma, you're not going."

Amantha caught the anxious note in her voice. "Winnie, I want to rest for a few days. There has been so much commotion lately—Trudy knows I can't stand any more.but that doesn't mean you should give up the masque. I know that you and Gwen were looking forward to it so much."

Godwina examined her face."But don't you want me to stay with you, mamma?"

Amantha looked down at her. "You are with me all the time, Winnie. I shan't mind if you are gone for a few days because I know you will enjoy yourself. I would not let you go with anyone except Trudy and Gwen. I know you will be safe with them."

"But, mamma, you would be here all by yourself and—it would be funny to be somewhere without you."

Amantha ran her fingers down Godwina's cheek and held her chin. "It will be just for a few days. You'll be so busy and so excited you won't really notice."

Godwina eyed her still. There was something odd here. What mamma said was quite true. She was less concerned about how frightened or unhappy she herself might be; she would not be alone since she was sharing a room with Gwen. The prospect of being part of the masque, after all, when she had become resigned to missing it, was delightful. But she didn't like the idea that perhaps her own enjoyment might be bought at mamma's expense. With a calculation that she did not really recognize, she began, "Papa wouldn't like it —"

Suddenly there was a flash of Amantha's dark blue eyes. With as much sternness as she could display, Amantha said, "Your father is no longer here, Winnie. We must make our own decisions. Now tell me: do

217

you want to go with Trudy and Gwen tomorrow?"

Accepting her challenge, Godwina said, "Yes."

"Well, then, let's go and pack your bag."

* * *

The next morning Mrs. Heston watched from the doorway as the carriage departed. Amantha had already gone back upstairs. Mrs. Heston felt very uneasy, uneasy because Mrs.Starratt was going out of town and she was left alone to cope with the mistress. The mistress was certainly not her usual self, had not been since her return from the States. For one thing, she had not sent for the other servants, even though the house-keeper had hinted that the house needed to be restored to its normal condition. It was difficult to manage just with the housemaid who came in for a few hours each day. There would be bound to be visitors who would have to be received. Mr. Shenstone had been a very important man. The bowl for callers' cards filled up every day. Someone should be attending to them. The master would have been outraged if he could have known about that. But the mistress made no effort. Matters just drifted from day to day with no decisions made. The difficulty was in getting the mistress's attention. Mrs. Heston felt resentful at having to assume greater responsibility than was rightfully hers. Of course, the master's sudden, unexpected death had been a dreadful shock. But the mistress had always been in charge; she knew how the master wanted things done and was vigilant to see that her orders were carried out. Mrs. Heston had never been in a better place. There was satisfaction in living under a well-run regime; it gave one confidence. But now all that was gone. The mistress gave no orders, had nothing to say beyond commonplaces, seemed oblivious of the problems that would eventually have to be solved.

The housekeeper stood for a while looking up the stairs where Amantha had gone. Then, giving up the puzzle, she went down into the basement.

Amantha, with a last wave to the carriage, climbed the stairs to her

218

sitting room. There was a pale sun that lit up the trees and shrubs in the garden and the walls of nearby buildings. She sat down in the chair by the window and for awhile thought of nothing in particular, lost in the listless nothingness that filled so many hours for her at night and in the day. Slowly she tried to rouse herself to coherent thought. There were things she should do. One was to write to Aunt Katherine, who undoubtedly worried about her. Godwin had invested money for Uncle Ralph, so now Aunt Katherine was quite well off. But she would never be able to persuade her to come to London for a visit.

It seemed to be a foregone conclusion that she and Winnie would continue to live in England. Mr. Weatherbee would be sure to protest if they moved very far away. But Trudy was right; she could not bear to live in this house, so she must find a smaller one, suitable for the style of living that would be theirs. Winnie's music must be the paramount concern.

With a sigh of weariness she leaned back in her chair. She could not drive herself to dwell for long on these practicalities. She drifted into the vacuum that had formed where the center of her life had once been. Her mind reached back to herself in Baltimore when she had met Godwin. It wandered back and forth, outside her control, hovering constantly on Leonie, seeing Godwin ever as the manipulator of her life.

Leonie. Forcing herself back to the present, she worried at the problem: should Leonie be told about Godwin's death? By whom? Certainly the Chevalier would have seen the news in the French papers. Or had she gone so far away from the world that even Godwin's death was a part of what she had left behind and was therefore now irrelevant?

It was too difficult for her to decide now and perhaps it was not something for her to decide. Everything now, when she tried to pin it down and examine it, seemed remote, strange, unconnected to her. There seemed no validity to anything she had done, anything that had been done to her, in the course of her life since she had left Aunt Katherine's house as Godwin's bride. There was no one she could explain all this to

219

and therefore no one who could give her any sort of counsel, who could even understand the mainsprings of her life.

Except Leonie. And Leonie was as lost to her as Godwin.

Her immersion in this scattered review was so deep that Mrs. Heston's knock on her door roused her to total blankness. It was no longer daylight, darkness lay beyond the window and the room was shadowy. She was unable to respond to the knock. Mrs. Heston opened the door and walked across the room to light the lamp. Seeing her seated by the window, she exclaimed, "Oh, ma'am! Are you ill?"

Amantha, blinded by the light, shook her head and raised her hand to indicate No.

Mrs. Heston came toward her, "You gave me such a start, ma'am! I could not find you anywhere in the house when I came up to turn the lights on in the hall. I thought you must have gone out without letting me know. Have you been here all the while?"

Amantha raised her hands to her head. She was aware of Mrs. Heston's anxious solicitude as she stood waiting for her to speak. At last she was able to say, "I'm sorry to have alarmed you. I have not felt the need of anything and the time has passed more quickly than I realized." Her voice was low.

"You've had no lunch nor tea. You must be faint. Let me fetch you a tray."

She bustled out of the room before Amantha could reply. When she returned with the tray Amantha was pacing slowly about the room. Poor lady! Mrs. Heston thought. The master was an admirable man in many ways but she had sometimes wondered whether he did not drive his wife a little too hard in the running of the household and the management of their social activities. He had been demanding; there was no doubt about that, and now the mistress was lost without him.

She set the tray down on a small table and looked at Amantha. "Ma'am," she coaxed, "will you sit here?" She thought, if I go out of the room, she will forget to eat.

220

Amantha, making an effort, sat where she indicated and ate some of the cold chicken and aspic, while Mrs. Heston stood silently by. Later that evening Mrs. Heston returned and suggested that perhaps Amantha should go to bed and, when Amantha agreed, helped her undress. It was on the tip of her tongue to say that Eugenie, Amantha's French maid, at least, should be sent for to come and attend her, but another glance at Amantha's withdrawn face silenced her.

In the morning she brought a tray up to Amantha's bedroom. It was a pity, she thought, that Miss Godwina was not there; she would have roused her mother to go through the normal daily actions. But then, poor child, she needed some relief from the gloom created by her father's death and no doubt the mistress was right to send her off with Mrs.Starratt. It was all she could do to persuade the mistress to dress and go to her sitting room. Every time she entered the dressing room she saw that painting propped up on a chair. Perhaps it comforted the mistress to see the child's likeness, though it was obviously the picture of a girl older than Godwina. She wondered how many days she would be left to watch over the poor lady.

* * *

It was a quiet, grey London afternoon. Amantha, pacing about her sitting room tried hard to focus her thoughts. She had lost track of time but she was vaguely aware that she had been alone, except for Mrs. Heston's periodic appearances, for more than one day and night.

She had struggled with the pent-up flood of remembrance that had assailed her ever since she had the news of Godwin's death. Her mind had gone up and down the corridors of memory, pursued by the dread of disaster that had fastened on her in the stormy Atlantic crossing and came to a climax in Aunt Katherine's house when she had been unable to prevent Godwin from going down to Godwin's Chance. When she had first heard that he was dead, all feeling had been stilled in her till slowly she

221

realized that with Godwin's disappearance from the world an immense emptiness opened in her own existence. Godwin and Leonie. Without them there was no meaning in what she had endured. There was only the child left and she must not allow the child's life to be damaged by what had happened in bringing her forth.

The knowledge that there was no one to whom she could speak of the ambivalence of her feelings about Godwin had paralyzed her will and her ability to respond to what lay about her. She saw herself from the outside; felt shame and compunction that she could not respond to Aunt Katherine's kindness nor thank those who came to commiserate.

She knew that some, like Trudy, pitied her for her loss not only of Godwin's care and protection but also of his bodily presence, his power to assuage her own sexual desire. How could she explain to anyone that, when lying acquiescent in his arms while he claimed his right to possess her body, she felt a deeper hunger that could never again be fed? She stopped by the tall-backed chair and placed her hand on it. Yet even now the reality of Godwin was fading in her consciousness — Godwin who had governed her daily existence, Godwin who had provoked in her love, rage, resentment, despair —leaving behind a vague but powerful and everlasting sense of failure, of nothingness. In what had she failed? She remembered herself on the loggia at the Villa Margherita, in her youthful ardor and untried self-confidence, assuring Leonie that happiness was obtainable, that happiness could exist, that happiness would inevitably be achieved even in the circumstances that faced them.

Through the travail of these last uncounted hours, beneath the surge and conflict of memory and desperate self-reproach, there had lain the image of Leonie, seen as if under a veil of water, fluctuating, but growing ever more vivid. It had in fact grown so vivid that it constantly distracted her from the effort to clear her mind of the contemplation of what had happened and could not be undone; had distracted her from the need to think out and take up her new responsibilities. She must turn away from that image if she was to return to a normal life.

But a vast rebellion swelled in her heart. Throughout the years she had obeyed the command to suppress her own desires, the natural bent of her heart and mind. She had done so under the urging of a vague hope that eventually there would be a resolution of the dilemma in which she had been so unexpectedly thrust. There seemed now to be no such hope; she had only been self-deluded. Perhaps Leonie had been right. Leonie had said that it was the Devil who had so skillfully ruined her own life. The Devil certainly seemed to have triumphed over Godwin's Goddess of Reason.

Leonie. She found herself gripping the chairback in a frenzy of despair. Trying to regain self-control, she wondered if she had cried out. If so, there was no one to hear.

There was a knock on the door and Mrs. Heston came in. Mrs. Heston had learned not to rely on her knock being answered or even perhaps heard. She came into the room warily. The mistress had said that she would see no one and indeed Mrs. Heston did not think her to be in any condition to do so. But the gentleman had insisted and she recognized him as someone who had been a guest of the Shenstones. He would accept no refusal. He must see Mrs. Shenstone. She had hesitated, looking at the lady with him, dressed in widow's weeds, with a heavy veil. Something about that mute figure prompted her to go up the stairs to the mistress's sitting room.

She was astonished when she entered and saw Amantha standing in the middle of the room, facing her. She was pale and grim-lipped but her eyes were no longer vague.

Amantha asked peremptorily, "What is it, Mrs. Heston?"

"Ma'am, a lady and gentleman are here who say they must see you. Oh, I do know that you have said you will see no one—" She faltered and stopped.

"Don't they say who they are?"

"No, ma'am. They are French people."

Amantha's eyes widened and she walked quickly past her across the room to the door. On the landing she looked down the well of the broad, curving two flights of stairs to the vestibule. For a moment she stood transfixed and then she ran down the stairs, her feet scarcely touching the treads, to the figure dressed in black standing there in the half-light of the overcast afternoon.

From the landing Mrs. Heston watched in fascination as Amantha flung back the heavy veil from the woman's face and caught her in her arms. It was in complete silence that the two women stood embraced, without moving. But where, wondered Mrs. Heston, was the gentleman who had brought this lady? She walked slowly down the stairs, pausing to peer through the fanlight over the door. There was no cab at the curb. He was gone.

* * *

When she could speak Amantha, slipping into French, said, "You are here — you are really here. Tell me that you are so that I can believe it."

Leonie's voice was hoarse. "Yes, I am here, Amanthe."

Amantha felt her sway in her arms. "Come, come with me."

She held her against her as they slowly mounted the stairs, stopping every few steps. At last they reached Amantha's bedroom and she guided her to an armchair and eased her into it. Mrs. Heston, alarmed, had followed them up and now hovered in concern. Amantha turned to her. "Will you prepare a tray and bring it up, Mrs. Heston? I think Mme. de Brieux needs something to eat and drink."

Mrs. Heston, relieved at the normal tone in Amantha's voice and recognizing in it the mistress she had thought lost, and reassured also because this strange lady had a name known to Amantha, left the room with a light step to obey her order. As she went out of the door she glanced sympathetically at Leonie, who sat with her head thrown back and her eyes closed.

"My darling," said Amantha, removing the black hat and heavy veil and releasing the mass of pale blond hair, "you have had a terrible journey. You are exhausted."

The clear grey eyes opened into hers. Oh, I shall drown in them! thought Amantha, catching her hands and kissing them. Leonie drew her head to her and kissed her lips. Her own were tremulous with fatigue and she sank back in the chair. Amantha began to unfasten her dress, pulling it down off her white shoulders. Leonie wore no corset; she is so thin, thought Amantha, there would be no purpose to it. She got up and fetched a dressing gown and, coming back, stripped off the rest of Leonie's clothes, tenderly fondling the soft, flaccid breasts as she did so. She wrapped her in the pale blue robe and braided her hair into a single plait that hung over her shoulder. All the while Leonie sat passive under her touch, as if grateful for the love it expressed.

As Amantha finished Mrs. Heston arrived with a large tray. Coming through the door, which Amantha held open for her, she came to an abrupt stop and stared at Leonie. Leonie, now sitting upright, gazed at her with wide open eyes. Mrs. Heston, regaining her self-possession, put the tray down on the table beside Leonie's chair and turned to Amantha with a questioning look.

Amantha said, "Mme. de Brieux will be staying with me, Mrs. Heston."

Flustered, Mrs. Heston asked, "Shall I prepare a bedroom, ma'am?"

"No," said Amantha, glancing at Leonie. "I shall attend to her here. In a little while, when I ring, bring hot water and towels to my dressing room."

Mrs. Heston left them, staring once more at the woman in the armchair. Surely, she thought, as she closed the door, this lady must be related to Miss Godwina on her father's side. She had heard that Mr. Shenstone had had a French mother.

Amantha pulled a chair close to Leonie and sat down. She raised a cup of tea to Leonie's lips and Leonie drank.

Amantha asked, "How did you get here?"

Leonie's musical voice was low pitched but no longer hoarse. "It was Louis de Montbrun — the Chevalier. He saw the account of Godwin's disappearance in the flood in the newspapers. He waited for a few days because there was a delay in declaring him dead, since his body could not be found." She stopped and raised her hand to caress Amantha's cheek. "My poor little one. How terrible it must have been for you." She paused again before she went on. "He understood at once that he must let me know, so he came to my house in the Auvergne. He did not hesitate to intimidate my servants and force his way in. I was alarmed when I saw him stride into the room where I sat. He has never approved of what I have done and his disapproval made him fierce. To me his voice was very loud. It assaulted my nerves, so that at first I could not understand what he said." Leonie continued her languid caress of Amantha's head. She went on, "You see, ma petite, I spent my days and nights in silence, except for my piano. I scarcely spoke at all to my servants and they did not talk unless I spoke to them. So Louis' voice, so masculine, so vigorous, shattered this quiet. Finally I understood that he was telling me that he brought very serious news about Godwin. I knew at once that Godwin must be dead. Louis described the circumstances. I asked him if he knew anything about you. He said he had inquired of the people in Godwin's Paris office and they said you were returning to London. I said I must go to you, that you would need me. I felt a frisson of horror at the thought of what it must mean for you."

Leonie stopped speaking, her eyes closed and her hands were still. Then she said, "Louis said I must come with him at once, at that very moment. He did not wait for me to pack any clothes. All I could do was to put on my widow's dress and veil. He took me to Paris to stay with Amelie, his wife. I cannot remember anything of that journey except the noise of the train and the uproar of the mass of people who filled the train stations. When he was sure you were back in London he brought me across the Channel and directly to your house here."

"He did not wait to speak to me," said Amantha.

"No. I'm sure he has gone straight back to Paris. He does not like to be separated from Amelie. He knew you were here to receive me. Your housekeeper had gone to fetch you. He had done what he needed to do. Oh, mon coeur, what a terrible journey! You cannot imagine how the noise, the people pressing all round me, harrowed my nerves!"

"If you had sent for me, I should have come at once."

"Oh, no! I had to come to you. Louis understood that." Leonie looked at her with a faint smile. "Madame, you still have responsibilities which you cannot drop at a moment's notice."

The gentle mockery in her voice filled Amantha's heart to bursting with joy at the recollection of the playfully sardonic Leonie in the house in the Auvergne. Before she could speak, Leonie, as if her mind also had reverted to that time, said, "Do you know, Amanthe, in the stillness of my house in the Auvergne I could hear your voice. It waited for me in every corner wherever I went in the house, as if you had left it there for me."

"Oh, my darling!" Amantha buried her face in Leonie's shoulder.

Leonie clasped her in her arms, talking softly in her ear. Finally Amantha raised her head. "He has always come and sought to console me about your cutting yourself off, as if he knew you meant a great deal to me."

"Louis? Of course, mon coeur. He and Amelie have known me since before I married. They guessed from the very beginning what had passed between Godwin and me and what role you were to play."

In Amantha's mind there arose the memory of the dinner party at the Villa Margherita when she had first met the Chevalier, had first realized what lay between Godwin and Leonie. She said, "He never let me have the least suspicion that he knew."

"He would not, ma petite. That would violate his code of friendship. He knew you would have enough of a burden without his bringing it to light. He was very resentful of Godwin —so much so that he found it

227

difficult to maintain an outward friendship with him. But he did so for my sake."

Amantha, lost in the flood of memory, knelt beside Leonie's chair and hid her face in Leonie's breast. She could hear the soft throb of Leonie's heart. Leonie made no attempt to rouse her, until Amantha stirred in her arms. Then she said, with gentle firmness, "Come, you must tell me about your ordeal. You must unburden yourself to me."

Amantha sat up. She felt choked by the recollection of the events in Baltimore. She said, hesitating, "I do not know where to begin. There is so much that I must tell you about Godwin, about my life that you do not know."

Leonie put her hand under Amantha's chin and raised her head to look in her eyes. "Mon coeur, yes, you must tell me all that. He was difficult I know. What he could not resolve in himself he burdened you with. I comprehend that."

"He could not forget you, Leonie, though he pretended that he did. He forbade me to speak of you. He tried to keep Winnie out of his life because she reminded him of you. Oh, my darling —"

"What a penance for you!"

"He was very confident in the last months, as if he felt he had triumphed in everything he did. But he was very upset when he heard about the damage by the storm at Godwin's Chance. The Chevalier told you about the storm, didn't he?"

Leonie nodded.

"He insisted that he must go there at once. We had a bad crossing on the ship. He was absorbed by the idea of going to see the damage. He would scarcely wait when we got to my aunt's house in Baltimore." Amantha's voice faltered. "I had a dreadful fear — I tried to keep him from going there — he would not pay any attention to me — oh, Leonie, perhaps you could have prevented him!" She raised her head to look at Leonie, despair in her eyes.

Leonie shook her head. "Amanthe, he was Godwin. It was his nature

228

to do what he wanted to do. He was certain he could conquer every obstacle, everyone and everything that might stand in his way. He would not be thwarted by anyone."

"Except you."

"Amanthe, do not torment yourself. He wrung everything out of you. You know that." Leonie put her hand behind Amantha's head and held her still. "There is much that you have stifled in yourself because you could speak of it to no one — perhaps because you think you should not admit it to yourself. Tell me, Amanthe."

Amantha, her eyes cast down, struggled unsuccessfully to find words.

Leonie said, "You are free of your bondage to him and yet you cannot rejoice in your freedom. You feel now that you are to blame because you could not love him as you think you should have. But it was he who destroyed your love."

Amantha sank back against her shoulder and Leonie caressed her. Amantha said, her voice muffled, "I cannot say this to anyone but you. I cannot admit that I tried to cherish him as I should have and that I failed." She raised her head to meet Leonie's eyes again. "Even if he had not thwarted all my efforts, even if he had been truly loving to me, I could not have put him in first place. It is you, Leonie, who fill my heart and soul. There is no room for anyone else."

Leonie caught her head in her hands. "Of course. How could it be otherwise? That is not something to grieve over, mon coeur." The steady gaze of the clear grey eyes anchored her own wavering spirit. She subsided once more into Leonie's arms.

* * *

As Amantha lifted the cover of the chafing dish on the tray and began to feed her the omelet it contained, Leonie said, "Your housekeeper seems astonished by me."

"That's because of the likeness between you and Winnie."

"Ah, the child! Where is she?"

"She is with Trudy. Trudy is an old schoolmate of mine who is now married to an Englishman. She has a daughter Winnie's age and they are great friends."

Leonie's eyebrows were raised briefly.

Slowly, between the forkfuls of omelet she lifted to Leonie's mouth, Amantha sought to explain the Starratts, Fairacres and the Elizabethan masque. Leonie listened attentively and said nothing.

Amantha said, "I let her go with Trudy because she really wanted to be in the masque with Gwen and because I was having a very bad effect on her. She was becoming the victim of my own despair and I had to put a stop to that."

Leonie smiled. There was again a hint of gentle mockery in her eyes. "The good mother. How fortunate the little one has been."

Amantha looked at her in surprise. "Fortunate?"

"What would have happened to her if she had not had you?" Leonie's smile was now ironic.

Amantha caught her hands. "Leonie, she is the image of you— oh, if you could know how her likeness to you has ravished me over the years. But she has also been herself, her own little person. Now she is no longer just a child — your image. She has your gift and to her music is the meaning of life, the reason for being. Godwin saw you in her as I did, but he strove to deny it. He was not sympathetic to Winnie's efforts to follow her bent, to develop her musical self. What I must do now is to see that she has the chance to live the life she wants as a musician."

In her earnestness Amantha gripped Leonie's hands tightly. Leonie flexed her fingers to loosen her hold and free them. She lay her hand on Amantha's cheek. She said, "It is Tante Melisande's legacy, Amanthe. She made me heir to her property but she left me a greater inheritance and that is also now the child's. Do not worry about that. I will see that she does not suffer as did Tante Melisande. And also that she does not neglect her legacy." There was a glint in Leonie's eyes. "Godwin made you her guardian, didn't he?"

"Yes, she is my ward — if I do not marry again —" Amantha's voice broke on a note of desperate hilarity.

Leonie caught Amantha's hand raised with the fork and held it. "Quelle blague! Amanthe, don't be fearful any longer. I am here now. You need not fear the future."

Amantha's voice was shaky as she put down the fork. "The future is no longer empty — barren — oh, Leonie!" She broke down in tears and Leonie comforted her. When she recovered she said, "Godwin told me some time ago that she would be my ward, but I could not be certain that he had not made a change. He often did not tell me of his actions."

Leonie was sitting very straight in her chair and gazing at her sternly. "When he tried to take her away from you — when I came to you in Paris — afterwards he came to see me at Rapallo before he returned to you. It was then that I told him that he must never make such a threat again, that he must let you decide what should be done about her."

Amantha overcome by the memory, was silent. Seeing her distress, Leonie went on. "He never admitted that to you, did he? Of course he would not. But that is what I required of him. He owed you that much. What he owed me and I him could never be settled between us."

Amantha heard the trace of scorn in her voice. "He was kind when he came back to me after seeing you. He never again tried to force me to do anything about Winnie that I did not want to. But I was often anxious. I did not know when he might assert himself again, and I knew I would not be able to reach you after that, that I would be alone." She gripped Leonie's hands again, choking on her own recollection.

"Mon ange, she is your child. I gave her suck for a day. She has grown up in your arms."

She sat back in the armchair while Amantha moved the tray away. The last of the daylight had gone. Beyond the windows, where the curtains were not drawn, it was dark. Amantha said, "My darling, I think

231

you should go to bed and rest. Come with me into my dressing room and we can get ready."

She helped Leonie get up from the chair and steadied her as they crossed to the door and went into the dressing room. She rang for Mrs. Heston and while they waited for the hot water and towels, Leonie moved slowly about the room until she stopped in front of the painting propped on a chair.

She spoke over her shoulder, "Where did you get this?"

"It is you, isn't it?" Amantha asked, stepping to her side and beginning to tremble.

"Bien sur." Leonie put her arm around her waist. "What is this? Why are you trembling?"

Amantha pressed close to her. "How can I tell you how much I have wanted you — wanted the warmth of your body, something more than insubstantial memory?" She tried to control her voice. "I found the painting among some rubbish in a shop. It is all I have had of you, except for the images in my mind. It was like finding a spring of water in a desert."

Leonie gathered her into her arms and wiped the tears from her cheeks with her fingers.

Amantha caught her hand and kissed it. Oh, those fingers like no others, whose touch she had dreamed of compulsively. Suddenly aware that Leonie felt the strain of bearing part of her weight, she straightened up and said, "Everyone thinks it must be Winnie though obviously the girl is older."

Leonie glanced at the painting again. "I was fifteen. My mother had died of consumption. They sent me to spend the summer with my Uncle Edouard in Brittany. There was a colony of painters near his house. They were imitators of the Impressionists who were raising such a scandal in the art world of Paris. My uncle was intrigued by them and let some of them come and paint in his garden. There was one woman — it was very unusual for a woman to be among such a group as painter and not only as a model. I suppose she was not altogether respectable. But she wanted to

232

paint me and my uncle permitted her to do this sketch. Years later, when I was more sophisticated, I realized that she was enamored of me, but then I knew nothing of such things. I knew I yearned for something, someone, but I did not know what or whom. Very likely the woman understood this and so she went away — vanished, leaving her painting behind. My uncle liked it and had it framed."

"She never finished it."

Leonie looked again at the painting. "I think it got too much for her — to keep gazing at me — and so one day she disappeared."

"Poor soul," said Amantha, "never to find you again."

Leonie laughed. "Mon ange, I can have only one lover. Come, kiss me."

They stood for a brief moment in each other's arms, until there was a knock on the door and Mrs. Heston came in with a tall can of hot water and towels.

A while later, Leonie, bathed and soothed, lay in the bed with her eyes closed, asleep or simply resting, Amantha thought. The bedroom was lit only by the glow of the coal fire in the grate. Amantha sat in the armchair in her dressing gown. She had sat there for some time contemplating what lay ahead of her. She was daunted by the demands that confronted her, but now at least she had regained the courage to deal with them. There were the expected visits of condolence by Godwin's business associates, the people who represented the charities and educational and art institutions he had supported, the emissaries of governments and large commercial enterprises, the many ordinary people he had befriended. There were also the sessions with lawyers and trustees concerned with Godwin's financial affairs. Mr. Weatherbee had suggested that, since as a woman she would understand nothing of the subjects discussed during the latter, she delegate him or one of his partners to act for her. But Amantha, aware that to do so would diminish her control, declined his suggestion. Perhaps she could not understand the intricacies of these matters but she knew Godwin's habits of mind and require-

233

ments and she would recognize whatever would most concern him. This was the last duty she owed him: to see that his affairs were wound up with the efficiency and dispatch he would have demanded.

Godwin. She was at peace with his memory now. She knew she could trust herself not to do anything with his property that he would not want nor allow anything to be done or said that would diminish his reputation. She also did not disguise from herself the fact that some of his most characteristic traits lived on in Winnie and that in the future she would have to deal with them. But Winnie would have the advantage of receiving all the love she could give her.

She would have to find a more suitable house. She had told Mrs. Heston to send for the other servants — especially Eugenie, to dress her hair and Mme. de Brieux's. Mrs. Heston, overjoyed at the prospect of a return to a normally functioning household, had exclaimed, "Oh, ma'am! Everyone will be delighted!" And she must send for a seamstress to come and make some dresses for Leonie; until then Leonie must wear her clothes.

Chiefly she must protect and nurture Winnie — and reconcile her to the presence of Leonie in her life. But that, she thought, she need not worry about; she was certain that Leonie would have the key to Winnie. And Trudy. The moment that Trudy laid eyes on Leonie she would know the rest of the story.

"Amanthe."

At the soft call from the bed her preoccupations fled. There was nothing now except the reality of Leonie's presence; everything else dropped away out of her consciousness. She sprang up from her chair and went to her. As she leaned over the bed Leonie reached up under her dressing gown to take hold of her round, firm breasts. The remembered touch of those thin, nervous, life-stirring fingers shot through her, erasing the anguish of longing. She cast off her dressing gown and slid between the sheets, seeking Leonie's welcoming hands on her naked body. Leonie's exhausted body was revitalized, soft and warm and seductive in

234

the bed. The years vanished. This was the downy bed in the house in the Auvergne and she was experiencing for the first time Leonie's teasing fingers seeking out the tender, eager places that had waited for this moment. This was the blue satin bed in the boudoir of the hotel de Brieux, Leonie's arms banishing the fear of abandonment.

They lay pressed together the length of their bodies. Amantha's fingers sought over Leonie's belly, remembering the blue-veined swelling that had made her cautious, tentative. Now there was no need for caution. Then Leonie's fingers released the pent up desire that had been stifled in her for so long, and afterwards Leonie rolled her over and taught her again the exquisite luxury to be enjoyed as Leonie claimed her own share of desire fulfilled.

Amantha lay for a few minutes quiet while a series of images rose and faded before her eyes: the first glimpses of Leonie in Paris, dazzling her, teaching her to speak, dress, act; Leonie on the shady loggia of the Villa Margherita, the sunny garden beyond, awakening the love that lay inchoate in her heart; Leonie in the midst of the violent clash of emotions in the old house in Paris — anger, the bursting out of deeply repressed desire, their joint ecstasy in the blue satin bed.

Suddenly, out of nowhere, panic came and seized her, a wave of black horror, of dread she could not escape. She flung herself on Leonie, sobbing, "Don't leave me again, Leonie! Stay with me! I cannot endure it all again —!"

Leonie exclaimed, "Amanthe, what is the matter?" She rolled Amantha over on her back and lay on top of her. "Hush, hush," she commanded. "I will never leave you again. You belong in my arms. Don't frighten yourself so. Be tranquil, my treasure. Have I not come to you when you needed me?"

Slowly, under her caresses, Amantha grew quiet. She looked up into Leonie's face. "Yes, yes," she said, drawing a deep breath and closing her eyes as her senses drank up the sweetness of Leonie's kisses. Fatigue and awareness that she had at last reached her safe haven in Leonie's calm, gentle grasp stole over her. Sleep inexorably claimed her as she heard Leonie's voice saying, "Mon coeur, mon âme — my heart, my soul."

The Sarah Aldridge Novels

The following books are now exclusively
offered only through A&M Books.

A&M
B O O K S

P.O. Box 283, Rehoboth, Beach, DE 19971.
(302) 227-2893.